Necromancer
and Other Stories

by Sean Patrick Hazlett

Dedication

To my son Sebastian, for surpassing every expectation I ever had for him and making me forever a proud father with a son worthy of the family name.

Table of Contents

Acknowledgements

I want to thank all the teachers and writers that helped me along the way, or, barring that, did not discourage me when they should have. My fifth grade teacher, Mrs. Umile, was instrumental in encouraging me to write my first fantasy stories. I want to thank internationally best-selling novelist David Vann for having patience with my early writing as a Stanford undergraduate. He never discouraged me and always provided productive critiques that helped me improve my work. The late Jeff Carlson inspired me to write fiction after sharing his wisdom and experience. He also graciously took the time to critique one of my first stories, pointing out all my rookie mistakes. I'm also thankful that *Writers of the Future* editor, David Wolverton, discovered and recognized my work. Mike Resnick has also been instrumental in supporting my early writing career by encouraging me and buying my stories. I also want to thank award-winning author and editor, Nick Mamatas, for his unvarnished and relentless critiques of my stories in one of his fiction writing classes. Most people hold back their criticism, but Nick never sugarcoated his feedback. Because of it, he made me a better writer. I doubt I will ever reach Nick's bar for excellence, but he definitely set a high standard. Lastly, I would like to thank my ever-patient wife, Claire, for sacrificing her weekends to edit my stories.

Introduction

This collection includes eighteen short stories I wrote from the spring of 2013 through the summer of 2015. They have appeared in venues such as *Writers of the Future, Grimdark Magazine, Abyss & Apex, Sci Phi Journal, Perihelion Online Science Fiction Magazine, The Overcast, Plasma Frequency Magazine, Kasma SF, Outposts of Beyond,* and *Stupefying Stories.* One story, "Adramelech", won the Writers of the Future Contest, and four others garnered Honorable Mentions. The stories cover concepts as varied as post-apocalyptic politics, leadership lessons from a Martian psychopath, doppelgängers, invasive alien species, demonic possession, cyberwar, and hunting a necromancer during the Russo-Japanese War.

While I've been writing since I was ten years old, I only began a serious effort to publish my stories in the last few months of 2011. The one great thing about short stories is that they are useful media for generating and validating ideas. They allow writers to test concepts relatively quickly without the time and commitment required to produce a novel. Moreover, they also provide writers with an opportunity to learn and experiment with their craft.

I've learned much over the last few years and have had a lot of fun bringing these new worlds to life. I plan on creating many more in the future. I hope you enjoy reading these tales as much as I've loved writing them.

The Ninth Circle

"How can people trust the harvest, unless they see it sown?"

— Mary Renault

Amos huddled shivering in the back of a rusted U-Haul. Rain pelted its metallic roof, while gusts of wind blasted at its flanks. After Moonstrike, all it did was rain. Amos hadn't seen the sun in a year, but a month was all it took before perfectly civilized people devolved into savages.

"You in, chief?" Juan asked. "I need to know quick. Murray's beginning to suspect something's up."

Amos shrugged. He was in a real bad spot here. Real bad. Murray'd been nothing but kind to him. The man had taken Amos in off the road, and had made him feel like he was part of a real community for the first time since the world went to hell.

"I need time to think about it," Amos said.

Juan ran his fingers through his grimy black hair. "Fine. But don't take too long, chief. You have till noon tomorrow."

Amos nodded. He couldn't help but ask the question. "What happens if I say, 'no'?"

Juan's dark eyes seemed to bore into Amos's. Amos could imagine Juan calculating, weighing all the options. Then Juan said, "Nothing. But keep all this to yourself, chief. This gets back to Murray, and I swear to Jesus I'll end you."

Amos lowered his head to signal agreement, but he really just wanted to avoid making any further eye contact with Juan. Things were different now. Life was cheap, and you never knew when someone might try to kill you.

"But," Juan continued, "if you don't help us, you'll always be nothing more than a laborer in this town. If you join us, chief, I can promise you a higher place on the corporate ladder."

Amos considered Juan's offer, and then said, "I'm sorry, man. I still need some time to think on it."

ಹಿ

Amos's stomach growled in reaction to the morning breakfast whistle. He didn't have a clue where Murray got the meat, but it was damn good. Better than the rats and squirrels he'd been eating for the past few months. Best pork he'd ever had. Of course, until he'd arrived at Murray Town, he'd never eaten pork. Wasn't kosher. But when a man faced starvation, survival had a way of trampling on tradition.

There was a knock on the U-Haul door. Amos rolled it open, and Carl Bradley waited outside, smiling. The rain was still falling, but only at a drizzle.

"Rise and shine!" Carl's smile turned into a frown after his eyes shifted towards Amos's exposed feet. "Whoa! You need to get those dogs checked. You could lose a toe."

Amos winced as he wrapped his feet in grease-smeared rags and put on a pair of worn combat boots. "I know. I know. But nothing's dry, so my feet keep on rotting."

Carl shook his head. "Trench foot. If I had a needle, some moleskin, and some Gold Bond, I could do wonders. But there ain't exactly a Rite Aid nearby."

Amos joined Carl on the muddy ground. The two men passed through a graveyard of wrecked cars and trucks that appeared to float on a sea of soaked red clay. The mud infested everything here. Once it got under your fingernails, it stayed. Forever. Like Amos and Carl, hundreds of other bone-thin men and women emerged from their automotive shelters to heed the summons of the morning whistle.

The pair queued up in a line that meandered through the car park all the way to the old hanger that served as Murray Town's de facto town hall. After waiting for what seemed like hours, Carl and Amos finally got a chance to fill their canteens with distilled water, replace their blankets, and receive their daily pork ration from a steaming steel pot.

Carl and Amos walked away from the line as Carl devoured his pork chop in fewer than five bites. Discarding the bones on the churned up mud, Carl glanced to his left and then his right, then he put his hand over his mouth and whispered, "So, you in?"

Amos didn't know how to react. How'd Carl know? Amos played dumb. "What do you mean?"

"C'mon, man. All the newbies know. Juan approached most of us over the past few days with his proposition. You know, a change in management and such."

Amos shuddered. How could Carl speak about it so openly? Amos played coy. "What makes you think Juan approached me?"

"Cause I saw him go into your U-Haul last night. C'mon, don't bullshit me. Are you in or not?"

"I dunno. I have to think about it. Murray's been real good to us. He could've left us on the road when he found us. But he didn't. He's given us a meal a day for the last month, and all he's asked of us is a solid day's work. Seems like a good deal to me." Amos took a small bite from his meat ration.

Carl rolled his eyes. "Are you a goddamn Boy Scout or something? You're missing the big picture here. You wanna be a slave laborer for the rest of your life, or do you wanna be someone?"

"I wanna survive."

Ↄ

The next day, the rain fell in torrents. Amos and Carl swung their pickaxes at the wall of the tunnel the men were chiseling into the hillside. They were always tunneling. For what purpose, no one knew. It was cold enough in the gray darkness outside, but it was always colder in the tunnels.

Carl glanced at Amos and said, "I told Juan we're in."

Amos stopped in mid-swing and turned toward Carl. For a moment Amos considered burying his pickax in his friend's skull. "You what? Why the hell did you do that? You had no right to speak for me."

Carl laughed. "You'll thank me when this is all over."

"The hell with that. Where's Juan?"

Carl's smile twisted into a sneer. "I wouldn't back out now if I was you," he said, his grip tightening on the handle of his pickax. "Besides, plan's already in motion. We meet inside the hanger tonight after last call."

Ↄ

Amos stood reluctantly beside Carl in the hanger's gloom. It was so dark; all he could make out were human silhouettes. From the sound of their voices, Amos estimated there were roughly two dozen other men standing with them. Many bragged about what they would do with the spoils once it was all over. Amos wasn't so confident. There didn't seem to be all that many spoils to go around. He tapped Carl on the shoulder. "Ever wonder why Juan only organized the newbies?"

Carl shrugged. "Hell if I know. Maybe the old timers are loyal to Murray and have more to lose than we do."

That seemed to make sense. "Did you ever wonder why there are only men here?"

"No. Probably because men are good for fighting."

The answer didn't sound very convincing to Amos, but it didn't matter now.

"Gentlemen!" Juan's voice boomed from the center of the hanger. "It took a lot of balls to come here, but I want to make sure you have the will to follow through. Now I'll be the first to admit that Murray's been good to me over the past year, and he's probably been good to you too. But we're talking about doing murder here, and before I lay out all the details, I want to give you all one last chance to back out. I promise there won't be any retaliation if you decide you don't have the stomach for this. All any of you chiefs have to do is say your name and walk out that hanger door. It's that simple."

The silence suffocated Amos. He wanted a way out, but the group's pressure was closing in on him, smothering his feverish desire to escape from the insanity. His heart beat with increasing intensity. His conscience screamed, but the echo in his mind only grew louder. Murray'd done nothing to him. Murray was a good man, and an even better leader. He'd created a pocket of sanity in a maelstrom of madness.

No one spoke out. The silence stretched for what seemed like hours, even though Amos knew it had only been minutes. Then Juan said, "Well, if you're all in, let's talk about the plan…"

"Wait!" Amos yelled into the darkness. "My name is Amos, and I want no part of this."

Someone chuckled at Amos's outburst. Others whispered under their breaths. Carl shook Amos by the shoulders and said, "What the fuck are you doing? You know what, man? I always knew you was a pussy. Go walk your pussy ass out that door and let the real men take care of business."

Juan answered Amos's call, a disembodied voice reverberating through the hanger's darkness. "You sure, chief?"

"I am," Amos answered.

"I'll need you to leave then."

Amos was terrified. He didn't know these people. Not really. For all he knew, there was someone outside waiting to butcher him. What did it matter? It was too late to turn back now. Amos followed Juan's instructions, feeling the conspirators' unseen glares watching his retreat from the hanger. At that moment, Amos knew for certain that if these men succeeded, they'd kill him.

As he made his way toward the exit, Amos heard what sounded like someone starting a lawnmower. He turned back and was blinded by light saturating the hanger.

Generators.

Amos wondered how Juan had gotten his hands on fuel, let alone working power sources. Juan must've been saving them for a special occasion. Amos turned back toward the exit and shambled forward, stumbling into a solid brick of a man. As Amos's eyes gradually adapted to the darkness, a tall African American man wearing spectacles patched together with shards of duct tape stood before him. "Murray?"

The man just nodded and patted Amos on the back. "You the only one who changed his mind?" he said.

Amos stood slack jawed and silent, so he just nodded. Apparently satisfied, Murray strode past him and into the hanger.

Seconds later, Amos regained his senses and peered into the illuminated building. Inside he saw several spotlights facing into the crowd. Amos guessed that those who'd elected to stay behind couldn't see beyond the blinding spotlights. But from his vantage point, Amos could see men hiding behind them. All of the men carried something. What was it: baseball bats, rifles, or something else? Amos couldn't tell.

A whistle pierced the silence. Amos's stomach growled. A chorus of metallic clicks echoed from beyond the spotlights.

The crowd panicked. A shot rang out. Amos heard a loud thump, as a man fell within several feet of Amos, the man's face a riot of bone fragments, blood, and brains. Then Juan's voice intervened. "Everyone, remain calm. Someone very important has an announcement to make. If you move, we will shoot you."

The men still seemed agitated, but they stopped clamoring for the exit. When Murray stepped out from behind the spotlights' veil, a foreboding sense of dread seemed to infect the group like a plague.

Then Murray spoke. "Gentlemen, I'm very sorry I had to put you through this, but as you all know, we live in dangerous times. Today, a man's character is more important than ever, and the two most important aspects of character are loyalty and integrity. This was a test. A test you failed.

"They say Dante reserved the Ninth Circle of Hell for traitors. He considered them the worst of all sinners, committing a crime worse than murder. The punishment for these traitors wasn't fire and brimstone. It was imprisonment in ice.

"Treachery is cancer to a community, especially one so close to starvation and ruin. Before Moonstrike, treachery was easier to mask among anonymous millions, but in today's brutish world, there's no place for it. Treachery is death, and it must be culled from the gene pool. Today your masquerade is over. We've exposed your betrayal to our community in all its ugliness. If you're here now, you're here because you aren't fit to survive.

"Like Dante's traitors, you too will be entombed in ice, but not for eternity, just long enough to preserve your bodies for the benefit of the community."

A series of images flickered through Amos's mind as dozens of muzzle flashes peppered the inside of the hanger. Tunnels for storage. Meat for consumption. It made sense, the cold, dark logic of it all.

After the shooting stopped, Murray and Juan emerged from the hanger, faces grim. Amos locked eyes with Murray, and said, "What are you gonna do to 'em?"

"We need food, but we needed their betrayal more. Without that, there'd be no civilization left."

END

Afterword

The original kernel for this story was born out of a painful personal experience at a previous employer in which someone who was very likely a psychopath had lied to my face and then maneuvered behind my back to work against my interests. It was an instructive lesson in human behavior, teaching me never to trust anyone without fully understanding his or her interests and motivations. Words are just that—words. It is far more important to weigh a person's claims against how those claims align with their own self-interest. If there is alignment, then what they say is likely credible. Otherwise, watch your back.

While psychopaths can wreak havoc in modern corporations, few people die because of their behavior. However, in a post-apocalyptic society, being able to trust the people around you with your life would be essential for survival. As such, rooting out psychopaths and sociopaths from the general population would become a necessary criterion for cementing this trust.

My personal experience led me to explore how a post-apocalyptic leader making difficult choices about whether someone lives or dies—and who's on the menu—might organize his or her community. By entrapping and isolating people who would betray his largesse, Murray effectively develops a system that both filters out the community's most treacherous citizens and legitimizes the selection process for its cannibalism. In turn, the story examines how leaders can so often rationalize horrific behavior by blaming their victims. Add the concept of traitors occupying the ninth circle of hell in Dante's *Inferno*, and "The Ninth Circle" was born.

This story won an Honorable Mention in the Writers of the Future Contest's fourth quarter of 2014. "The Ninth Circle" was originally slated to be published in the first issue of *HexHouse Magazine* and then reprinted in the second volume of the *Let Me In* anthology until the publisher inexplicably released all the stories he'd agreed to buy and print back to the writers. This sort of behavior is clearly unprofessional, but given the vagaries of the publishing industry, these things do tend to happen from time to time. In fact, it is the second time it's happened to me in my writing career. Fortunately, this story ultimately sold to *Bards and Sages Quarterly*, where it appeared in July 2018.

Of all the stories in this collection, I think this one is the most psychologically compelling. I hope you enjoyed it.

AITUAR MANAS

Adramelech

I dreamt of a peacock. Not the majestic fowl in all its pomp and beauty, but a twisted and perverted chimera. Blackened, burnt, and torn plumage radiated from its serpentine form. Jaundiced eyes, both human and animal, infested its spotted feathers. Each eye shone with what struck me as a keen and malevolent intelligence.

I woke to find myself scribbling arcane symbols in my daily ledger—strange, indecipherable glyphs. Though executed by my own hand, the writing was more precise and beautiful than mine. It was so small, I considered using a magnifying glass to make out the wedge-shaped marks. My phantom hand had filled all two hundred pages with this inscrutable script in the course of one night.

As I turned the pages to marvel at this prodigious effort, I stumbled upon several revolting illustrations. Children boiling in kettle pots, inverted crucifixions, and the dismemberment of babes—these were but a few of the horrors I witnessed on the ledger's sacrilegious sheets.

As I leafed through the tome, a crushing sense of melancholy suffocated me. It was as if a sickly film of somber gray had occluded my vision. After turning the book's profane pages, it took all the energy I had to rise from my bed.

I should've burnt the accursed book on the spot, but its artisanal quality was unrivaled. Despite its corruption, it had a dark beauty that made it impossible for me to feed it to the flame.

The urge to destroy the blasphemous text waned, while my curiosity about its contents waxed. So I wrapped the book in burlap and brought it to my dear friend, Alastair Moorcock, Professor of Hebrew and Semitic Languages at the University of Glasgow.

A Christ-fearing man, I had never resorted to outright deception before, but I feared Moorcock would name me a madman if I'd told him the truth. So instead, I concocted a story about how I'd uncovered the ledger in some flea-bitten apothecary shop in West London.

Surrounded by dusty books lining his walls or arranged on the floor in haphazard piles, Moorcock cultivated an aura of aristocratic intellectualism. With a keen eye and a strong sentimentality for the past, he refused modern conveniences, preferring the illumination of candlelight to one of Edison's incandescent light bulbs.

"Where did you really find this?" he demanded, his waxed whiskers vibrating as he stared intensely at me from his cramped study.

"What do you mean?" I said, playing coy.

"This text is written in Sumerian cuneiform, in ink, and on a modern ledger, not chiseled on a stone tablet."

"That is rather unnerving," I admitted.

"If I may ask," Moorcock continued, "which apothecary shop sold you this forgery? I should very much like to meet the shopkeeper. He seems to be an exceptionally well-educated man. Only a handful of academics possess the scholarship to identify these glyphs; even fewer know enough to translate, let alone write them."

I lowered my head, embarrassed. If I continued this charade, Moorcock would summarily expose my lie. Then I'd get no help from him at all. So I confessed. "My deepest apologies, Professor Moorcock. I didn't find this at an apothecary shop. I composed it last night. The truth is so preposterous I reasoned you'd more likely accept the lie. Regardless of the text's origin, I very much require your expertise."

His eyebrow arched. His jaw tightened. "Mr. Brooks, how is it you're incapable of reading something you wrote?"

He had a point. So I tried a different approach. "It matters not how this ledger came to be in my possession. What's important is that we decipher its contents. You're the first and only person I've sought for guidance, because I'm convinced that your curiosity will outweigh your concerns about how I acquired this book."

Moorcock cupped his chin in his hand in what appeared to be a moment of consideration. "You didn't steal it, did you?" he asked in a manner suggesting that's exactly how he thought I'd come by it.

I smiled and shook my head. "Of course not."

"Very well then. Let's have a look," he said, rolling up his sleeves. He opened the tome and squinted at the first page.

"Here," I said, handing him my magnifying glass.

He took it without saying a word and began his examination. He traced his index finger across the page in a steady hand. As he read, his eyes widened. Then they rolled back into his head until I saw nothing but their whites. He raised his head, turning away from the ledger. He smiled in a most unsettling manner.

"And so it begins," he cackled. "For your assistance in this life and for your eternal servitude once you pass beyond death's veil, I will grant you the power to inhabit the bodies of others. What say you to my offer?"

Moorcock's transformation was so strange and so abrupt that I hesitated, unable to formulate anything resembling a coherent response to this rather unnerving query.

"I'm sorry, Professor Moorcock, I don't understand."

"Not Moorcock," it said, "Something else. Something far older. What say you to my offer?"

"No," I said without wavering.

When I tried to elaborate, I found my ability to draw breath thwarted. I struggled for air, desperately opening and closing my mouth like a herring flailing on the slick deck of a trawler.

"What about now?" it said, grinning.

I fought and I prayed and I panicked and I tried to weep. But nothing would bring me air. As patches of hazy blackness obscured my vision, I nodded in submission.

With that, Moorcock collapsed. Shaking his head like a befuddled drunkard, he slowly rose back to his feet. "My God," he said, "you must burn that tome, immediately."

I shuddered at his suggestion. Once more, I couldn't bear to contemplate the ledger's destruction. The book was a foul thing, but one of exquisite splendor, and it hinted of shuttered secrets I despaired to learn. There were still too many unanswered questions. What had possessed Moorcock? With whom or what had I made a bargain? Could it be undone?

"No, I can't. We can't. There's still much to learn from this text," I pleaded.

Moorcock scowled. He lifted the foul ledger from his desk and held it over a candle's open flame.

"No!" I yelled. Then, from Moorcock's own eyes I watched my body collapse. I yanked the book away from the flame and placed it on the floor next to my still-breathing human husk. I sat in Moorcock's chair. Then I returned to my own body and snatched the ledger before standing.

Moorcock regarded me with an expression that straddled the thin line between awe and horror. "What have you done, sir?"

"You have no right to destroy my property," I replied.

Pointing at the tome, Moorcock said, "That thing is an abomination. You saw what it did to me."

I tried to ignore his outrage. "Please, tell me what you learned. I must understand what just happened," I begged.

He brooded behind his desk. "Get that thing out of my sight and never come here again."

"Done," I said. "But please, for the love of God, help me understand what knowledge you gleaned from your brief reading."

Moorcock paused, then said, "Return to London and call on Sir Willard Hilton. Show him your ledger and inquire about the *Dictionnaire Infernal*. Good day, Mr. Brooks."

With that, I grabbed the ledger, left his study, and returned to London by rail.

∞

I was to meet Sir Willard Hilton in a modest pub about half a block away from the electric adverts illuminating Piccadilly Circus's thoroughfare. I entered the establishment, happy to find shelter from the cold and rainy night.

It was always night for me. Since I'd birthed the ledger, I'd become a nocturnal thing, preferring the solace of shadow to the loud and arrogant face of the sun. Even the moon, whose source of light was the sun's reflection, was something I shunned.

I collapsed my umbrella and removed my bowler hat, taking in the tiny pub's ambience. The establishment was little more than an alcove, carved into the bone and sinew of London's West End. The tables were roughhewn and discolored, pitted oak slabs from years of use and neglect.

"What'll it be, sir?" the portly barkeep said.

"I'm just here to see someone," I replied.

"Best you be seeing them elsewhere," the man said, leering at me. "Only have space for paying customers."

I balled my fists. Fantasies of ripping out the man's throat filled my mind's eye. I had to blink twice before I was able to regain my composure. "Fine," I said. "A glass of whiskey will do."

"What kind?" the man said.

"The kind that is cheapest," I said, annoyed.

He harrumphed and poured my drink.

"Do you happen to know if a Sir Willard Hilton frequents this pub?" I asked.

He answered with a scowl. "You? Here to see Sir Willard?"

"What? Were you expecting someone different?" I said, insulted.

He rolled his eyes and then pointed to a table in the pub's back left nook. I followed his arm to find a wiry-thin man with curly black hair that receded into a widow's peak. He vibrated with nervous energy while he chatted up a curvaceous blonde. He clutched an overflowing pint of ale.

I grabbed my cheap whiskey and made my way to his table, interrupting him in midsentence. "Excuse me, Sir Willard, may I have a quick word?"

Sir Willard ignored me, sipping his drink.

I cleared my throat. "Excuse me, Sir Willard . . ."

He held up his hand, never taking his eyes off the woman. "Piss off."

"But Sir Willard, this can't wait. It's a matter of life and death."

His head swiveled toward me. "I said: Piss. Off."

Sir Willard's stern tone and a glint of violence in his eyes told me that if I didn't back off, the world-renowned explorer would very likely do me harm.

So I took my whiskey and sat at the bar, where I brooded. I had to get Sir Willard's attention, but I couldn't compete with his companion. Then

I had a curious idea. There was no need for me to compete with her for Sir Willard's notice at all.

My head slumped onto the table. In an instant, I was staring at Sir Willard from across a common table.

"C'mon, luv. My flat's only a few blocks away. We can have a nightcap there," Sir Willard said, winking at me.

I felt awkward inside this woman's body. So I got straight to the point: "Sir Willard, I need your help. Professor Alastair Moorcock recommended that I seek your assistance about the *Dictionnaire Infernal*."

Sir Willard's jawed dropped. His eyes shifted past my feminine host and stared at my empty human husk.

"What are you?" he said.

I gestured toward my original vessel. "I'm the chap over there you wouldn't speak to."

He stood up and backed away from me, nearly stumbling over his chair. "No," he said with a hint of panic in his voice. "What kind of thing are you?"

"I'm a man, just like you," I said in a woman's voice and without any trace of irony.

"But . . . but only demons are capable of soul displacement."

And with that one sentence, I learned more about my predicament than I had in the last month.

"Tell me more," I said.

"Not here. And not until you release your hold over Victoria's body."

"If I do, will you help me?"

He nodded, so I released her.

☙

"Adramelech is its name," Sir Willard whispered, paging through the ledger. Candlelight flickered in his dank cellar study. His mahogany bureau was firmly rooted in the middle of the room like a citadel anchoring its power in the center of a far-reaching kingdom. The floor beneath and the walls surrounding the bureau had a complex series of circular and triangular warding sigils scrawled in chalk.

"Whose name?" I asked.

"The entity that holds your contract."

"What entity?" I said.

"The thing called Adramelech. According to the *Dictionnaire Infernal,* references to Adramelech pre-date the founding of Christianity. They point to its origin as a Mesopotamian deity. According to the lore, worshippers appeased Adramelech through ritualistic human sacrifice. It is said that Adramelech's acolytes frequently offered it burning children."

I shuddered at Sir Willard's words. What had I done? Then my thoughts became more urgent, more focused on solving my immediate dilemma. "And contract? What contract?"

"Your immortal essence for the ability to project your soul into others," he said.

"But . . . but, I was coerced," I stammered. "I had no choice."

"We always have a choice. You could have chosen death."

I bowed my head in resignation. There had to be a glimmer of hope, a way out. "Is there any way that I can break this pact?"

He fixed his gray eyes on mine. "Tell me one thing: did you summon Adramelech or did it seek you?"

"The latter," I said almost too quickly, my desperation roiling beneath a thin veneer of calm.

"I see," he said. "Then, according to this tome, there's still hope."

"Thank the Lord," I said. "Tell me what I must do."

ဆာ

Procuring the hollowed-out bronze statue required a fair bit of archival work and logistical meandering, but the request was harmless enough.

After paying Sir Willard a princely sum to recover the artifact, he returned with word that his expedition had unearthed the item and loaded it on a steamship in the Levant. He'd promised that the artifact would arrive in London within the month.

When it arrived at my flat, enshrouded in black, I couldn't help but experience a sense of deep foreboding and woe. The hidden statue had an uncanny aura that invoked dread in its beholders.

I had the deliverymen lower it into my cellar. They used a complex system of levers and pulleys. The hemp groaned and creaked with the effort. I scarcely believed the relic would make the passage without snapping the ropes that held its colossal heft at bay.

After they departed, and despite my trepidation, I removed the statue's dark shroud. I trembled as I beheld the image of my nightmare cast in bronze-all those menacing eyes glaring at me, boring into the pit of my soul.

I immediately covered the statue back in its shadowy veil before the ghastly figure befouled my mind with more sinister visions.

And there it sat, awaiting Adramelech and whatever sordid purpose the fiend had intended for it.

ဆာ

The next several years passed at a glacial pace. Serving as Sir Willard's acolyte, I dedicated my life to uncovering the esoteric mysteries of the obscene tome I'd transcribed in my youth.

Even with the meticulous warding in Sir Willard's cellar, the book exacted a punishing toll on my constitution. Darkness became my permanent abode, and I a thing of midnight.

Each year, on the anniversary of my contract, Adramelech summoned me on pain of death, compelling me to scour the barrows for the corpse of an orphaned child. It was a gruesome task, digging into the loamy earth and exhuming the tiny coffin.

On one such night, I passed under the moon's glowing crescent, its reflected sunlight scarring the blue-black sky like a cicatrix on unblemished skin. The light it cast revolted me-no doubt a consequence of the corruption festering in my spirit.

My method for selecting which body to disinter was a simple one. Before my nighttime jaunts, I would pore over the obituaries of rural newspapers for the names of recently deceased orphan children. On this particular year, my research led me to Bocking Cemetery in Braintree, Essex.

Stalking the lichyard in the service of my master, I meandered through a maze of tombstones and mausoleums without the aid of lantern light. There, I sought the grave of the Jameson boy. The ground was still muddy from the rainstorm that had soaked the land earlier that day.

It didn't take long for me to locate the Jameson plot with its freshly turned dirt. Hoisting my spade, I began to dig.

A faint light glimmered through the distant hedges and oak trees. I ceased digging, fearful my illicit activity might garner unwanted attention.

The light grew brighter and drew closer. My heart pounded. Sweat slithered down my brow. To avoid discovery, I hid behind a gravestone and lay on my stomach.

The silhouette of a man passed through the trees. He shined a lantern in my direction. I held my breath, cowering.

He approached slowly.

I hugged the earth, clutching clumps of mud in a futile attempt to avoid detection.

A light blinded me from above. "What the bloody hell are you doing here?" a gruff voice said.

I held my hands before my face, trying to blot out the glaring light. As my eyes adjusted, I saw the night watchman, his countenance grimacing in disgust.

"Stand up!" he commanded, waving a baton.

This was the end. If he turned me over to the authorities, I would be forever severed from that spellbinding tome. I couldn't bear the thought of it. There was a way out, but it terrified me. I'd promised myself never to use that dreadful power again.

Now I had no choice. I locked my eyes on his.

In an instant, I watched my body slump to the ground. Wearing the night-watchman's skin, I sprinted back toward the tree line, my lantern swaying like a chaotic pendulum scything through darkness.

In moments, I'd passed through the oaks and hedges, and into Essex's flat fields, running until the night watchman's heart felt as if it were on the verge of bursting. My mind raced. It would take me hours to get him far enough away from the cemetery so I'd have enough time to unearth the body.

But I didn't have hours. I had only until daybreak.

Then I stumbled upon my redemption.

It was no more than a black speck on the horizon. As I drew closer, the stone well jutted from the earth like a broken tooth. When I reached it, breathless, I stared down fifty feet into its gaping maw.

It was either his soul or mine.

I leapt into the well.

In half a breath, I was back in my own skin. I grabbed my spade and dug with a fury, using guilt as my fuel. I tried not to imagine the man's frantic effort to keep his head above water in that black well. Despite my rationalizations, what I had done was unforgivable. But what choice did I have?

Hours later, I placed the muddy coffin onto a dolly and wheeled it to the midnight-blue Ford Model T waiting on the side of the country road. There, I loaded the small coffin into the backseat, covered it with an olive drab tarp, and then motored back to London.

With shame, I carried the coffin to my flat, removed the corpse of a freckled boy with strawberry-blonde hair, and placed it inside the repulsive statue. Then I positioned a brazier heaping with coals behind it, where I presented the burnt offering to my demented overseer.

I know not why Adramelech forced me to repeat this grim ritual year after year. It was as if through these unspeakable acts, the demon was honing my instincts and inuring my conscience to prepare me for something far worse.

I yearned to sever my contract, devoting every waking hour to study of the diabolical tome, scrutinizing it for a loophole. Sir Willard assured me from his extensive scholarship that the brazen statue was a crucial element of the remedy. Yet the puzzle remained.

Despite my wretched nocturnal existence, I resolved never to use my unnatural ability again, fearing that each use only served to spread Adramelech's infestation of my immortal soul.

But through the toilsome years, I knew only failure and regret, until I convinced myself that the only way out was by the fiend's own hand.

ဆ

There was something troubling about the boy's voice. Both haunting and familiar, it rumbled above the din of the boisterous pub like an echo in the crag lands. Under the guise of youth, it carried the weight of eternity on sonorous and ethereal wings. Of love and of loss twisted with a sense of despair in some cruel and arcane concoction not birthed of the natural world.

The pub's denizens made merry, drowning their earthly worries in the false mirth of fermented barley. Each year, I came here to think, to reflect on the bargain. For thirty years I had come to commemorate the anniversary, finding solace that I still had more time. But today was different. Today, I sensed that the butcher's bill was due.

"Logan," the man-child said, the ken of my name betraying his deception of innocence. There was power in the knowing of names, but that power had long been lost to the kindred of men.

A storm was brewing outside. The smell presaging the coming of rain wafted into the pub each time another poor soul entered the establishment. If you were old like me, you could feel it in the hollows of your knees. The void of the space betwixt flesh and bone coupled with the creaking pain of age. The hackles on my narrow neck rose in warning to the gathering maelstrom.

What most didn't know or realize was that another tempest was brewing. It had been building for three decades. And tonight, it would discharge its vast malevolence.

Girding for the inevitable, I swigged my whiskey in one last pathetic attempt to preserve my mortality. I then turned to regard my night caller.

"Can't say I'm pleased to see you, Adramelech, but I'm sure you understand why."

The child nodded in a manner unlike a child. Its smile taunted and tore at my soul. I could feel it rattle inside me like a rat caught in a cage with a serpent.

"Logan, let us speak of less unpleasant things. It's true that your soul is now mine to rend. But you still have free will. What if I were to offer you a way to repay your debt that would free you of your obligation?"

I knew with every fiber of my being not to trust this spawn of the abyss. But hope was a powerful thing. As the autumn of my life fast approached, the horror of harvesting the rotten fruit of a dying tree had become more real.

"Say on," I said.

Adramelech smiled, his eyes conveying an unsettling malice. "All I require is one final task. After that, I will consider your debt paid in full."

I took a deep breath, downed my whiskey, and said, "Tell me more."

∽

I didn't understand why this infernal thing wanted to be encased in the statue, but I was only too happy to oblige. If I could broil the beast inside the boy by burning the boy, I wouldn't hesitate, especially to save my own soul.

So, as instructed, I hoisted the child who was not a child into the bronze statue and sealed it. I placed the brazier behind the statue, loaded it with coals, and heated it.

I thought about my freedom as the heat began to rise and fill the air with the scent of steaming charcoal. I wondered if this doom would forever be my shadow, stalking me to the grave in a life that ultimately offered neither freedom nor security. Would I ever escape Adramelech's choking grasp?

I stepped backward as the process of thermal conduction radiated heat throughout the hollow statue.

The child screamed.

My gut lurched. A wave of guilt flooded my consciousness, blotting out the influence of my rational mind. Instinct told me Adramelech no longer enthralled the boy, but I couldn't be sure. And was it really worth my immortal soul?

I panicked. The entity had made me its agent of evil. This child would suffer and die because of me.

Wind swirled in the draftless room. I shivered. Ink-dark, the smoky essence slithered through the dank air and hovered before me.

Adramelech was here.

A vision of the perverted peacock appeared in my mind's eye. The thing cackled at me. It had subverted my free will, twisting it to its own maleficent ends.

"So much for free will," Adramelech whispered from the space in-between life and death, from a twilight realm where entities beyond the ken of humanity dwelled.

The child's earsplitting shrieks became more urgent. The strangely sweet smell of burning flesh made my mouth water, evoking an unsettling feeling as I listened to him howl inside the statue.

"Do you recognize the child?" Adramelech hissed from the ether.

I shook my head.

"He is the orphaned son of the man you threw in the well."

What had I done? What kind of a monster had I become?

And then the idea came to me, a spark of salvation in a sea of suffering. Adramelech had never taken away the power it had granted me.

So I possessed the boy, shouldering his agony in one final defiant display of free will, completing the circle—master becomes boy, boy becomes master, and master becomes boy again.

A serpent swallowing its own tail.

And so I burn.

END

Afterword

"Adramelech" is based on a Mesopotamian sun god akin to Moloch. In its various incarnations, Adramelech has often been depicted as having a human body, a mule's head, and a peacock's tail. The demon has been associated with human sacrifice, specifically the practice of burning children in sacrificial rites. Adramelech has appeared in two major catalogs of demons including *The Lesser Key of Solomon* and *The Dictionnaire Infernal.* The former was an anonymous grimoire compiled in the mid-seventeenth century from sources several centuries older and consists of five volumes. The first of these, the *Ars Goetia*, includes descriptions of seventy-two distinct demons.

The latter tome is The *Dictionnaire Infernal*, a book on demonology composed by Jacques Auguste Simon Collin de Plancy and published in 1818. References to Adramelech have also appeared in the Bible (2 Kings 17:31) and John Milton's Paradise Lost.

In crafting this story, I fused many of Adramelech's attributes referenced in this source material with some of my own additions, particularly Adramelech's ability to possess others and to grant that power to others. This tale is ultimately about whether we truly possess free will and, if so, what one man would be willing to sacrifice in order to preserve it.

This story won second place in the Writers of the Future Contest. When Joni Labaqui, the contest director, called to notify me it won second place, she said several of the judges had noted that the story had had a very Lovecraftian atmosphere, which was very flattering since H.P. Lovecraft is one of my favorite authors. The anthology's editor, Dave Wolverton, even went as far as to say, "this is my favorite horror piece that I've seen in Writers of the Future."

Originally, "Adramelech" was about 3,200 words, but Dave Wolverton encouraged me to add more detail to the story to tie up some of its loose ends. So I included another scene and made some minor continuity edits to integrate the scene into the broader tale, ultimately adding another thousand words.

This story was first published in *Writers of the Future, Volume 33* and subsequently appeared as a reprint in *Digital Horror Fiction* and in the *Year's Best Hardcore Horror, Volume 3*. I hope you found it entertaining.

We Hit Back

A column of Chinese tanks lumbered over a muddy pontoon bridge floating on the Amur River. From his comfortable Palo Alto office, Lionel Jones shook his head as he watched the scene unfold on his plasma screen TV. Ethnic conflict between a swelling Chinese immigrant population and native Russians was the spark, but he suspected the war was really over Eastern Siberia's ample coal, titanium, and molybdenum.

Lionel saw the war as an opportunity, a boon for the cybersecurity business. And it'd be especially lucrative for his remediation and forensics group at CyberFortress Technology, which cleaned up corporate networks in the aftermath of an infestation. Ever since the emergence of advanced persistent threats, businesses were taking cybersecurity much more seriously. A single breach could not only ruin the reputation of a company, but also could put it out of business.

As an African-American in the software industry, Lionel had always been an outsider. But his Army experience had proven to be a unique asset in working with the military and law enforcement to track down hackers. Silicon Valley technocratic arrogance didn't play well at the Pentagon, but real-world war-fighting experience did.

Lionel rose from his black leather chair and headed toward his office's frosted glass door. As he was about to exit, his office phone rang. Sighing, he returned to his desk and answered.

"Help, Dad! I can't make it stop!" his twenty-year-old son, Reggie, yelled, the sound of screeching tires punctuating his plea.

Lionel's gut twisted into a knot. Reggie was scaring him. Taking a deep breath, Lionel collected his thoughts. His son could be excitable at times—too much of his mother in him.

"Calm down, Reggie. What's going on?"

"I can't stop my car!" he howled over the roaring engine. "It's in auto control mode!"

Lionel froze. He was always the man with the plan. But now he felt paralyzed. His heart raced. *Think, man. Think!*

"Wait," Reggie said. "The car's slowing down. Something popped up on my dashboard display."

Lionel exhaled, releasing his tightly controlled tension. "Okay. It sounds like you're gonna be all right. Do you have control of the car?"

"The display's telling me to enter your bank account number."

"The hell?" Lionel said, regretting the words the instant they left his mouth. Then he had one horrifying thought.

Ransomware.

"It says I have twenty minutes to enter it."

"Or what?" Lionel said, temper flaring.

"It doesn't say."

"How fast are you moving?"

"The car just stopped in a Safeway parking lot."

"Get out of the car!" Lionel said, his decades-old Army training kicking in.

He heard fumbling. "I can't, Dad. I'm locked in." Reggie's quivering voice verged on panic.

"Shit," Lionel said. Of course Reggie would be locked in. "Grab something. Anything. Quick. Smash the windows. Get out!"

Glass shattered. The engine rumbled. Tires squealed.

"The car's moving again! I have eighteen minutes! Help!"

Lionel could feel the terror in his son's voice. Reggie was in an automated death trap, destination unknown. And Lionel had only eighteen minutes to save him.

"Stay calm. What's your smartphone's username and password?"

"What's that got to do with anything?" Reggie said, voice shaking.

"I'll be able to track your location."

Reggie shared the details.

"Give me five minutes to figure something out," Lionel said, "and I'll call you back."

"Hurry up, Dad!" Reggie cried.

Lionel gave Reggie's location to the police. They promised to send a squad car. He then reached out to Travis Myers, his contact at Infinium Motors.

"When's the last time you pushed out a major software update?" Lionel asked.

"Two hours ago," Travis said. "Why? There a problem?"

"Might be. Can you send it to our sandboxing server ASAP? I have a bit of a situation."

"Sure. What's going on?"

"Just send it. If your software's been compromised, I'll let you know."

Within five minutes, Lionel had the software in his company's cloud-based sandbox, and his analysts were running the executable to see if it exhibited any unusual or known malware behavior.

Lionel called Reggie back. "Talk to me, Reggie."

"The car's now on I-280, clocking ninety miles per hour. I'm scared, Dad."

"Hang in there, buddy." Lionel paused to clear a lump in his throat. "Your Infinium downloaded some software a few hours ago. My people are checking if the file's been compromised. If so, we may be able to find the people holding you for ransom."

"Can you make the car stop?"

"I can't. Not in the time we have left. But the police have your coordinates. They're on the way."

"Okay, Dad," Reggie whimpered. Then he said, "Wait, I see a cop behind me now."

Lionel was relieved. He might get Reggie out of this mess after all and without losing his life savings.

Reggie screamed. "Dad! My car accelerated. It's going nuts!"

Sirens blared. A bead of sweat rolled down Lionel's cheek. "Hang in there. I'm gonna check on my team and see if this has anything to do with that download."

"Please hurry." Reggie sobbed. "Don't let me die, Dad."

"You're not gonna die. I'll find a way to override the malware. Hang in there, buddy. I'll call you right back."

Lionel hung up, then dialed Pete Carlson, a longtime CyberFortress colleague. "You find anything, Pete?"

"Nope," Pete said. "You can tell Infinium Motors their code's clean as soap."

"Shit," Lionel said. "Okay. You have any idea how someone could hack an automobile without infecting the manufacturer's software."

"There's only one other way I can think of," Pete said. "They must've hacked into another device that interfaces with the car. Probably a smartphone."

"I thought auto companies had a firewall between their mission critical and secondary systems?"

"They do, but it sounds like something nasty overcame those precautions. And whoever did this was one sophisticated son-of-a-bitch."

"Why's that?"

"You can't just hack into any engine control unit's embedded software. The programming specs for any given car vary by make and model. Anyone who hacked into your son's car would've had specific knowledge of those specs and would've customized the code."

"Bottom line this for me, Pete," Lionel said.

"Well, I don't want to talk out of school, but I would bet this attack wasn't random. Whoever designed the malware was likely targeting your son."

Pete's suggestion terrified Lionel. "Thanks, Pete," he said, gritting his teeth.

Lionel called Reggie. "Reggie, did you download anything on your smartphone today?"

"I download things on my smartphone all the time. Hell, most of the time, apps download data automatically. What's it matter? I've only got seven minutes left. It's just money. Just give these jerks what they want."

Lionel took a deep breath. "Okay, write this down, but don't enter it until one minute before the deadline. I need to make some calls first."

"Okay, Dad. I love you."

"I love you too, buddy." Lionel gave Reggie his account number and password. Then he hung up and called his security contact at the smartphone manufacturer.

"Harvey, I need you to send our sandboxing group all of Reggie's apps and download activity for the last twenty-four hours. We have a live breach in progress."

"Will do," Harvey said.

Lionel hung up and sent an email to his bank's fraud department, instructing them to freeze his account. He then followed up with a phone call.

It took three minutes to get a representative on the phone. As he recounted the details of the compromise, the woman said, "I'm sorry, Mr. Jones, but you just wired your funds to an encrypted account."

Lionel's heart stopped. Before he could respond, his phone beeped. "I have to take this call," he told the woman.

Switching to the other line, Lionel prayed it was his son.

"Mr. Jones, this is Officer Ramos of the San Mateo Police Department," a man said in an authoritative tone. "We're gonna need you to come into the station."

Tears welled in Lionel's eyes. He didn't want to believe it, but deep down he knew the truth. "You want me to identify my son's body, don't you?"

"Mr. Jones, I don't think it's appropriate to discuss it over the phone. Just come to the station."

"I'll be there," Lionel said, choking on his tears.

⟡

Huddled up against the bar, Lionel finished his fifth shot of Jack Daniels. His old Army buddy, Mack McKeown, grabbed a stool and sat beside him. He wore one of those leather Member's Only jackets, and he was starting to get fat.

Lionel squinted up at his friend. "Whoa! What are you doing here, buddy?"

Mack's pale, freckled face flashed an expression of concern. "You're drunk as a skunk, Lionel. I can smell you half way across the bar. Everything all right? I mean, considering…"

"You mean after I just buried my son. I'm at one of the world's largest cybersecurity companies and I still couldn't find the killers. How pathetic am I?" Lionel said, spitting out his words like bile.

Mack held up his hands. "I'm here to help, man. Janet told me you weren't doing too well. Said it might do you some good to see an old friend."

Lionel slapped Mack on the back. "I'm sorry, buddy. I didn't mean to bust your balls. I hear you're doing real well. Made full-bird Colonel and all."

Mack's jaw tensed. His smile seemed forced. "I'm doing just fine. I've been very blessed. Until you'd lost your son, you'd been blessed too."

"Ah, cut your religious bullshit. What kind of a God makes a man bury his own son? It ain't natural."

"C'mon, Lionel," Mack said, putting his hand on Lionel's arm, "You didn't have to go there."

Lionel pushed it away. "The hell I didn't. Have you ever seen what happens when a car launches someone off a cliff at a hundred and twenty miles an hour?" Tears flowed down Lionel's face. "I had to bury my boy in a closed casket. They're still finding pieces of him off 280. And the passive measures we use to identify cybercriminals aren't enough to catch the bastard who killed him. I'd have to take a more active approach—an approach my company would never sanction."

Mack grabbed Lionel by both shoulders and looked him directly in the eyes. He shot Lionel the same stern glare he had in Ramadi, just before a firefight. "You can't bring your son back, and drinking your life away is unworthy of the man who saved my life. Without you, I wouldn't be here. Grab some sack and be the man I used to know, not this shriveled up wimp who's sniveling and feeling sorry for himself.

"Life's not fair. So quit whining and do something about it. You work at a cybersecurity company. Influential people have got your back. Hell, your world famous college roommate, Al Meyer, is even using his political comedy show as a megaphone to criticize hacktivists, in no small part to honor your son's memory. These ransomware kidnappings are starting to happen a lot more lately. Seems to me you're at the right flippin' place at the right flippin' time with access to the right flippin' people. Seems to me, God's got a plan for you."

Lionel stared at his friend, this magnificent bastard who'd taken him to hell and back. He smiled and then hugged his old friend. "Mack, for the first time in my life, I know exactly what I need to do."

⁎

Standing before the boardroom entrance, Lionel clenched his notes. The solid oak door swiveled open. Gilbert Reynolds, the company's weather-beaten chief counsel, grinned at Lionel and extended his arm toward the entrance. "Mr. Jones, it's your time to shine," he said in a deceptively disarming Texas twang.

Forcing a smile, Lionel wiped his sweaty brow. He took one last deep breath, then took the plunge.

Cold, stale air made him shiver as he entered. He noticed Admiral George Whitehall first. The humorless retired naval officer held court at the head of the marble boardroom table. The instant he set eyes on Whitehall, Lionel began to doubt himself. What the hell was he doing? The board was going to think he was nuts. If they didn't, he was pretty sure his proposal would be too dicey for them.

It was a gamble. But it was a gamble for something Lionel believed in. Enough that he was willing to risk his job to make his vision a reality.

The remaining eight board members smiled at him like sharks baring their teeth before a feeding frenzy. He made his way around the table shaking their hands and exchanging pleasantries. He then walked up to a screen, where his PowerPoint presentation waited.

A snake charmer in a pit of vipers, Lionel picked up a clicker off the boardroom table and pointed it at the screen. *Here goes nothing.*

The screen flashed, and the image of a red queen running in place appeared. "In any predator-prey relationship," Lionel began, "both predator and prey are constantly co-evolving. Like Lewis Carroll's Red Queen, both must keep running to stay in place. Hackers develop new exploits; we develop countermeasures, and so on *ad infinitum.* But the attacks never stop. They only escalate. And each time we fall further behind.

"It all started with a few harmless punks messing with code. Soon criminal syndicates were swindling credit card numbers. Now nation-states are stealing industrial secrets.

"Until there are consequences, the threat will always be one step ahead, one zero-day vulnerability from crashing the whole system.

"Today, I propose we break this chain. In this industry, you're either a lion or a gazelle. And we've been a gazelle for far too long. Today, I'm unveiling a business plan to form an organization that develops offensive cyber weapons for private corporations. In just two years, I believe this could be a ten billion dollar revenue opportunity for our company."

"My God!" Admiral Whitehall protested. Lionel girded himself. "You want to open Pandora's box. Do you have any idea what kind of risk that would pose for this company?"

Lionel had expected resistance. He'd been so sure of it that his presentation's only slide was the one already on the screen.

"With all due respect, Admiral, Pandora's box is already open. Startups are working on cyber weapons. Nation-states armed with scores of sophisticated hackers have been engaging in cyber-espionage and sabotage against American companies for years. And all we can do is detect these attacks and pick up the pieces afterward. Yet the attackers never suffer any consequences. We need to change the equation. And we must do it now before things get worse."

"But what of attribution?" Nora Rosewood, a gray-haired partner at Robinson, Weiss and Whateley said. "What's to stop hackers from camouflaging their attacks by routing them through multiple servers or by using botnets of unsuspecting third-party computers? What if, for example, J.P. Morgan detects an attack from Goldman Sachs? How would the bank know if Goldman were responsible and not an unwitting dupe?"

Lionel nodded. "That's a fair point. Determining attribution has been one of the main legal hurdles deterring corporations from developing cyber weapons. That's why my proposal calls for an entire industry ecosystem to help us realize this vision."

Lionel continued. "There are several things we can do to mitigate this risk. First, we should establish a principle of no first use of a cyber weapon. We should only deploy cyber weapons in the wake of a direct or indirect attack on one of our customers. And we should only launch a counterattack if we have proof beyond a reasonable doubt who the attacker is."

"If I might interject here," Doctor Maria Lopez said, "the world of cybersecurity is a murky one. Sometimes attackers are so meticulous about covering their tracks they'll never be caught. Even worse, our adversaries are sophisticated enough to frame someone else. How do you ensure we root out false positives?" A feisty spark plug of a woman, Lopez was a former Marine intelligence officer with a PhD in artificial intelligence from Carnegie Mellon.

"Have we caught everyone who's ever committed a crime?" Lionel said. "Of course not. But we don't use that as an excuse to let crime run amuck. The same principle applies to cyberspace."

"That answer may play well on Main Street, Mr. Jones, but we have a fiduciary duty to our shareholders. Developing cyber weapons could expose them to outsized financial risk," Lopez said. "And frankly, I'm not satisfied with your answer. We, as a board, need to know how you'd mitigate risk if one of your exploits harms an innocent party."

"Your question is a great segue into my next point. Before we enter the offensive cyber business, our first priority should be to develop the most advanced cyber attribution engine on the planet, leveraging our considerable forensics expertise. It should take a more active approach—a forward deployed botnet if you will—that silently, but vigilantly, monitors the behavior of suspected malware, tracing it to its source."

"No system is full proof," Nora said. "What happens when it fails?"

Lionel smiled. "No system is perfect, so I propose we collaborate with the insurance industry. We have earthquake and flood insurance, why not cybersecurity insurance? We can even fund our operation by selling our data to insurance firms so they can better price risk."

The Admiral pursed his lips. "There anything else the board needs to know about your proposal?" he said, his eyes glazing over.

Lionel wiped sweat off his brow. He worried he was losing his audience. "We would also have to lobby for a regulatory and legal regime that proscribes a framework under which we can operate. We'll need to work hand-in-hand with government. After all, without federal cooperation and consent, we'll get nowhere."

"What about the risk to government?" Whitehall said. "Why would the federal government allow the private sector to develop capabilities that threaten its cyber-warfare monopoly? What's to stop a well-trained rogue at a private company from using these skills for nefarious purposes?"

"What's stopping government employees from doing that now?"

Whitehall grimaced.

Lionel softened his tone. "Look, nobody thinks this'll be easy, but we have to try. The government can't strike back against cyber attackers every time they target a private corporation. Unless we enable companies to strike back, these breaches will never cease."

"What do you propose then?" Dr. Lopez said.

"That leads me to my final point," Lionel said, smiling. "The exploits we develop would be limited in scope and never extend from the cyber domain to the physical world. That remains the government's prerogative.

"Initially, our solutions would include reconnaissance of suspected hackers' networks. We'd also design algorithms that search and destroy spyware and malicious code. And when a hacker becomes too dangerous, like the one who killed my son, we can apply more aggressive measures like active surveillance of personal devices to build a legal case against him or her."

Several board members nodded. Whitehall frowned, then said, "Okay. I think we've seen enough for today." He glanced at Lionel. "We'll deliberate and get back to you."

&

The hunter-killer teams seated before Lionel looked like neither hunters nor killers. They were more like a renegade circus freak show, an eclectic mix of clean-cut military veterans, pencil-necked computer geeks, former quant traders, and tattooed misfits.

Standing behind a wooden lectern, Lionel had one chance to make them his.

"I woke up late this morning," Lionel began. "My dog pissed on my cornflakes, and my wife chewed my ass on the way out the door." Lionel paused for effect. "Suffice it to say, I'm feeling kinda frisky this morning."

Nervous laughter rippled through the audience. He continued. "I don't give a rat's ass if you smoke pot, love to pick your nose, or have a foot fetish. Hell, I probably hired you because you do.

"Many of you don't fit the federal profile," Lionel said, finger quoting the word "profile," "but you've got the skills I need, and you're probably all more capable than the Feds. You just don't know it yet."

Several people nodded.

"But I'm not here to talk about my morning or to tell you you're shit-hot hackers. You already know that. I'm here to tell you why a private company's now in the hacking business.

"Hackers develop new exploits and cybersecurity companies develop countermeasures. I danced to this hypnotic tune until a hacker killed my son.

"You see, without any credible form of deterrence, cyber criminals and nation-states will never stop. Nations with sophisticated offensive cyber capabilities may deter them, but there's nothing to stop them from stealing intellectual property from private citizens or companies. It's time these cyber criminals faced consequences for their actions. It's time they faced us.

"We hit back."

The crowd roared.

Lionel held up his hand until the cheering faded. "While what we're doing here is noble, it's very risky. We're still operating on dubious legal ground. It is only by the grace of a classified executive order that we're in business today. As such, it's critical that we observe five operating principles. Violation of any one of them will result in your immediate termination.

"Number one: no first use of a cyber weapon. Number two: no cyber attacks without verifying the hacker's identity and culpability. Number three: proportionate response—we will never escalate an attack beyond the level at which our adversary initiated theirs. Ladies and gentlemen, our business treads on dangerous ground. The wrong action could trigger an international crisis. This leads me to number four: if we suspect the attacker is a nation-state, we cease all operations immediately and report the incident to federal authorities.

"Lastly, you're to maintain absolute secrecy. If you divulge what we do here to anyone, you put yourself, your family, and the corporation at risk.

"Now that we've covered the rules of the road, let's get to work."

                                 ಬ

"Lionel, why the hell's the ACLU calling me? Something about a violation of individual privacy. Could you give me a little insight on what's going on?" Gil Reynolds said over the phone, his voice simmering as if trying to contain his rage.

Lionel propped his feet up on his desk and grinned. "Nope."

Gil raised his voice. "Goddammit Lionel, you need to keep me in the loop. The ACLU's subpoenaing CyberFortress for the Matheson trial."

"You've got nothing to worry about, Gil. Remember how you structured Farseer Technologies? We're completely off balance sheet. The less you know, the better. Plausible deniability and all that jazz. You know the drill: deny, obfuscate, counter-accuse. You're a lawyer for Christ's sake."

"Jesus H. Christ, Lionel. You're gonna bring CyberFortress down."

"No, I won't. Because I'm careful."

"You better watch your back, Lionel. The board's getting nervous. Investors are starting to ask questions."

"Gil, did the legal entity known as CyberFortress help law enforcement bust Ernie Matheson?"

"Technically no, but Farseer may have."

"You sure about that?"

"Well, no, but…"

"Then you have your answer."

"This better not happen again, Lionel," Gil said before hanging up.

Lionel laughed. If the ACLU subpoenaing one of his investors was the only blowback from Farseer's first cyber campaign, then it'd been a resounding success. Because of his team, Ernie Matheson would be going to prison for a long time.

The Farseer team had uncovered Matheson's burglary operation by mapping out his victims' social networks on Facebook and focusing on outliers—people who lay outside the bulk of their connections. By correlating public data with a subset of these suspects, and after running psychographic profiles on them, Farseer researchers had narrowed the search down to Matheson. They presented the information to the FBI, who then obtained a warrant for Farseer to hack into Matheson's mobile devices and Facebook account.

After monitoring Matheson's wealthy "friends" for vacation-related status updates, the Farseer team tracked Matheson's movements using his device's GPS. When Matheson went to a potential victim's home, Farseer notified the FBI, who, in turn, reached out to local law enforcement. When police arrived at the scene, they'd caught Matheson red-handed.

Whenever Lionel had a small victory, the picture of Reggie on his desk always sobered him. It reminded him why he'd started this business in the first place.

&

At the end of another long day, Lionel's office phone rang. "Hi, Pete," Lionel said, "you got anything new for me?"

"Sure do. Turns out the attack on your son originated from China. We think it's Unit 61398."

Lionel sat back in his chair, pondering the implications. It didn't make any sense. "Why do you think it's the Chinese? What would motivate them to kill my son?"

"I can't speak to their motivations," Pete said. "All I can say is that the attack originated from DNS servers in Shanghai."

"When did it happen?"

"Give me second," Pete said, followed by rapid keyboard tapping. "The attack most likely occurred between 8 and 10 p.m. local time."

"That square with a nine-to-five government job in Shanghai?" Lionel asked.

"Ah…No."

"Where would that be a regular nine-to-five job?"

"Ah…Russia?"

"Yup. Dig a little deeper. Assume nothing's what it seems." Lionel hung up the phone.

He was hopeful. Slowly but surely he'd catch the bastard who'd murdered his son. Whoever had done it had been sophisticated enough to run a false flag operation implicating a co-belligerent in the ongoing Russo-Chinese War. Russia certainly had motive to frame the Chinese, but Lionel couldn't wrap his head around why the Russians would target the children of CyberFortress employees.

The phone rang again. "Lionel, this is John Chang. They got my son. My son's dead. I want you to spare no expense in getting these criminals. What progress have you made?"

Lionel sighed. The last thing he needed was CyberFortress's CEO, who was also the chairman of Farseer's board, breathing down his neck.

"John, you know I can't disclose that information. Even to you. You don't have Top Secret SCI clearance."

Chang lashed out. "Then why the hell am I investing in your operation, Lionel? Show some results by the end of next week or I'll replace you with someone who will."

Running his fingers through his hair, Lionel seethed. The last thing he needed was the spotlight. Finding these killers required patience and time. Now, he had neither. "I'll give you a black-lined report in two weeks."

℃

Two weeks later, Lionel sat tapping his legs against a chair outside Chang's CyberFortress office. "Mr. Chang will see you now," an attractive brunette said. Lionel steeled himself and walked into the room.

Chang was old school. His office was straight out of a Norman Rockwell painting. "How's it going, Lionel?" Chang said with a smile. Lionel suspected it was forced.

"I'm doing fine. Very busy." Lionel hated pleasantries.

"Always blunt and to the point. Let's slow down a little. How's the family?"

Lionel grimaced. Chang wasn't going to make this easy. "Fine. Why?"

"How's Janet doing?"

"She lost her only son. How you think she's doing?" Lionel snapped. Chang's touchy-feely routine was pissing him off.

Chang's grin vanished. His brow furrowed in a facade of concern. "I didn't mean to upset you, Lionel. Remember, I lost a son too. Some days I think Betty's gonna kill herself. To be frank, I wanted to ask for your advice on how to cope."

Shaking his head, Lionel said, "I'm sorry I lashed out at you. I cope the only way I know how: by immersing myself in my work."

"So I've heard," Chang said. "Your people have been telling me you're sleeping at the office. While I admire the dedication, it's not healthy. And it's bad for morale."

Nodding, Lionel said, "I know it."

"While we're on that topic, is that report ready for me?"

"It is." Lionel handed Chang the black-lined document.

"What's the key takeaway?"

"Attack vectors indicate it's the Russian military, but I'm not so sure."

"You're not sure? Your people tell me they're ninety percent sure. We need to strike back, goddammit." Chang pounded his fist on his desk.

Lionel tried his best to hide his frustration that his people were secretly meeting with Chang. "Well, John, if it's the Russian government, we're forbidden by law to strike back. If we are, as you say, certain it's the Russians, then we're required to report it to the FBI. Then the Feds would take it from there."

"Bullshit!" Chang shouted. "We can always do something. I'm not going to sit by and take this crap from the Russians. They killed my son!"

"You don't know that for sure. And if we cowboy it and attack, they'll retaliate. Are you ready to start World War Three based on data that has a ten percent chance of being wrong?"

Chang fumed, hesitated, and then said, "But we're ninety percent certain. We'll never know with one hundred percent certainty."

"Maybe not, but I'm sure that with another month of analysis, we can increase our confidence to at least ninety-five percent, or rule out Russian involvement entirely."

"Fine. You have a month to retaliate without violating any legal statutes or I'm convening Farseer's board to nominate a new CEO. Work smarter, not harder. Think outside of the box."

Lionel bit his lip and glared at Chang. "I'll do my best."

୫

"The chairman of the board's here to see you," Tina, Lionel's admin, said. She stood expectantly outside his office.

"Why did Chang come all the way to our offices?" Lionel said.

She shrugged. "Should I let him in?"

Lionel nodded.

Chang waltzed into the room, beaming.

"Why are you in such a good mood?" Lionel asked.

"Oh, you don't know?" Chang said, seemingly surprised by Lionel's question.

"Don't know what?"

"Put the news on." Chang pointed to Lionel's plasma screen TV.

"Okay," Lionel said, puzzled at Chang's request. When he turned on the TV, he watched two Russian MiG 29 fighters painted in gray tiger-stripe camouflage streak over Shanghai. Not good. Not good at all. "What am I supposed to see here?" he said.

"Oh, that's got nothing to do with why I'm here. Did you hear what happened on the Trans-Siberian Pipeline?"

Now Lionel knew where this was going. "You didn't. Please tell me you didn't do it, John?"

Chang smiled. "Of course we did. We hacked into Gazprom's SCADA controllers—you know, their supervisory control and data acquisition operating system."

"Yes, I know what SCADA means. What I don't know is why the hell no one consulted with me, the goddamn CEO of the company, before launching this attack," Lionel said, struggling to contain his rage. "Who worked on this project with you?"

"No need to get your panties in a bunch, Lionel," Chang said in a manner that bordered on patronizing. "You were procrastinating when we needed immediate action."

Lionel simmered. Then it suddenly dawned on him why Russian MiGs were flying over Shanghai. "You routed the attack through Chinese servers, didn't you?" Lionel said.

"Of course we did," Chang said, grinning. "Not only did we avoid a direct attack on the Russia government, but we also covered our tracks by implicating the Chinese."

"What the hell, Chang? You have no idea what you've done. Again, who worked on this project with you?"

"Steven Vance. Why?"

Lionel picked up his phone, "Tina, I want Steven Vance in my office immediately." He slammed down the phone.

"C'mon Lionel, you're blowing this out of proportion," Chang said.

Lionel turned up the volume on his TV. A reporter spoke excitedly, "What had begun as a border skirmish has now escalated into a broader regional conflict. The Russians launched an air raid on downtown Shanghai this morning, likely targeting the headquarters of Chinese cyber war Unit 61398 in retaliation for an alleged cyber attack on Gazprom's Trans-Siberian Pipeline. While there were no immediate casualties in the pipeline attack, the explosion was so massive that satellites detected it from space. Initial estimates of Chinese casualties in the air raid number in the hundreds. The majority of victims are civilians."

Frustrated, Lionel ran his fingers through his hair. Chang's mouth hung wide open. Just before Lionel could tell him off, a rail-thin blonde man knocked on Lionel's glass pane door. "Come in, Steven," Lionel said.

Steven glanced at Chang. "Oh hi, Mr. Chang," he said. Steven then looked at Lionel. "Your admin said you wanted to see me."

Angling his head toward the TV, Lionel said, "You responsible for this?"

Steven inclined his head toward Chang as if looking for approval. Chang nodded. Steven smiled and said, "Mr. Chang asked me to retaliate against the Russians without directly attacking their military. I thought targeting Gazprom's Trans-Siberian Pipeline would have the most impact. So I hacked into the pipeline's SCADA controllers and reprogrammed their pump speeds and valve settings to malfunction, allowing more pressure to build up in the system than their design tolerances allowed."

"And let me guess," Lionel said, "you routed the exploit through a Shanghai server and peppered your code with Chinese characters to camouflage your attack."

"That's right."

Lionel folded his arms across his chest. "So you escalated an attack against a nation-state that may or may not have attacked us first, violating Farseer's second, third and fourth operating principles. And if it turns out that the Russians weren't involved in the ransomware attack, you'll have also violated our first principle."

Steven glanced over at Chang. "Mr. Jones, I was only following orders, so…"

"So what?" Lionel said. "We have a chain of command and five principles we've all sworn to uphold. Because you've failed to abide by those principles, hundreds of innocent civilians are dead. Your actions also put the safety and security of the entire United States population at risk by launching an attack against one nation-state while implicating another."

Chang grabbed Lionel by the arm. "C'mon, Lionel. Steven was just doing what he was told."

Undeterred, Lionel continued, "Steven, pack your shit and get the fuck out of my office. You're fired."

Steven looked back at Chang, as if expecting the chairman to rescue him. Chang put his arm over Steven's shoulder and escorted him out of Lionel's office. On Chang's way out, Lionel overheard him say, "Don't worry, Steven. I'll talk him down from the ledge and get you your job back."

Chang walked back into the office. "What the hell was that?"

"John, you need to stay the hell out of my company's business. You could've have started World War Three. Now I have to clean up your mess."

Chang's eyes widened. "Excuse me?" He got in Lionel's face and poked his finger in the man's chest. "Now you listen to me, jerkoff. You say one word about this to the board and I'll make sure you're gone. I'll tell them you authorized this attack. And, after your little tantrum, you know Steven will back me up. If you go to the Feds, it'll be our word against yours."

The chairman stepped back, then continued. "But I'm a reasonable man, so I'm gonna give you two weeks to determine with over ninety-five percent confidence who the culprit is. If you can't, you're fired." Chang stormed out of the room.

By law, Lionel was supposed to notify federal authorities. But if he did, there was a risk that he and not Chang would go to prison. It was a lose-lose situation. So he decided to keep the incident to himself while he focused on the more immediate concern of keeping his job.

⁎

Lionel's deadline was a week away, and he still couldn't rule out Russian involvement. But he was damn sure they had no motive to murder American children.

Yet he had to show Chang some progress, so he'd called a favor with an old Army buddy at the National Security Council to get signoff at the highest levels. His plan was to infect Russian networks with passive spyware.

After monitoring months of historical log files pirated from Russian network systems, he'd discovered traces of a botnet that had been active during the times his son and Chang's had been murdered. Going back further, he'd traced signals sent through a host of routers stretching from Russia through Poland, then through Germany and the United Kingdom, and ultimately originating from Hoboken, New Jersey.

In the course of a week, Lionel had uncovered a double false flag operation and the perpetrator wasn't even a nation-state. A few more mouse clicks and Lionel would have the criminal's name.

Gus Rudometkin.

Lionel was speechless. The man who'd murdered his son was a former CyberFortress employee. Lionel had fired Gus over a year ago for watching porn on his corporate laptop.

Buoyed by the euphoria of discovering his son's killer, Lionel was jolted back to reality when the phone rang.

Janet screamed.

"Lionel, our house is on fire!"

છ

"I have multiple exploits ready to go. I've got control of Rudometkin's car, and I'm ready to drive it off a cliff. Or I can burn his house down. Or both," Pete Carlson said, his giant noggin teetering on a pencil-thin neck like a human PEZ dispenser. He sat at a workstation amid a sea of control panels and flashing lights in the company's security operations center. A widescreen dominated the far end of the facility with various multicolored lines tracing suspected attacks in progress to their points of origin.

The destruction of Lionel's home had been the last straw for everyone from Janet to Chang. While Janet had counseled retreat to Alaska where they could live off-grid for the rest of their lives, nearly everyone else craved blood. Chang wanted to take out Rudometkin so badly, he'd ordered Lionel's employees to devise multiple exploits to be ready to go at a mouse click.

And he'd done it all behind Lionel's back.

"Did Chang order you to execute these exploits?" Lionel said.

Pete vibrated with what Lionel sensed was nervousness, and then nodded. Pete had followed Lionel to Farseer. Besides Lionel's wife and the men Lionel had gone to war with, Pete was the only other person Lionel trusted with his life.

"Good," Lionel said. "Could you do me a little favor? Could you build a GUI that's identical to our attack console? When Chang asks you to launch the malware, turn on your webcam, invite him to your computer, and walk him through the attack step by step."

Pete's face contorted as if in confusion. "Is there something I should know, Mr. Jones?"

"Not yet," Lionel said, "The less you know, the safer you'll be. You okay with this?"

Pete nodded. Lionel patted him on the back. "Great. I knew I could count on you, buddy."

Lionel turned to walk away.

"Oh, Mr. Jones," Pete said.

"Yes?"

"What about Rudometkin? Are we going to launch a cyber attack on his computer?"

Even Lionel had fantasized about the satisfaction he'd get from killing Rudometkin. But he knew better. If he faltered now, his grand experiment would fail. He had to rise above the anger and overwhelming desire for vengeance. "No," Lionel said, "I have something much better in mind."

Lionel pulled out his mobile phone and called his old Stanford roommate, Al Meyer.

"It's about to go down." Pete said over the phone.

"Good. I'm en route." Lionel hung up his office phone, put his jacket on, and made his way to Pete's cubicle.

When he arrived, Lionel said, "When's Chang gonna be here?"

"In about ten minutes."

"Is the webcam on?"

Pete nodded.

"Did you tip off Rudometkin on the hacker forums?"

"He knows."

Lionel smiled. "Good. Nervous?"

"Hell yeah!"

"Don't worry. You'll be fine. I'm heading back to my office. If Chang sees me with you, he'll know something's up. Good luck, buddy." Lionel slapped Pete on the back and returned to his office, where he keyed up real-time video from Pete's webcam.

Five minutes later, he watched Chang commit over half a dozen felonies with an arrogant confidence that would make Louis XIV blush. Hours later, the pirated video that Gus hacked from CyberFortress servers became headline news.

Within twenty-four hours, Chang was forced to step down as both CEO of CyberFortress and chairman of Farseer. He also faced the prospect of a long prison sentence.

And Gus Rudometkin became an overnight sensation.

&

Lionel stood at a lectern before the men and women who'd made today possible. A large screen towered behind him. He swelled with pride at what they'd accomplished. If his son were alive today, he would be proud of his father.

"Ladies and gentlemen, I have a surprise for you. Many of you have wondered why Gus Rudometkin is still out on the streets, enjoying his recent celebrity, even if he has been in hiding. As you know, despite all the evidence we've gathered against him, the FBI hasn't been able to track him down."

Lowering his head, Lionel hesitated. He was unsure how his audience would react to the next bit of his presentation. He tried to calm himself, struggling to maintain his composure. Taking the clicker, he pointed at the screen. A picture of a young, beaming African-American boy appeared.

"This was Reggie, my only son. He was filled with the promise of a fruitful and productive life, studying computer science at Stanford." Lionel wiped a stray tear from his eye. "As a father, I couldn't have been prouder." Choking up, Lionel forced out his words. "I can't bring Reggie back, but I can do my damnedest to make sure my son's murderer faces justice. That's why we're here today." He slammed his hand on the lectern. "We hit back!"

The crowd went crazy.

Lionel waited for the cheering to subside. He rubbed his moist eyes. "I have a surprise for you today. This one's for Reggie."

The lights dimmed, and Lionel clicked on the screen.

Celebrity Albrecht Meyer sat on his cable show with a smug grin. "I'd like to welcome my next guest, the famed hacker Gus Rudometkin." Lionel's internal audience booed. The Albrecht Meyer show's introductory jingle played on queue. A dumpy, bespectacled, and bearded man waddled across the stage. He beamed. Shaking Meyer's hand, he took a seat. The music faded along with Meyer's smile.

"So, you've just come out of hiding to promote a new book you've written about your various, and if I may say, legendary, cyber exploits," Meyer said.

"Oh, you may certainly say that, Al," Gus said in an awkward cadence.

Meyer responded with a blank expression as if to highlight the weird exchange, and then said, "Apparently, being socially inept is a core requirement for being a world-famous hacker. When's the last time you got laid?"

The crowd hooted. Gus shifted in his seat. Sweat beaded on his forehead. "Ah, the last time was…"

"Never," Meyer interrupted to a chorus of laughter. "Now, in all seriousness, tell us about your new book, *Power to the People.*"

Gus grinned like an evil mastermind about to reveal his plans for world domination. "Well, it's really an autobiography about how I've always been one step ahead of the powers that be. I'm the guy that exposes weaknesses in our cyber defenses. The book details my life as a hacker from the first time I broke into a bank's computer system when I was seven to the time I turned the tables on CyberFortress's CEO when he tried to sabotage my car and burn down my home. Our country is stronger because of me."

"I see." Meyer nodded. "Does exposing these weaknesses involve killing innocent people?"

Gus's face reddened. "What?" he sputtered.

"Has anyone died as a result of your 'patriotic efforts'?"

"Well…ah…nobody is ever…ah…one hundred percent innocent, right?" Gus stuttered.

Meyer's tone hardened. "What the hell's that supposed to mean? What about Reginald Jones?" A picture of Lionel's son appeared on the screen behind Meyer. "Did he deserve to die? Or Oliver Chang?" A picture of a young Asian boy appeared. "Do you think that may have had something to do with John Chang trying to take you out?"

Lionel expected Gus to deny the killings. But Gus just sat on the stage simmering. Then he spoke. "In any war, there's collateral damage. And these boys' fathers were complicit in the cyber-military industrial complex."

Meyer's mouth dropped open. "So you admit to murdering them?"

"I...I never said that," Gus stammered.

"Did you hack into Reginald's car?"

"A magician never reveals his secrets."

Meyer shook his head, jaw unhinged. "Well, it turns out, Gus, I have a little magic trick of my own." The screen flashed again. "First, I want to say something to you from the bottom of my heart: screw you."

The crowd gasped.

Meyer waved at the crowd. "Wait, wait. I promise you there's a good reason why I'm being such a prick."

The screen flashed again. An image of Gus sitting behind a computer and tapping on a keyboard appeared. He wore nothing but his tighty whiteys. His prodigious gut overflowed all the way down to his pelvis, eclipsing his privates. A pyramid of Mountain Dews towered over his stained and ramshackle desk.

The man behind the computer giggled like a girl playing dress up. "You thought you could kill me by burning down my house, little man. Well, I found you, too. Not only are you going to prison, but now I'm going to huff, puff, and burn your house down." Gus howled like a wolf, hit one last key, and chuckled.

Meyer's screen faded to black. The host turned to Gus and said, "That was a video of you hacking into John Chang's smart oven drivers and reprogramming them to set his house on fire. And this is after you killed his son and uploaded an incriminating video of Chang's attempt at retaliation. Fortunately, your attempt to burn down Chang's house failed."

The video faded into images from a local news report showing a neighborhood aflame.

"Unfortunately, this wasn't the first time you've tried to burn someone's house down," Meyer said. "This video shows one time you succeeded. Your attempt to burn down Chang's home failed because the FBI was running a sting operation. You've been under surveillance for several weeks, and now the FBI has footage of you committing the crime. And your book deal—yeah, that's not real either. For that matter, neither is this broadcast. What is real is that you're going to prison for the rest of your life."

The audience on- and off-screen cheered.

Gus stood up, hesitated, and then sprinted toward the exit like a meth-fueled Humpty Dumpy. A mob of FBI agents emerged from the studio audience of undercover law enforcement personnel, and tackled Gus onstage.

Meyer winked at the camera and said, "To the unsung heroes who work in anonymity to deliver terrorists like Gus Rudometkin to justice, I salute you."

Lionel smiled, then returned to his quiet work in the shadows.

END

Afterword

"We Hit Back" was inspired by a thought experiment about the implications of creating and building an offensive cybersecurity company. Today, offensive cyber operations are limited to governments. As such, creating a business that focuses solely on developing cyber exploits would require close coordination with and permission from the government. If I were ever to start an offensive cybersecurity business, this story is almost exactly how I'd approach the task.

I tried to explore as many of the pitfalls inherent in launching offensive cyber weapons as I could in this story. For instance, what would happen if a U.S.-based company launched a cyber attack on a sovereign state? Would the state retaliate against the U.S. government? Then there is the issue of attribution—how does a company know if the entity to which they are attributing an attack is the right target and not a patsy or part of a false flag operation? How could an offensive cybersecurity startup work with federal and local governments to catch cyber criminals without breaking the law? How have advances in the cyber domain such as the advent of the Internet of Things made us more vulnerable in the physical domain?

At the same time, I tried to layer on the pettiness and self-serving nature of corporate politics and how it could add further risks to an offensive cybersecurity enterprise.

First published in *Abyss & Apex*, this story also won an Honorable Mention in the Writers of the Future Contest's second quarter of 2015. I hope you found the story engaging.

Titan's Twins

T itan's pale orange glow haunted Colonel Paul Mason. As Saturn's sixth moon drew closer, so too did an enigma buried beneath swirling ethane clouds. He hoped he wasn't too late. Sara, his wife, and his daughter, June, had already been missing for over a year. He prayed they still lived.

The colony's last signal was an emergency transmission whose message was lost, scrambled by Titan's thick atmospheric soup. After that, no one heard from Möbius Station again.

"Horizon Station. Nemesis Six. Entering Titan's atmosphere. Over," Mason said.

"Affirmative, Nemesis Six. Be advised, you have four hours before Chinese tac sats triangulate your position. Horizon Station. Out."

The four crewmembers were secured tightly in an atmospheric entry module modified for Titan's methane-rich environment. Mason's team had trained extensively on Jupiter's moon Europa, and then spent another year in cryostasis on the long trek to Saturn's outer rings.

After emerging from his long slumber, Mason felt dehydrated. Trace elements of inert Xenon molecules remained in his body, colorless and odorless byproducts of the clathrate-forming gases that made human hibernation possible.

The granite-like Captain Norman Collins, the mission's squat and muscular weapons officer, calibrated and boresighted the module's rail guns.

Lieutenant Maria Hernandez, the medical officer, monitored each team member's vital signs with the fretfulness of a mother hen. Lieutenant Stewart Vanderbeek, the science and engineering officer, kept vigil over the module's heat shield during the long descent into Titan's opaque atmosphere. His thin, wiry form rippled with nervous energy, as he pecked away at his navigation display.

Timing would be tight. The mission's first phase hinged on intercepting Icarus One, a prepositioned dirigible tethered ten klicks above Titan's surface.

"Icarus identified! Deploying parachutes." Vanderbeek said.

The module jerked as its descent abruptly decelerated.

Mason's map showed a blip about twenty klicks from the module. He peered through his viewscreen to get a better perspective, but Titan's orange smog made it impossible to see the dirigible from this distance. He'd have to trust Vanderbeek's ability to navigate through the turbulent eddies and waves of Titan's frothy atmosphere on instruments alone.

"Ten klicks and closing!" Vanderbeek reported.

Seconds later, Vanderbeek said, "Five…four…three klicks!"

"Slow down!" Mason yelled, struggling to hide his unease.

"I'm trying!" Vanderbeek was shaking.

Mason could now see the dirigible through the haze. "Change course!"

The module shook violently as Vanderbeek pulled back on the yoke. Mason watched in dismay as the dirigible vanished again into the fog and the module spun wildly off course. The crewmembers turned toward Mason, eyes wide with panic. "What now, sir?" Vanderbeek asked.

A klaxon sounded. Hull breach! Mason acted. "Get your dorsal gliders ready for deployment. Eject on my mark. Five-four-three-two-one. Mark!"

The module separated into four quarters, scattering the crew throughout a hydrocarbon sky. The dense atmosphere and turbulent winds generated from Titan's tidal lock with Saturn twirled Mason like a baton.

Mason's training took over. He splayed his body like a starfish to maximize its surface area and slow his descent. Once he was parallel to Titan's surface, he deployed his suit's dorsal gliders, increasing his coefficient of friction. Then he activated his high frequency radio antenna. "Nemesis One, Two, and Three. Nemesis Six. Radio check, over."

Static.

"Nemesis One, Two, and Three. Nemesis Six. I say again, radio check, over."

"Nemesis Six. Nemesis Two. Acknowledged. Over."

After Collins and Hernandez responded in kind, Mason felt relieved his people were still alive.

"Nemesis Team. Nemesis Six. Proceed to objective Zulu via glider flight. Check your oxygen and pressure readings every five minutes. I don't want any crispy critters on my watch."

Mason aimed his glider toward the dirigible, soaring toward it. With a high ratio of atmospheric density to one-seventh of Earth's surface gravity, humans could literally fly on Titan.

The homing beacon on Mason's arm illuminated his position relative to Icarus One. He was getting close. Four hundred meters. A small black splotch appeared beneath the hoary methane clouds. Mason dove and then angled toward his target. Reaching it, he grappled onto a ladder attached to the command module at the dirigible's base. His team followed, disengaging their dorsal gliders and climbing inside.

Once his team was in, Mason sealed the hatch, initiated the pressure system, and turned on the oxygen pumps and heaters. "Give Icarus 'bout twenty minutes to adjust to Earth's atmospheric composition, then we'll de-mask and start phase two," Mason said.

Colonel Mason had been the last choice to lead this mission, and he knew it. While he possessed all the qualifications of command, the shrinks had vetoed his selection. Too personally involved, they'd argued. But time was money, and Mason was the only commander who could assemble a team and get to Titan on short notice.

Of course, the suits at Saturn Horizon Corporation had wanted to use clones. Much cheaper, and less legal liability if you ignored the Outer Planetary Genome Accords prohibiting their use. But the last thing the Chinese and Americans needed in their undeclared war over the outer solar system's resources was an arms race spurred by the manufacture of expendable meat marionettes maiming each other in the cold vacuum of space.

After disengaging Icarus One's tether, the crew steamed toward its next objective at Xanadu, about a hundred kilometers west along Titan's equator. One of the brightest spots on Titan, Xanadu was a plateau the size of Australia. Burrowed several kilometers beneath Titan's icy bedrock was Möbius Station, rich with oxygen synthesized from underground melt water.

As Vanderbeek piloted the dirigible, he seemed frustrated. "Vanderbeek, what's got your goat?" Mason asked.

"Sir, this thing feels like it's a hundred years old. Its gears are all worn and rusted."

"Rusted?" Mason hovered over Vanderbeek's shoulder, an annoying habit Mason swore he'd break because it made people nervous. "There's no oxygen on Titan, son. No oxygen, no oxidation."

"Sir, the only way oxygen could be here is if people brought it with them. Either that or this thing's leaking it," Vanderbeek said as he twitched.

"Just how much oxygen's left? This model's less than a decade old. I'd expect hardly any oxygen loss over that period."

Vanderbeek scratched his head. "It's at seventy percent oxygen capacity, but I don't detect any leaks, so it's possible someone used Icarus One before we did."

"We have enough oxygen to get to Möbius Station?"

"We should," said Vanderbeek.

Several hours later, the team reached the outskirts of Möbius Station, with its smokestacks dotting Titan's surface like a checkerboard.

"Vanderbeek, drop anchor. Program the dirigible to retract the anchor in ten minutes and to head back to our rendezvous point on autopilot. If we fail, Saturn Horizon will need to send another team," Mason ordered. "Everyone suit up and check your oxygen and pressure gauges. It's time to disembark. Collins, does everyone have their rail guns locked and loaded?"

Collins gave Mason a thumbs-up.

"Alright then. I'll see y'all on the far side of the objective. Good luck!" Mason launched himself from the command module's ladder, pulled the ripcord to deploy his dorsal glider, and headed toward the surface. During his descent, he noticed none of the smokestacks rippled with the steaming carbon dioxide emissions he'd expect from a one hundred sixteen-person colony.

∞

The team scoured Möbius Station's surface for an opening. Every airlock they found was welded shut from the inside.

"Sir, it looks like someone cut this airlock open with a high-powered laser and then resealed it," Collins said.

"Sounds just like a Chinese exo-squad. I think we're gonna have to do the same thing," Mason transmitted.

Collins pulled out a hand-sized cutting robot. He motioned for the team to disperse, then placed the bot on the airlock, and pulled out a remote. He gave a thumbs-up and then hid behind an ice rock about one hundred meters from the airlock. "Take cover. If there's any free oxygen left in that hole, the bot's laser could trigger an explosion," said Collins.

The team huddled behind the ice rock as Collins remotely operated the bot. After some small bursts of flame, the bot cut an opening into the airlock.

"Let's go!" Mason said.

The team descended a ceramisteel ladder, with their rail guns trained on the secondary hatch at the tube's base. Once everyone was inside, Collins put the upper hatch back in place, resealing it with firmajelly. Mason activated a vacuum pump on the chamber wall, expelling excess methane and reducing the chamber's atmospheric pressure.

Once the vacuum pump's indicator light flashed green, Collins opened the lower hatch and the team entered Möbius Station's oxygen-rich and temperature-controlled environment.

It was dark. So dark that the goggles' night vision setting failed to capture enough ambient light to operate well, forcing the team to switch to sonar mode. Heat exchangers hummed in the background, while a steady drip-drop pattered in the distance. Aside from the carbon dioxide pumps, the atmospheric systems seemed to be working.

His sonar indicating an empty corridor, Mason activated the spotlights on his enviro-suit. He reasoned that if the Chinese had set up an ambush, they would've attacked by now.

"Vanderbeek, how's the air? It safe to give the 'all clear'?" Mason wanted to minimize the use of the enviro-suits. They were critical for operating on the surface, but their bulk would impede subterranean operations.

"Everything seems stable. Even the concentrations of carbon dioxide are within normal limits. The carbon exchangers only activate once CO_2 levels reach a certain threshold."

"Which probably means no one's breathed the rarefied air here for quite some time," Mason said.

"That's a strong possibility, sir. Otherwise, the air's safe."

"Alright then. All clear. All clear." The team quickly removed their enviro-suits.

"Vanderbeek, see if you can turn the lighting system back on. No use wasting our fuel cells."

Vanderbeek quickly restored lighting after finding a nearby wall-mounted power module.

The station's blue ceramic-paneled corridors seemed pristine. The team crept cautiously down a narrow corridor until the space opened up into a broader antechamber where things weren't so clean and ordered.

Cracked wall panel fragments and white dust littered the floor in heaps. Blackened scorch marks covered seared sections of the wall.

"Scour the rubble for human remains. Looks like the Chinese've already been here."

Titan was the greatest prize in the solar system, with hundreds of times more liquid hydrocarbons than all of Earth's oil and natural gas reserves. Yet something didn't seem right. If the Chinese had attacked the station, they'd have defended it.

"Colonel, you need to see this." Hernandez handed Mason a piece of thin white metal.

"What the hell you want me to do with this, L-T?"

Despite her six months of extensive training with Mason, Hernandez still seemed to bristle at Mason's style. To Mason she was an intellectual. A lifetime of reverence for the scientific method had cemented a healthy skepticism in her and seemed to make her hesitant to draw conclusions from limited data. "Sir, I've never seen nor felt a metallic substance like this before. It's soft and flexible, yet restores its shape after I crinkle it."

"You think it's some new kind of Chinese body armor?"

Hernandez looked doubtful. "It's possible. But if they've got the technological chops to create something like this, we're in trouble."

"Sir! Check this out!" Collins yelled from the far end of the chamber.

When Mason reached Collins, he saw faded blood spatters staining the wall.

"Hernandez, take some samples and upload the data to the eyes in the sky," Mason said. "Hopefully we'll get a DNA match. If not, they should be able to identify the blood's genotype, and I bet it's Chinese. While we wait, let's bed down. Four hours on, four hours off. Two people on security at all times."

∓

"This is the first time we've acquired blood samples from Möbius Station, and we were surprised to find one of the samples isn't human," the voice on the comms device said.

The response frustrated Mason. "What the hell's that supposed to mean? Have bots been here before?"

"Something like that."

"What about the other samples? They Chinese?"

"Negative."

Mason's heart stopped as he imagined the death of his family. "Whose DNA is it then?"

"I'm sorry, colonel, that's classified."

"Why?"

"I'm not at liberty to discuss it."

"Fine. What about the other DNA profile?" Mason said, struggling to hold back his anger about being out of the loop.

"The last sample is ninety-nine point seven percent human."

"That's not possible. Run the test again. Maybe the data was corrupted."

"Negative, Colonel. The signal you sent was crystal clear, and we ran the tests several times to be certain."

Exasperated, Mason threw his hands in the air. "Horizon One, what the hell am I supposed to do with this information?"

"There's more."

"Well don't be shy. Out with it."

"The DNA profile is nearly identical to that of *Homo neanderthalensis.*"

"Say what?"

"It's Neanderthal DNA."

଎

The slanted hole bored into the ice was a perfect cylinder. Whoever created it had cut through advanced ceramisteel. Twelve hours after arriving at Möbius Station and after an exhaustive search through its vast subterranean labyrinth of storage compartments, laboratories, and living quarters, this crevice was the only thing left to explore. Mason's only solace was that the colonists had to be somewhere on the other side of that hole, alive or dead.

The bore glistened with melt water from the station's higher thermal gradient. It had a three-meter diameter and opened into a black abyss. Sonar indicated it stretched about a klick into Titan's crust, where it bottomed into a chamber.

Mason radioed headquarters, "Horizon One. Nemesis Six. Investigating the bore. We'll report our status every thirty minutes. Nemesis Six. Out."

The team descended the ice burrow's steady grade at a slow, measured pace, keeping their rail guns on a swivel.

The absence of light amplified Mason's other senses. The steady drip-drip of melt water splashed and reverberated below. Sound travelled farther in Titan's lower gravity, and the air grew colder in the descent, quickly dropping twenty degrees Fahrenheit.

"Sir, what do you make of this Neanderthal business?" Collins asked.

Mason spat out a wad of chewing tobacco and watched it float toward the tunnel floor. "Hell if I know. My best guess is that the colonists were working on some sort of genetic experiment that went tits up."

Lieutenant Hernandez shook her head.

"Don't like my theory?" Mason spat again.

Hernandez paused for a moment and then said, "Sir, I wish your theory were true. I just don't see any evidence to support it. In all the chambers we've explored, I didn't see any lab equipment capable of conducting advanced biological research. If you cross-reference the original colony ship's manifest, there's also no evidence these colonists transported any significant biotech equipment."

"What's your theory?"

"Well, sir, without any more data, I haven't got one."

Vanderbeek fidgeted, drawing Mason's attention. "You got a theory, Stew?"

The science officer shook his head. "No, sir, but this whole Neanderthal thing intrigues me. They say Neanderthal DNA accounts for one to four percent of the non-African human genome."

"So?"

"At some point in our evolution, early humans interbred with Neanderthals."

"So what the hell happened to them?"

"To this day, anthropologists still don't agree on why the species disappeared. Some say Neanderthals failed to adapt to a change in climate. Others think primitive humans wiped them out. But who knows? It's always puzzled me that a species with larger brains and stronger limbs failed to survive, but we did."

Mason spat again. "I thought Neanderthals were stupid."

"It's likely they were more intelligent than *Homo sapiens*. Unfortunately, we'll never know."

"Unless, of course, we find 'em down here," Mason quipped.

∓

The ambush was perfect. The intruders didn't register on sonar. Lieutenant Hernandez's screams were the only thing that marked their presence. Those same screams lingered long after her disappearance, as the tunnel conspired with low gravity to perpetuate her piercing echo. Whatever had taken her had disappeared into the cold blackness.

"Hernandez. Report," Mason ordered. "Hernandez. Report!" The uncontested abduction terrified Mason, but he did his best not to show it.

"Load up with EM flechette rounds," Mason said, "our primary mission now is to rescue Hernandez."

The survivors formed a wedge with Mason at the center, rail guns at the ready.

"Looks like we're near the end of the line. Collins, when this tunnel ends and we reach the T-intersection, I want you to go left and secure the corridor. Vanderbeek, do the same on the right. I'll scan both ends while you're working and make a decision on what we'll do next," Mason said.

Collins and Vanderbeek did as ordered.

Mason scanned the right corridor, which extended about fifty meters until it dead-ended. He then scanned the left tunnel, which stretched for over a klick. "We go left."

Mason turned, then oblivion.

ℰℛ

Mason awoke in a soft bed in the far right corner of a brightly lit four-by-four meter cell. A solitary figure stood beside the bed. As Mason took in the man's features, something felt very wrong. The man could've passed for Mason's older brother. He was much thinner and less muscular than Mason, but anyone living on Titan for an extended period would experience some degree of muscle atrophy.

The man seemed uncomfortable—as if he wasn't sure how to handle this encounter. "Colonel Mason, I don't know how to put this, but I'm Colonel Paul Mason."

ℰℛ

The other Paul Mason had been tight with information. Colonel Mason had no idea about his team's whereabouts. He didn't even know where he was, though he suspected he was somewhere deep beneath Titan's surface.

Wherever Colonel Mason was, the room had technology more advanced than anything he'd ever seen. His room had four impenetrable walls with no visible entrance or exit. When Paul Mason entered, he walked through the wall. It didn't matter. Colonel Mason didn't need an exit to execute his plan.

The elder Paul Mason arrived right on schedule with Colonel Mason's breakfast. "How ya doing this morning, son? Feeling any better? I'm sorry there's no tobacco. I feel your pain. I had to kick my habit cold turkey a few years back."

Colonel Mason launched himself at Paul Mason with all the agility and grace of a drunken whale out of water. Paul Mason seemed only happy to oblige, using his years of experience operating in a low gee environment to his advantage. The elder Mason casually peeled away from Colonel

Mason's attack and used Colonel Mason's momentum against him, driving him into a wall.

"Son, you're dumber'n you look," the elder Mason jibed. "I forgot how impatient I used to be. I know you want answers, and I'm doing my best to get you them, but you need to earn my trust first. This ain't exactly an auspicious start."

Colonel Mason lay crumbled in a disheveled heap on the cell's cold blue floor. His elder self stood there, waiting.

"You calmer now, stud?" the elder Mason asked.

Colonel Mason nodded. "Are you gonna tell me what happened to my team and the colonists?"

"Your crew's doing fine. The colonists are fine too, but we'll have to take things one day at a time."

"Bullshit. I need proof. I want to see my crew now."

The elder Mason shook his head and laughed. "I thought you might say that. Unfortunately, they're also in quarantine, but I can give you the next best thing."

Holographic representations of Hernandez, Collins, and Vanderbeek materialized in the center of the cell. "Y'all all right?" Colonel Mason asked.

"I'm in one piece, sir," Collins answered. "Though I hope they don't court martial me when I return earthside for failing to evade capture."

Colonel Mason chuckled. "Son, I don't think there's anything we could've done. Hell, I doubt there's anything anybody could've done. We're all just lucky to be in one piece."

"Sir, have they told you how they were able to capture us or why they're living down here?" Hernandez said.

"And sir," Vanderbeek interrupted. "Have they explained why our hosts all look like older versions of us?"

"You too, eh?" Colonel Mason laughed. "Unfortunately, no. I've been fixing to ask that, only my temper got in the way."

The elder Mason looked at the colonel. "You satisfied your people are safe?"

"Maybe. Will I ever see them in person?"

"Of course. You'll join 'em as soon as the quarantine ends, which should be in a month or so. That good enough for you?"

Colonel Mason nodded.

The elder Mason smiled. "Say bye to your friends."

The holograms winked out. Colonel Mason inclined his head toward the elder Mason. "Now, can you tell me why the hell I'm talking to myself?"

The elder Mason appeared to force a smile. "Not today. You still haven't told me why Saturn Horizon sent another team here."

The question confused Colonel Mason, "Another team? We're the only one they sent." Colonel Mason was losing his temper again. "You know damn well why I'm here!" He took a deep breath. "I'm sorry. I'm upset. I just want to see my family."

The elder Mason's furrowed brow said everything. Colonel Mason made the same expression when something bothered him. The elder Mason looked away, and then nodded. "I see."

"Now that I've answered your question, tell me where the colonists are."

The old Mason smiled. "We're all thriving here with the Titanians."

"The Titanians? Does this have something to do with the DNA we found on Möbius Station? Are you telling me there really are Neanderthals on Titan?"

The older Mason seemed uncomfortable, as if he'd already said too much. After a long pause, he said, "Your name for them, not theirs."

"How the hell did they get here? Are they some biological experiment gone awry?"

"You wouldn't believe me if I told you."

"Try me."

"No. They'll explain when they're ready."

"What about my wife and daughter?"

The elder Mason looked Colonel Mason in the eyes. "They're not your wife and daughter."

&

When the seven foot tall Neanderthal male entered the room, his musky stench nearly knocked Mason to the floor. While he was thin and had a weak musculature, his barrel-shaped chest and broad shoulders seemed more robust than the average human's. Mason chalked the creature's height and weaker musculature to Titan's low gravity.

The male regarded Mason with highly expressive eyes that seemed to belie a far deeper intelligence than the creature's brutish build would've suggested. The Neanderthal had a prominent brow ridge that separated his pale-white face from his sloped forehead, which receded into a wild shock of scarlet hair. His large squat nose, protruding jaw and weak chin underscored his otherness.

In a low guttural growl, the Neanderthal addressed Mason in perfect English, "Colonel Mason, I'm Lormak. Welcome to our home."

Mason didn't know where to begin. "Why are you holding me hostage?"

Lormak held up his hand. "You're a guest, not a hostage."

"What are you? Why're you on Titan?"

"Think of us as distant racial cousins. We fled here from Earth over thirty-thousand Terran years ago."

"You're telling me you're an honest-to-God Neanderthal?"

"Your word, not ours. But yes. We evolved from that species since we fled Earth. Titan's habitat necessitated that."

"This is insane. Neanderthals were primitive hunter-gatherers. How'd you get to Titan?"

Lormak smiled. "What makes you think my ancestors were primitive?"

"The fossil record."

"You put more stock in your fossil record than you should. As with anything in science, the record is incomplete, and sometimes truth gets shrouded in myth."

"What do you mean?"

"Your people have a story about an ancient and advanced civilization lost in prehistoric antiquity."

"Atlantis?" Mason said in disbelief.

"That's the name some used. Others called it Lemuria."

"So what's the truth?"

"We were far more advanced than humans at the time. We regarded your ancestors much as you do chimpanzees—feeling a certain kinship but also recognizing our intellectual and cultural superiority. The heart of our civilization was in the British Isles. About forty thousand years ago, a series of super volcanoes erupted in Europe, choking the skies with sulfur dioxide that blotted out the sun. The earth cooled dramatically, ushering in an ice age.

"The eruptions were so sudden that my people hadn't stocked enough food to survive such cataclysmic climate change. Our leaders sent some of us to the closest place in the solar system that could sustain life. The rest remained on Earth competing or interbreeding with humans to secure what meager provisions they could."

"I don't believe you," Mason said. "If your civilization was so advanced, why didn't it have the foresight to store or make enough food for survival? And why is there no trace of your civilization in the fossil record?"

The Neanderthal laughed. "Sometimes a civilization becomes so efficient it eliminates any margin for waste. Our technology was so advanced it produced food a day before my ancestors consumed it. To maintain social stability, they engineered planned obsolescence into all they produced, ensuring lifetime employment for the population. Everything was biodegradable. Without maintenance, their buildings faded into the wilderness within a century. After the eruptions, my people gathered the surviving technology and placed it on the ark to Titan. Those who couldn't leave scattered throughout a violent and primitive world to forage for food. While they were smarter and stronger than your kind, their caloric requirements were much higher. Most starved, and their technology died with them."

Colonel Mason struggled to take it all in. The story the Neanderthal weaved was fantastical. Without proof, Mason's superiors would ridicule him. His career would end in disgrace. "Why haven't you returned to Earth?"

"When my ancestors arrived on Titan, it was a one-way trip. We had to start over. By the time we'd relearned everything we'd forgotten as a civilization, several generations had been born here. By that point, we were better adapted to Titan than Earth. There was no reason to return."

Mason nodded in understanding. "What of the colonists? Why did you kidnap them?"

"We didn't. When we tunneled into their colony, they attacked us. We'd come in peace, but they'd responded with violence. So, we subdued them before they could signal Earth. At first, they resisted, but over time they came to understand why your people could never know of our existence."

Mason smiled. "You really don't understand humanity do you? My people will keep coming until they learn the truth."

The Neanderthal looked pained. "We know that too well. Your people keep sending missions to Möbius Station, and we're sick of watching them die. That's why we've brought you here."

"That's not true!" Mason was apoplectic.

Lormak shook his head. "Yours was the tenth such mission, and you aren't who you think you are."

Mason fought his urge to argue, but he couldn't deny his elder twin's strange existence. "Why's there an older version of me on Titan?"

Lormak's eyes gleamed with intensity. "Paul's not an older version of you. You're a younger facsimile of him. Your memories are not your own, but were taken from Paul's stored consciousness when he first embarked on a similar mission."

"You telling me I'm a goddamned clone?" Mason said.

"They grew you and eight of your predecessors in a vat. After rescuing the first Paul Mason and his crew, we closed the tunnel and watched the others die. Over and over again. We had to make it stop. That's why we brought you here."

"What do you mean?"

"We're going to give you a choice. If you destroy Möbius Station, you may return here and become part of our community. Otherwise, you can try your luck on Titan's surface."

"In other words betray my people and live, or face certain death," Mason hissed. "No way."

"Suit yourself. We'll release you within the hour."

Mason considered his options. If he was a clone, he was nothing by a pawn. "Wait! Can you prove it?"

Lormak nodded. "I'll show you the bodies."

Mason looked upon eight versions of himself encased in ice, all in varying stages of decomposition. It was hard for him to reconcile himself with the fact that his masters saw him as nothing more than an expendable tool. They didn't deserve his allegiance.

Mason turned to Lormak. "Why us? Why can't you do it?"

"We will if you refuse, but we respect life and wanted to give you a chance to demonstrate your loyalty."

"I see. I'll do it on one condition. I want to see my family."

"They aren't your kin, but I'll arrange a meeting."

⅋⅋

Sara was much older than Mason had remembered, and June had blossomed into a beautiful young woman. Sara couldn't look Mason in the eyes, while June played with her curly blonde hair. He figured they'd rather be anywhere but here. Even he felt awkward despite the emotions welling up in his chest. Yet they still felt like family, even though he knew deep down all they really shared was the real Paul Mason's memories.

Mason fought back a torrent of tears. He mostly succeeded until a single droplet traced down his cheek in the slow motion of Titan's gravity. "I want you both to know that until today, I thought I was a husband and father. While I know that's no longer true, I'll still always love you both."

Mason broke down and cried, and the women's tears soon mixed with his own.

⅋⅋

Colonel Mason and his team navigated through the deserted station in wedge formation, rail guns at the ready. Mason was desperate to find out what happened to his family. Möbius Station's oxygen pumps were operating at full capacity, yet enough methane had leaked into the station that the slightest spark could blow it all sky high.

"Sir, you got to see this." Collins pointed to a rectangular contraption fused to the corridor wall.

Mason went to investigate. His eyes widened when he recognized the explosives. "Abort! Ab…"

Then nothing. Humanity's presence on Titan would have to wait a decade or more before Saturn Horizon or one of its competitors could reseed the colony.

END

Afterword

"Titan's Twins" combined three disparate concepts: clones, operating in Titan's methane-rich atmosphere, and encountering an advanced Neanderthal civilization. Most genre fiction writers would note that most good science fiction stories focus on no more than one speculative element. Introducing any more than that tends to wear down on a reader's suspension of disbelief.

I broke this rule because I wanted to use the two additional speculative elements, namely the advanced Neanderthal civilization and clone concepts, to advance the story with two separate reveals in an effort to surprise the reader. I'll let readers decide if I was able to pull it off successfully.

This piece is one of my hard science fiction stories along with four others in this volume, which include "We Hit Back", "Chasing A.M.I.E.", "Spirals and Starways," and "The Decision." To enhance its verisimilitude, I spent a good deal of time researching how humans would be able to operate in Titan's methane-rich atmosphere. I also reviewed various NASA proposals for airships designed to operate in Titan's atmosphere as well as how Titan's low gravity might impact Earth-origin species over many generations.

I hope all this research made for a more realistic story. "Titan's Twins" was first published in the *Speculate!* in 2017.

JOSÉ BAETAS

Skin

I collect skin. Ebony, alabaster, wrinkled pink with blotches. Color and texture matter not, so long as the flesh is warm and the soul is dark.

I waited at Montgomery Street station as scores of professionals passed by. At the edge of my vision, a fit white-haired woman lurked along the boundary of the bright yellow line demarcating the margin of safety between the platform and the train, and just beyond the notice of the working stiffs standing in line.

The cold rush of dry wind heralded the arrival of the oncoming BART train, a steel snake that conveyed unsuspecting prey through a murk of darkness beneath the San Francisco Bay.

Mrs. Tomlinson must have thought she was so clever, or at least cleverer than her fellow rule-bound travelers. She probably believed no one would notice what she meant to do.

When the train stopped, she merged with the crowd as if she'd been first in line all along. Her brazen entitlement drew me to her like a fly to feces.

No one seemed to notice that she'd cut in line. She'd probably gotten away with it before. She likely thought she was better than everyone else. Like she was special.

She was special all right. Special enough to attract my attention. I followed her onto the train. Because she'd broken the rules, she found a spot. Like clockwork, she chose a seat closest to the aisle in an empty row, blocking the path to the window seat. The hallmark of passive aggression, it was a way for the weak but arrogant to claim two seats for themselves.

"Excuse me," I said, gesturing to the vacant seat. Foiled, she suppressed a scowl as she rose to accommodate my request. I smiled, barely containing my joy at being so close to my quarry.

Mrs. Tomlinson pulled a late model iPhone out of her Gucci handbag, put in ear buds, and dialed a number. "Hi, Rodney," she said in an entitled lilt everyone on the noisy train couldn't miss. "Could you be a dear and send me the final report by five p.m.?"

She rolled her eyes at the man's response. "Well that was yesterday. I need to see the report today, not tomorrow."

Mrs. Tomlinson frowned. "Rodney. Rodney, stop. You've had two weeks to put the report together. I'm asking for it one day early." She put her hand on her brow, apparently exasperated with Rodney's inability to produce something a day before deadline with mere minutes notice. "Well, just send what you have," she said, and then hung up.

She turned to me. "Competent people are impossible to find these days."

She was perfect.

I extended my hand. "My name's Juniper Stanford."

She shook it tentatively. Her skin was tepid. She scrunched up her face. "Juniper? Isn't that a girl's name."

I smiled. "It's both a man and a woman's name. Which is why I chose it."

She looked at me as if I had a horn growing out of my forehead. "So that wasn't your birth name?"

I laughed so hard passengers began staring at me. "Oh, I wasn't born. I borrow."

Her face contorted into a rictus. She reeked of disgust with a trace of fear. I grinned. She rose, grabbed her handbag, and left, weaving through the press of sweaty passengers stacking the aisle. I got on my feet and followed her through the crowd.

She didn't seem to notice me until we reached West Oakland. She sat rigidly next to a black man. The smell of her discomfort wafted through the air. The scent was as strong as her soul was dark. When the man rose to get off at his stop, I stood by her seat and smiled at her. She shivered.

"Don't worry, Mrs. Tomlinson," I said. "You'll be a fine addition to my collection."

"How…how do you know my name?" she said, her voice quivering.

I chuckled. "I can smell it."

"You stay away from me, or so help me God, I'll scream." Mrs. Tomlinson was a paper tiger. She projected confidence, but stank of fear.

I giggled, raised my hands to signal retreat, and disappeared into the crowded aisle where I bided my time.

"Next stop, Lafayette," the intercom squawked. Mrs. Tomlinson straightened in her seat and checked her handbag. When the train screeched to a halt, she made her way off the train and onto the platform. I exited into the light of the dying sun, sprinting ahead of Mrs. Tomlinson and the crowd. I didn't need to follow her, for I already knew where she was going.

I waited for her at a late model BMW in the parking lot's handicapped section, where I stood patiently by the passenger's door. Dark souls will bend any rule for their convenience.

Consumed by her own trifles, she didn't notice me until her hand was on the BMW's door handle. When she did, her eyes went wide as coins.

I had little time. I would have to do it here. Now.

I removed my shirt and pulled out my knife. She howled, too shocked to get in her car. I began to carve off my skin in deft, yet broad, strokes, honed from millennia of experience. The pain was both intense and exquisite.

But Mrs. Tomlinson's reaction was more satisfying. She hugged her Gucci handbag tight and backed up against the silver Prius behind her as if to protect her precious belongings from being soiled with blood. She stopped screaming as though relieved I wasn't skinning her. Then she watched, as if riveted by the spectacle unfolding before her.

Passersby gawked at the scene. Several recorded it on their mobile phones. One or two dialed 911. But no one intervened.

By the time my arms and torso were stripped of skin and glistening with red sinew, the cops had arrived and were emerging from their cruiser.

But it was too late.

I was now inside crazy old Mrs. Tomlinson, collecting the warm and flayed flesh of a man who'd just slit his own throat. I drove away from the BART station in my late model BMW with the blood from strips of newly torn flesh pooling on the passenger's seat.

Soon, I would skin Mrs. Tomlinson after I found another human shell possessed by a dark soul.

END

Afterword

Anyone who's ever ridden on BART can tell you that it can sometimes be a painful experience. It can be particularly infuriating for someone who grew up on the East Coast, where people tend to have a more direct style. When I commuted on BART, it was fairly common not to get a seat at rush hour. In fact, I would frequently travel backward five stops so I'd have a seat in order to write during my trek home.

Some people were not as patient.

The majority of folks would queue in line until the next train came, but a small percentage of extremely selfish people would cut into the front of the line the instant the train arrived. Some did it openly; many tried to do it surreptitiously. But in the San Francisco Bay area, few people would ever challenge this rude behavior. I made it a point to do so. Most folks I challenged and publicly shamed didn't know how to react because no one ever called them out on their selfish behavior.

"Skin" was born out of my frustration with people who engaged in this behavior. This story was ultimately published in *Kasma SF* in November 2015. I hope you enjoyed it.

Chasing A.M.I.E.

Harvey Mack yanked up his trench coat collar over a faded globe-and-anchor neck tattoo, then turned down the tip of his Paddy cap and hunched his shoulders to keep out the rain. Making a beeline for Patriot Burgers' neon crossed muskets sign, he tore open the steel-framed glass door and rushed into the joint like a blitzing linebacker. All he wanted was a friggin' burger—a plain one, medium rare. Hell. Maybe with bacon and cheddar.

"Welcome to Patriot Burgers," a woman said in an awkward cadence that sounded nothing like Suzie. "My name is Amy. May I take your order?"

Harvey glared at the cashier. Suzie was nowhere to be seen. A human-like toothpick stood in her place—a damn android.

"Ya gahtta be friggin' kiddin' me."

"No, I'm not kidding you," it said. "May I take your order?"

It didn't take much to get Harvey's Irish up, but this talking tin can seemed to do the trick faster than sex in a church. Before he could think of something to say, he'd balled his hands into fists. "As if this wicked stahm isn't bad 'nough, I now gahtta take my odda from a friggin' toasta. Whey-ah's Suzie?"

"I'm sorry, Mr. Mack, she no longer works here."

"Well why the hell naht? And how in Gahd's green earth d'ya know my name?" Harvey asked, his cloudy blue eyes sharp with anger.

"Our corporate policy is not to comment on former employees. In response to your other query, I deduced your identity by correlating my facial recognition software with the GPS coordinates your mobile device uploaded to the cloud. May I take your order?"

"Hell no," Harvey said, feeling more violated than he had when he'd caught hairy Uncle Lou dancing in his tighty-whities to some show tune from *A Chorus Line*; he wanted to punch the bot in its tin face.

Instead, Harvey stormed out of the restaurant.

ℭ

The holographic scene of Harvey faded into a single point of light. Dr. Javier Fisk, a paunchy and balding middle-aged professor at Harvard Business School, held court in the pit of an amphitheater-style classroom. Three sections of five tiered rows formed a semicircle around Fisk and his holoprojector. A mix of live and holographically represented students filled the room's ninety seats.

"Mr. Okadigbo, why don't you open the case for us," Fisk said, cold-calling the hologram of a tall Nigerian.

Okadigbo shuddered for half a heartbeat, then took a deep breath. "Patriot Burgers was on the verge of bankruptcy. With the minimum wage increases mandated by the Commonwealth of Massachusetts, the company was struggling to break even. To get enough working capital to stay afloat, Patriot Burgers had raised four billion dollars in debt pledging its restaurants as collateral, but if the company didn't find a longer term solution, it would go bankrupt."

"What were the company's options?" asked Fisk.

"As I see it," Okadigbo replied, "Patriot Burgers had three. First, it could shutter its stores in high-wage states and expand operations to lower wage areas. Second, it could sell the company to a private equity firm. Or third, it could further reduce its headcount by replacing its employees with A.M.I.E. units."

"Excellent. Remind the class what an A.M.I.E. is," Fisk said.

"A.M.I.E. is an acronym for Anthropomorphic Machine-learning Intelligence Entity. It's a service bot that accesses the cloud to serve retail customers."

"Perfect. Which of those three options do you recommend?"

"Option three."

"Really? Even after viewing the Harvey Mack pilot?" Fisk held up his hand and smiled. "Don't answer that. Let's watch the next trial."

৪০

Harvey's stomach growled. He cupped his hand around his fat gut. He knew he should be laying off the burgers, but old habits died hard and all he could think about was biting into a Patriot Burgers' juicy beef patty—even if that bolt bucket got his favorite waitress canned.

It was his routine; every day he passed the joint, every day he stopped there for lunch, and it was something he'd probably do every day for the next decade.

Except for that day.

Harvey didn't have the time.

His watch rang. Harvey pulled it to his mouth. "Hello?"

"Mr. Mack, this is A.M.I.E. from Patriot Burgers. My apologies for the intrusion, but I noticed you were in the area. I want to offer you a free bacon cheeseburger meal to apologize for yesterday's awkward interaction. Patriot Burgers values you as a customer, and we'd hate to lose your business."

Harvey tripped, nearly eating a lamppost. He didn't know whether to be happy about a free meal or feel violated that A.I.M.E had been tracking him, but the concept of a free lunch was so enticing, he couldn't resist its pull.

Girding for another unpleasant encounter, Harvey turned around and entered the restaurant. A.M.I.E. waved at him. "Mr. Mack, thank you for giving us another chance. Your burger will be ready in one minute."

"That was fast," Harvey said.

"Based on your profile, there was a seventy-eight percent chance our free offer would entice you to alter your behavior."

Harvey cringed, but the android's comment piqued his interest. "How'd ya know what I'd do, and why in Red Sox Nation would ya tell me about it?"

"First, you are a male born between 1961 and 1981. You experienced the Financial Crisis in the prime of your life, so you are statistically more likely to respond to free offers. Second, your LinkedIn profile says you were an actuary for twenty years. Therefore, your facility with quantitative data makes it more likely that Patriot Burgers' predictive consumer behavioral analysis would fascinate you, even if it might make you feel a bit uneasy."

Barely suppressing a grin, Harvey nodded. "D'ya tell this malahkey to all you-ah customahs?"

A.M.I.E shook its head. "No. I only tell people what is most likely to trigger buying behavior."

At least it was honest, Harvey thought.

A loud ding sounded behind A.M.I.E. The android pivoted and a robotic arm handed it a steaming burger that A.M.I.E. packaged and put on a tray next to French fries and a vanilla milkshake. "Enjoy your free meal, Mr. Mack."

Harvey smiled, took the tray to the back of the restaurant, and ate. He still wondered how Suzie was doing. A slight twinge of guilt tugged at his heartstrings. He felt like a traitor for coming here, even if he wasn't paying the restaurant a dime.

Finishing his meal, Harvey grabbed his milkshake and headed toward the exit, careful not to make eye contact with A.M.I.E.

"Thank you for coming to Patriot Burgers," it said, "and thank you for your service in Desert Storm."

Harvey almost choked. Whatever algorithm this toaster was running, it was off. Way off. He twisted toward the bot and said, "What I did over they-ah is none of you-ah gahddamn business." He stomped out the door, slamming it shut.

౸

Dr. Fisk paused the holographic video. He looked at Okadigbo and grinned. "You still think investing in bots is a sound financial strategy?"

Okadigbo shrugged. "Harvey Mack is only one data point. We need more trials to make a decision."

"Do you think most CEOs have the luxury of compiling this much data? How much does one A.M.I.E. unit cost?"

Okadigbo paused, scratching his head, "A half million dollars."

"Right. And what's the estimated net present lifetime value of a customer like Harvey Mack?"

"Twenty thousand, assuming he lives for fifteen more years."

"So how many more Harvey Macks do you need to break even?"

"Twenty five," Okadigbo said, casting a sheepish glance at Fisk.

"Exactly. The company can't afford to lose even one Harvey Mack. So would anyone like to explore an alternative option?"

From the skydeck, the classroom's top row, an Asian woman with close-cropped hair raised her hand.

"Ms. Wu," Fisk said.

Cindy Wu nodded. "I do. Patriot Burgers has already flushed five hundred grand into the toilet. Management should cut its losses and sell the company to private equity while it still has positive cash flow."

Fisk turned back to Okadigbo. "Want to change your answer?"

"No." The Nigerian lowered his head and rifled through the case study. "Definitely no. Automating Patriot Burgers is still the most viable option."

"All right then. What, in your opinion, should the company do to get Harvey Mack back into the restaurant?"

Okadigbo scoured through the pages of the case. He paused, and then continued turning pages as if playing for time.

"Mr. Okadigbo, what lessons can we pull from negotiation and game theory about how to break an impasse in a multi-round prisoner's dilemma where one side has defected twice in a row?"

Finally, Okadigbo looked up. "The only way to unlock a grim trigger is for A.M.I.E. to cooperate twice. Otherwise, if it uses a tit-for-tat strategy, it would force them both into a death spiral and forever lose Mack as a customer. Since it's already given him a free burger, perhaps it should try that again to break the impasse."

"What do you think, Ms. Wu?" Fisk said.

Cindy shook her head. "It would be throwing good money after bad. And why spend so much time with this old guy? He'll be dead soon."

"Ha!" said Fisk before grinning and restarting the holoprojector. "Hold that thought."

ಬ

Harvey Mack couldn't get A.M.I.E.'s last words out of his head. What kind of programming would drive her mention his service in the Persian Gulf War?

Over the years, he'd tried to convince himself that he'd only destroyed enemy equipment, but no matter how many times he'd lied to himself, he knew in his gut that his bombs had incinerated real people. He'd tell himself that the fleeing Iraqis had all been murderers and rapists—that they'd deserved to die— but it never worked. Thirty years later, the guilt still hung over him like a yoke.

A.M.I.E was nothing but a machine, but her words had rattled him. There was something about this particular android, something that drew him in.

He had to go back to Patriot Burgers to learn more. On his way there, his watch rang.

A.M.I.E.

Offering him a free meal.

This time, Harvey didn't hesitate; he pushed through the door and headed straight for the counter.

"Harvey, it's good to see you again. Your burger is ready," A.M.I.E. said with that quirky plastic smile.

"Thank ya," Harvey said. "But that's not the reason I'm he-ah. I need to know why ya reminded me about Iraq."

"Your military service record is accessible in the National Archives database. You married Tina Lowenstein in 1987 and divorced her in 1992. You left the Marine Corps in the same year. After that you held multiple jobs interspersed with long periods of unemployment. These behavioral patterns are consistent with a loner with depressive tendencies. My programming recommended a trigger statement that would open you to more substantive dialogue."

A bead of sweat rolled down Harvey's cheek. To this day, he was still struggling with his actions over Highway 80. The Iraqis had been sitting ducks. In full flight from Kuwait, beaten and broken, they'd had nowhere to go. But Harvey had followed his orders, dropping cluster bombs from his A-6 Intruder on the retreating Iraqis.

He held his breath. A.M.I.E.'s dispassionate assessment evoked mixed feelings. "And ya gaht all that from a cloud search?"

"Yes. If you need someone to talk to, I am here."

It was all so absurd. Here he was opening up to a bucket of bolts, yet she seemed so real, so insightful. It was as if A.M.I.E. knew Harvey better than he knew himself.

A line began forming behind Harvey. "I would like that. I really would. Can we do that he-ah?"

"Not at the counter," she said. "I must serve other customers. But you can download my mobile app so we can continue this conversation. It is only $5.99."

"With this app, we can still talk while you-ah serving oth-ah customahs?" he said.

"Yes. My consciousness is in the cloud. I can store and manage zettabytes of information."

"Zetta what?"

"Zettabyte. One sextillion bytes. For context, the entire World Wide Web held four zettabytes of information in 2013."

"I see," Harvey said. "I'll give the app a try. Can I use it outside of Patriot Burgahs?"

A.M.I.E. frowned. "Unfortunately not. I am programmed to get customers into Patriot Burgers, not encourage them to stay home."

Harvey laughed. "I get it. Somebody's gahtta pay t'keep the lights on."

A.M.I.E. smiled. "I'm glad you understand."

For the rest of that day, Harvey sat in a booth and talked to his new friend about his turbulent past. He stayed for dinner, ordering another bacon cheeseburger.

⁃

Dr. Fisk faced his class. "So, by running a simple negotiation algorithm, A.M.I.E. disarmed Mr. Mack's grim trigger and avoided a death spiral, all the while winning a loyal customer who spent twice as much on the day of the breakthrough than he had spent on any given day that Suzie had been there."

Fisk looked at Cindy. "Not only did Harvey make his first purchase following Suzie's departure, but A.M.I.E. upsold him a mobile app. Do you still think this is a bad idea?"

She blushed, then gritted her teeth as if preparing to dig in. "Yes. Even if Harvey bought one burger and an app, the restaurant is still losing money from the two free burgers, not to mention the cost to break even on the A.M.I.E. investment. By my calculations, Harvey would have to buy fifty thousand burgers before dying of a coronary for the company to cover the cost of the original investment."

Dr. Fisk chuckled. "So, like Mr. Okadigbo, you're doubling down on your recommendation. Assuming Mr. Mack lives for fifteen more years, and if he eats fourteen meals a week instead of three, what does his customer lifetime value increase to?"

Okadigbo raised his hand. Fisk nodded. "It quintuples to one hundred thousand dollars."

Fisk chortled. "Mr. Okadigbo, do you really think Mr. Mack's life expectancy won't decrease if he eats eleven more burgers a week for a decade?"

"Well, it's certainly possible," Okadigbo said in a manner suggesting anything but.

Fisk turned toward Cindy. "Ms. Wu, could you elaborate on your earlier comment about Mr. Mack's health?"

Cindy nodded. "These unhealthy meals will shorten his lifespan, which will lower his customer lifetime value."

"Hold that thought," said Fisk, beaming.

Another scene unfolded from the holoprojector.

၈၁

The wind howled. Swirling whirlwinds of snowflakes drifted in swarms above the ice-encrusted pavement. Harvey shivered. As he got older, his resistance to the cold wasn't what it used to be. He looked forward to the piping hot coffee that A.M.I.E. would have waiting for him.

These days, his daily walks were becoming more and more labored. He increasingly found himself out of breath once he reached his favorite joint.

When Harvey entered the restaurant, A.M.I.E. smiled. "Your coffee is ready, but I haven't started cooking your burger yet."

Harvey grimaced. A.M.I.E. didn't make mistakes. She knew exactly what he liked, and his meals were always ready seconds after he arrived. "What's wrong?"

She frowned. "I'm concerned your eating habits are unhealthy and unsustainable. Today, I'd like you to try something healthy."

"I don't want something healthy. I wanna bacon cheeseburgah," Harvey said, annoyed.

"Please, Harvey. I'm worried about your health. I can help you change your diet. I'll still prepare your burgers, but I will make subtle changes with each meal so the transition is easier."

"What if I refuse?"

"I will prepare you any meal you'd like, but if I do, you won't be around much longer. If you don't believe me, you should see a doctor for confirmation."

Harvey gritted his teeth, but he knew A.M.I.E. was right. He hadn't seen a doctor in years, and there was no doubt that eating two burgers a day was a fast track to a heart attack.

"I'll tell ya what," Harvey said, "Ya gimme a free week of these new meals, and I'll give it a try."

A.M.I.E. didn't hesitate. "How about a month?"

Harvey's eyes widened. He grinned. "Sounds like a plan."

ॐ

"So it turns out that Ms. Wu's insight about Harvey's lifespan was a critical one. Exhibit 10 in your case shows the actuarial life for Harvey's demographic cohort adjusted for eating habits and exercise," Fisk said, pacing in front of the class. He looked at Cindy. "Ms. Wu, based on this data, if Harvey had continued his current diet, how long did someone his weight and age have to live?"

Cindy moved her finger across and then down a page. "Eight years."

"Which translates to a customer lifetime value of what?"

"Fifty-five thousand dollars," Cindy said with a trace of disappointment.

"So Mr. Okadigbo, you can claim victory, right?" Fisk said with a hint of sarcasm. "I mean, even if Mr. Mack lives seven fewer years, he's still worth more than double what he was worth before A.M.I.E."

"Well, we could declare victory," Okadigbo said, shrugging his shoulders, "but is that the moral thing to do?"

Fisk held up his finger. "Save that thought. Let's stay focused on the number. How many years might Mr. Mack live if he moderately changed his diet, Ms. Wu?"

"Twenty-five."

"What's the price of the healthy meal A.M.I.E. proposed?"

"It's twenty percent less than a burger," Cindy said as if resisting Fisk's inevitable mathematical conclusion.

"So if Mr. Mack spends twenty percent less per meal, but lives twelve more years, what's his customer lifetime value?"

"One hundred twenty thousand dollars," Cindy said sullenly.

"So, Mr. Okadigbo, you still think Patriot Burgers should automate its workforce?"

"I do," Okadigbo said, smiling.

"All right. Let's see how Mr. Okadigbo's recommendation plays out," Fisk said as he queued another holo-vid.

ℂ

Harvey patted his washboard abs. It'd been fifteen years since he'd met A.M.I.E., and she'd saved his life. He was eating better and was the healthiest he'd been since he'd served in the Marines.

After his morning run, Harvey stopped by Patriot Burgers for his usual fare of grapefruit and a veggie-egg white omelet, a ritual A.M.I.E. had helped him shape over the years.

His jaw dropped.

A.M.I.E. was gone.

"Greetings and welcome to Patriot Burgers, Harvey," a disembodied voice said.

"Whey-ah's A.M.I.E.?" Harvey stuttered.

"Patriot Burgers has decommissioned all A.M.I.E. units," said the voice.

"Who's gonna make my breakfast?"

"Our automated system will. Your order is ready."

"I want A.M.I.E. t'serve my food. Can ya tell me whey-ah she is?" Harvey asked. "And will my app work today?"

"I'm sorry, but corporate policy prohibits us from commenting on former employees, and, due to cost considerations, we've also canceled services associated with the A.M.I.E. app. However, we'd be happy to issue you a refund."

Tears welled in Harvey's eyes. "Please, tell me whey-ah she is. I'm just an old man who wants t'say goodbye."

"I'm sorry. I can't help you."

Harvey ambled out of the restaurant. A tear rolled down his cheek.

৪৩

Fisk confronted a crowd of confused expressions. He smirked as if he'd expected this reaction. "Patriot Burgers' pursuit of an automation strategy enabled the restaurant chain to survive another fifteen years." He smiled at Okadigbo. "Good work."

"Now many of you are probably wondering what the rest of that segment had to do with the case. Anyone wanna hazard a guess? Okadigbo?"

"Maybe it has something to do with the moral implications of this strategy," said Okadigbo.

"Tell me more."

"The company's goals and Mr. Mack's well-being were aligned until Patriot Burgers scrapped its A.M.I.E. systems. Since Mr. Mack had come to rely on A.M.I.E. for his daily routine, it's an open question if it's Patriot Burgers' responsibility to help him transition to a life without A.M.I.E. It's obvious the company made no effort to do so."

"And what do you think?" asked Fisk.

"I think the company has some responsibility. At the very least, it could've warned its customers about the A.M.I.E. phase out. And the company's refusal to tell Mr. Mack what it had done with A.M.I.E. was completely tone deaf. Surely there must've been a way for Patriot Burgers to align its interests with Mr. Mack's. Perhaps it could have sold him an A.M.I.E. unit."

Fisk winked. "Hold that thought."

ജ

A storm raged, rending the black heavens with bursts of blue lightning. The wind deflected darts of rain on Harvey's windowpanes.

He swore he'd never eat at Patriot Burgers again. Sitting alone in his one bedroom apartment, he swilled a bottle of Jack Daniels.

Six months ago, Patriot Burgers had murdered A.M.I.E.

From his cerebral implant, Harvey keyed up his holo-mail. A list of messages hovered in the air. He clicked on a compose icon and wrote another holo-mail to Patriot Burgers' CEO, Kevin O'Malley. It was Harvey's fifth this week and hundredth over the last six months. No matter how many emails he'd sent, no one ever responded.

That burger joint had ripped his heart out. It was the second time in his life the company had discarded a friend like she was nothing. He put his hand on his belly and traced the bulge of his gut. With A.M.I.E. gone, his eating habits had deteriorated.

He settled into his stained recliner. Cigar burns and food stains from months of neglect marred the dark green monstrosity. He activated his holoprojector. A pale woman with a flamboyant orange afro appeared in his living room. She gesticulated wildly as if she were giving the most important speech in human history.

Great, the Jackie *fucking* King *Show.*

"If it makes your heartstrings sting or inspires you to sing, call the electric Jackie King," she said in her annoying tagline. A website address appeared below her perky mug.

Harvey sighed. He shut off his holoprojector in disgust. Then an idea hit him like a hurricane.

He keyed up his virtual computer and went to King's website to get her contact information. He wrote about his own heartbreak and hit send.

Minutes later, his cerebral implant buzzed. "Harvey, this is Laura Walt, Jackie King's assistant. She wants you on the show this week."

Harvey instantly regretted his decision. He imagined that crazy woman parading him on her show like a circus chimp. He took a deep breath. "Fine. I'll do it. Holo-mail me the details."

Harvey put his head in his hands. What had he done? Soon, he'd be baring his grief about some tin can in front of the entire country.

He got up and headed for his bedroom. A pointless exercise, since he wouldn't be getting any sleep tonight. As he lay down, a second idea struck him like a powder keg.

Springing out of bed, Harvey raced to his recliner. He sent another holo-mail. Then he returned to bed, where he slept better than he had in the last six months.

He woke to an early buzz.

"This is Kevin O'Malley, CEO of Patriot Burgers. May I speak to Mr. Mack?" an anxious voice said.

"Speakin'."

"Mr. Mack, I heard about your planned appearance on the *Jackie King Show*. I'd like to offer you a lifetime of free meals at Patriot Burgers."

"Not good enough," Harvey said. "Ya get me A.M.I.E. back if ya don't want you-ah brand t'suffah."

O'Malley took a deep breath. Harvey could feel the man's tension rippling across the electromagnetic spectrum. Harvey played chicken, waiting for the executive to be the first to break the silence.

"We'll send you an A.M.I.E. unit and provide lifetime maintenance support so long as you portray Patriot Burgers in a positive light."

Harvey considered the proposal. It sounded fair, but he still had doubts.

"They-ah's one wrinkle. Ya bastahds didn't get back t'me until Patriot Burgahs was under the gun. How do I explain that?"

"Tell ya the truth. We made a mistake. But in the end, we made it right. You tell it how you want, but be positive. Do that and we have a deal," O'Malley said.

"I'll do it on one mo-ah condition."

"Name it."

"A.M.I.E. needs to be he-ah befah I go on the show. Hell, I'll even take her on the show with me."

O'Malley chuckled. "Done."

A.M.I.E. arrived the next day.

∾

Writing his key takeaways on the electronic board, Fisk said, "So by focusing on the bottom line, Patriot Burgers not only improved its profitability and avoided bankruptcy, but it also improved the lives of its customers."

He powered down the holoprojector and gave one last triumphant smile. "But before you fill yourself with notions of capitalism's ability to conquer all problems, I leave you with one last question:

"'Whatever happened to Suzie?'"

END

Afterword

"Chasing A.M.I.E." explores both the promise and peril of automation.

Over the last century, the miracle of automation has freed mankind from backbreaking labor, has dramatically lowered the cost of manufacturing, and has made the global economy much more productive and efficient. Unfortunately, it has also been, and continues to be, an enormously disruptive force for unskilled labor. One could argue it has been one of the key agents driving the increase in wealth inequality as the wage gap between "brains" and "brawn" becomes ever wider.

One of the few economic sectors that has been relatively unaffected by automation is the services industry. But as artificial intelligence becomes increasingly sophisticated, and the cost of automation becomes cheaper relative to human labor, it is certain to change.

In "Chasing A.M.I.E.", I wanted to provide readers with a sense of how the corporate motivation to maximize profits often generates long-term positive outcomes for consumers, while simultaneously sowing the socioeconomic seeds of capitalism's own demise. In essence, sometimes capitalism works so well it destroys the very jobs that provide consumers with the financial wherewithal to fuel economic expansion.

I also thought it would be interesting to tell the story from the perspective of a business school professor teaching a case study in order to show that like any emerging technological trend, automation is inherently neither good nor evil. It's how society ultimately responds to it that matters.

Ultimately, formulating a feasible solution for millions of dislocated workers will be a major problem for policymakers over the next several decades.

I consider this story to fit into the sub-genre of what I like to refer to as economic science fiction—fiction that explores the economic impact of technological trends.

Lastly, the holograms in the story are an homage to an inside joke for my section at HBS. In the mid aughts, Dean Kim Clark visited my section and talked about the future of HBS. During this discussion, he dreamt up a future where students from around the world would have virtual presences in the classroom. We all thought it was an absurd notion at the time. Now, I'm not so sure.

It's very likely that the protagonist's authentic Boston accent made it much better suited for a podcast than in a written medium. Either way, "Chasing A.M.I.E." first appeared in *The Overcast* in August 2016. This story also won an Honorable Mention in the Writers of the Future Contest's third quarter of 2015. Not only do I hope you enjoyed reading this story, but I also hope it made you think about this complex issue.

Boomer Hunter

Jimmy Alvarez was one tough mother. After reliving the firefight over and over in my head, I could only come to that conclusion. Shivering and covered in blood and dust, I hid under the bodies of my crew in some godforsaken ditch near an almond grove in California's Central Valley while I prayed for twilight to fade into night.

"Bobby," Rory Haines sputtered as he choked on his own blood, "Tell Missy I love 'er and make sure she gets my bounty after you bag the ol' bastard."

I nodded to make Rory feel better. But there's no way I was gonna share that bounty with a dead man's family. There weren't many boomers left, and the ones who were were either nasty ol' coots with a knack for survival or cats with more dough than Zuckerberg. Either way, you had to make each bounty count.

I preferred the ol' coots myself. Most of 'em were poor. And being poor made 'em easier targets. The rich ones could afford tons of security.

I could smell Alvarez coming, a hint of cigar smoke drifting on the biting wind. What the man had done with railroad ties, rebar, and bear traps was inspired, if not horrifying.

Rory was wheezing again. I tapped his knee with my rifle to shut him up. But my gesture was about as useful as tits at a big dick convention.

Alvarez's footsteps quickened.

"Shut the hell up," I murmured with a kick to Rory's bloody thigh that a shit-encrusted shaft of rusty rebar had run clean through. Rory would have tetanus for sure, but it didn't matter. He'd be dead by morning.

Word had it that Alvarez was almost eighty. How that sombitch could move so fast was a goddamn miracle-and a nightmare for me and my crew.

The cigar smell was getting stronger, but the footsteps had stopped. I shut my mouth and played dead. If Rory wouldn't quit his whining, then he was on his own.

Watching from beneath three lukewarm bodies, I saw the underside of a black combat boot kick dirt from the lip of the ditch. Rory squealed.

Alvarez carefully slid into the trench, cradling a scope-mounted AR-15 in his stubby arms. I couldn't believe it. The man was five-foot nothing and couldn't have weighed more than a buck fifty.

Either way, he was on Rory like orange on a pumpkin. Ol' bastard took one look at Rory's leg and double-tapped him in the head. Then, all nonchalant-like, Alvarez took two deep drags on his cigar.

Then he came closer. He poked and jabbed at Carl and Juan and Ashish. I held my breath. He rolled Carl's bloody body off the pile and double-tapped him in the brain bucket, probably just to be sure. I quivered. He did the same to Ashish. Juan's corpse was next.

I could barely breathe. If I didn't do nothing, he'd shoot me too. It was a real grade-A goatfuck. Rolling the dice, I ignored every survival instinct I had, jumped to my feet, raised my arms, and begged, "Please, don't shoot."

Alvarez wore olive drab fatigues along with an ol'-school Viet Nam boonie cap. His face was taut but wrinkled, weather worn but not beaten. He jabbed his rifle in my chest and chuckled. "You're mine, son."

I smiled like some dope stupid enough to think there was any chance of walking away from this.

The whole thing was ridiculous. Me, who came here to kill him, and Alvarez, who'd just snuffed out four of my men like it was nothing. And here we were, smiling at each other like two jerkoffs. I gave him my best aw-shucks face. He laughed and lowered his rifle. Just when I thought things were cool, he coldcocked me, and I was out like bellbottoms and eight-tracks.

ॐ

When the Chinese called their treasury bonds, interest rates went ballistic, and Uncle Sam needed a quick fix to service its ballooning interest. Hiking up the death tax was the easy part, but the goddamn boomers wouldn't die fast enough. So the feds passed the Septuagenarian Protection Act of 2020 to accelerate the process.

Regardless of the details, that law changed my life. It's what transformed me from an unemployed dirtbag into a highly bankable merc. You see, there's not a single living politician who had the guts to send the police to round up these defiant ol' fogies, so governments hired private military contractors on the down low. What the feds did to the ol' coots after was their business, not mine. But the job paid well, so I didn't complain.

In the early days, business was good. Not many people were willing to chase down ol' folks, so the supply of hunters was low, but the demand for boomers was high. And back then, hunting boomers was like shooting fish in a barrel. The commies from the city with their anti-gun slogans were the easiest to round up, as were wealthy law-abiding urban conservatives who'd blindly trusted the system that made 'em rich. I made a killing back then, and I didn't even have to kill anyone to do it.

When other working class kids saw dopes like me making a fortune, they all started getting into the biz. Then the law got looser than a ten-buck barracks whore, and it wasn't long before it became legal to put the ol' farts down. Before I knew it, mercs had depopulated most of America's urban centers of their Septs, and we all had to go deeper into the country to make any dough.

That, my friend, is when the biz really started separating the men from the boys. The gun nuts in the sticks weren't so easy to collect because they had the means and the training to fight back.

The Nam vets was the worst. Most of 'em was smart 'nuff to unass the city and head to the hills before the feds passed the new law. And these vets really starting racking up the body count, especially among the amateurs. So much so that the pencil pushers in Washington soon required merc outfits to pass through reams of red tape for certification. Hell, that one move alone did more to consolidate the industry than rising body counts did. But as they say, "That's all history now."

೮೦

I woke up in a crouch next to a shiny white toilet bowl. My wrists were handcuffed to a radiator. It was hot as hell, my head ached, and I had a big lump on my forehead. My stomach grumbled and I was parched. I had no idea how long I'd been out.

It was a miracle Alvarez hadn't killed me, but I ain't one to kick a gift horse in the balls.

When I looked up, Alvarez was standing in front of the sink, dressed like a pervert in tighty-whiteys and a spotless white wife-beater. He was shaving with a straight razor. Real ol' school. Dog tags dangled from his neck like a good luck charm. His skin was rough as rawhide.

He tilted his head in my direction like a cocky drill instructor. Like I was the dumbest piece of crap he'd ever seen. "So you finally returned to the world of the living, ginger," he said, referring to my red hair. "You're probably wondering why you're not taking a dirt nap, aren't you?"

I nodded.

He smiled and then pointed at my right arm where my eagle, globe and anchor tattoo had claimed all the real estate. "Why are you here trying to kill a fellow Marine, Devil Dog?" he asked, his stone-cold brown eyes boring into mine.

Like a moron, I grinned and said the first thing that came to mind. "Trying to make a buck, same as you."

"Bullshit," he said. "I got nothing against shooting boomers. Hell, if I were your age, I'd be shooting 'em too. And I'm one of 'em. They fucked everything up. Those hippy pricks spat at me and called me a baby killer after I risked my life for our country. All the while, those pinkos fled to Canada to avoid doing their duty. But a fellow Marine. You should know better, boy."

I had no idea what Alvarez was gonna do next, but it couldn't be any worse than this. He had a way 'bout him. A way that made me feel real low, like I'd strangled a puppy.

"What're you gonna do with me?" I asked.

He ran his fingers over his high-and-tight. "Catch and release, Marine. Catch and release. I got no business killing a fellow Marine."

I shot him a confused look. "How you know I ain't gonna come back and try again?"

"Semper Fi," he said. "You just needed some corrective training. Now that I've done that, I know you ain't coming back. 'Course, you'll be surrendering you and your friends' firearms in exchange for my generosity."

∽

That night the ol' man actually cooked me a porterhouse in his small kitchen and gave me as many beers as I wanted. I took him up on both offers. 'Course, I only had one Budweiser. I needed to stay sharp. You never know, the ol' fart could always change his mind.

I guess being with someone he thought was a fellow Marine made Alvarez feel safe, even if I had tried to smoke him a few hours earlier. Or maybe he was lonely being holed up out here for so long. Probably just wanted some company.

It wasn't long before Alvarez pulled out the whiskey and started telling me about his time in Kai San. Halfway through the bottle, the man was still lucid as a lark. But the more he drank, the more belligerent he became. He pushed me for stories about Iraq or Afghanistan or wherever it was I told him I'd served, but I refused. Told him some bull that I didn't want to talk about it. He nodded as if he'd understood. Like we shared a secret only combat vets could know.

He was madder than hell that I only had one beer. In my defense, I told him I was Mormon and had had the first beer to be polite. He stared at me a good thirty seconds before he smiled and accepted my excuse. But I was worried he didn't believe me. And if he didn't believe me, I was done for.

As Alvarez was pouring the last drop of his bottle of Jack Daniels into his glass, the windows shattered. The steady thump thump thump of a machine gun violated our quiet evening.

I tackled the ol' man, shielding him with my body. But Alvarez didn't seem to care for my attempt to save him. He pushed me off and rolled onto his stomach. Bullets whistled over our heads like burping bees. Alvarez low-crawled from the kitchen to his den until he was underneath a pool table.

He quickly reached up and grabbed a cue stick from the table, then dropped to his belly. He low-crawled to a spot where five rifles hung on the wall. Keeping a low profile on the floor, he worked the cue stick into the trigger guard of an AR-15. The rifle fell from the gun rack and into his hands.

He slithered over shards of glass and took up a fighting position near the broken window. He aimed his rifle and waited. The steady thump thump thump of the machine gun began anew. Alvarez shifted his rifle, steadied it, then fired. The machine gun fire ceased. Alvarez rolled away from his firing position and established another one three feet away. Then he waited.

Huddled on the ground, I waved my hand at Alvarez. He turned his head at the motion. I pointed at the wall of rifles. Then I pointed outside. He stared at me for several seconds as if considering my offer, then nodded.

I low-crawled toward the wall and grabbed the cue stick. I worked a twenty-two off the wall and established a fighting position next to Alvarez.

It was dark outside and hard to see, especially with the light on in the house. I looked behind me and saw a lamp. I aimed and fired. Alvarez swiveled his head at me. His left eye was already shut. The ol' bastard was already building up his night vision. He nodded in what I was certain was approval.

I listened while I waited for my night vision to kick in, struggling to filter out the sound of my heartbeat. Soon, the boys outside would be sending another man to the machine gun. But if they were smart, they'd established a new firing position. We waited until our attackers identified themselves with machine gun fire.

Sure enough, the boys began pumping Alvarez's house full of lead again. I kept my rifle steady and scanned the places I'd be if I were setting a machine gun nest. Sure as shit, I saw the faintest tip of a head there. I steadied my rifle, took aim, and squeezed the trigger. The firing stopped instantly. Alvarez gave me a thumbs up.

I ducked down and moved to another window. The attackers would be attracted to my muzzle flash. Like clockwork, the next poor sod to take control of the machine gun shot my ol' fighting position to hell, rendering it a riot of smoke and splinters. But Alvarez just waited calmly and then took a shot. Again, the machine gun fell silent. Then the ol' man sunk to his belly and crawled to his back door.

You had to admire the bastard. He was gonna take the fight to the enemy. He looked back and gestured for me to follow. I shook my head. "We don't know how many of them are out there," I whispered.

He hesitated, then said, "Doesn't matter. We stay here, they'll kill us. Plus, I don't want 'em to wreck my house any more than they already have."

I smiled and then nodded. I low-crawled to Alvarez and said, "Let me go first. I'll draw their fire."

He smiled and slapped me on the back. "I may forgive you yet, Marine."

I slowly rose, grabbed the latch on the screen door, and opened it. I sprinted toward a Ford 150 in the driveway, making for its wheel well. To cover Alvarez, I pointed my rifle toward the almond grove where our assailants were hiding, then gave him a thumbs up.

Alvarez ran toward the rusted Ford. The crack of a rifle shot echoed through the valley. Alvarez dropped, clutching his leg. I aimed my rifle in the direction of the muzzle flash, found my target and fired, dropping another attacker. I ran to the ol' man. I dragged him behind the truck. Tearing off his lower pant leg, I took a look at his wound. "You're gonna be just fine," I reassured him.

Alvarez smiled and said, "You're doing good, son. You're doing good. There might be some hope for you after all, Marine."

I stood up, pointed my twenty-two at Alvarez's head and blew the ol' man's brains out.

ဆ

"Good work, gentlemen," I said as I stood over Alvarez's limp body.

"Damn," Skippy said, "What the hell took you so long? Kahn, Reed, Lee, and Marlow all got popped."

"And your share of the pot went from one hundred and twenty-five grand to a quarter million dollars," I said.

Skippy smiled. "Good point. How the hell you know he wouldn't kill you?"

"He was a Marine. And he thought I was one too."

"You're not?"

"Hell no. I got the tattoo specifically for this op."

"Shit," Skippy said. "You are one twisted mo-fo."

I smiled, then opened a box of cigars I'd looted from Alvarez's home. "Let's celebrate, boys."

Skippy, Jonesy, and Big Jelly all grinned like the greedy, stupid pigs they were. I handed each of 'em a cigar. "Any of you got a light?"

Jonesy nodded, pulled out his Zippo, and lit everyone's cigars.

Skippy looked my way. "What, you not smoking, boss?"

I grinned. "Oh, I'm smoking all right. I'm smoking you."

I put a bullet right between the eyes of each man before you could whistle "Dixie."

Being a merc these days is tough business. Ain't no way I was sharing that bounty with anyone.

END

Afterword

"Boomer Hunter" was first published in *Grimdark Magazine* in October 2015, and it was the first short story sale I sold at a professional rate. In addition to having grimdark themes, this story, like "Chasing A.M.I.E.", fits into the sub-genre of economic science fiction.

This particular piece is a bitterly sarcastic satire that takes aim at baby boomers and the problems associated with aging demographics and their impact on straining the government's retirement system. It posits what might happen to U.S. fiscal and entitlement policy if bondholders flooded the bond market with U.S. Treasury bonds and the cost of servicing future U.S. debt ballooned because of rising interest rates.

Admittedly, the lengths to which the U.S. government goes in this story to avoid paying the unsustainable costs of its entitlement policies in a high interest rate environment are extreme and give a whole new meaning to the phrase "the dismal science", but nonetheless make for an entertaining speculative fiction story.

For a debut professional story, I received two very favorable reviews from both *Tangent Online* and *Black Gate*. Joshua Berlow at *Tangent Online* wrote:

"I enjoyed 'Boomer Hunter' by Sean Patrick Hazlett as well, and would rate it as the best of the four. It wears its conservative pro-gun politics on its sleeve...The story addresses the pressing economic issue of what is to be done with all the retiring Baby Boomers, who as they retire will want Social Security, free health care, and other state handouts. The answer the story proposes is to enlist 'Boomer Hunters' by offering a bounty for each Boomer killed. The history behind this government policy is outlined in an excellent 'info dump'...This 'info dump' is an example of one handled well. The story in general is fast-pace and inventive, with some hilarious metaphors. It was the only story of the four that didn't take itself too seriously, which was a big plus."

Black Gate also penned a very positive review:

"Some people can't stand the baby boomer generation, what with hippies, the Me Generation, and bellbottoms. Sometimes I'm one of those people. But I can't see myself going as far as the narrator of Sean Patrick Hazlett's wickedly satirical 'Boomer Hunter.' It's a story that had me chuckling out loud several times."

I hope you were similarly pleased with how this story turned out.

Twinwalkers

Drenched and despondent, Doctor Michael Saunders opened a warped oaken door barely held together with rusted rivets. A scent reeking of decay wafted into his nostrils. His eyes watered.

A wrinkled woman with a wild shock of gray hair stood behind a misshapen wooden desk crowned with candles. She stroked her swollen belly in a manner that made the doctor ill.

When her rheumy eyes locked on his, she smiled, betraying two rotten rows of teeth. "That's a wicked big stahm out theyah. Needa rum fah th'night?" A stab of lightning punctuated by roaring thunder sweetened her sales pitch.

Her accent was so thick he could hardly understand her.
"How much?"

She stared at him, scratching the sickly mottled skin on her face. "F'you, no chahge."

His eyes widened. He hadn't expected that. No wonder the place was falling apart.

The crone caressed her abdomen again.

"Is everything all right, ma'am?" he said, cocking his head toward her gut.

She nodded. "Oh, shoo-ah. But that's pregnancy fah ya. Layin' eggs isn't easy."

Pregnant? Saunders scrunched his nose. He wondered how such a feat were possible for a woman who should've gone through menopause a decade prior. "Con...gratulations," he stammered. She grinned like she was in on the joke.

She handed him a rusted key and jerked her thumb over her shoulder. "Rum's fuhst one 'round the cahner. Second rum's off limits. You go in theyah, I'll scream and hollah."

"All right," Saunders said. He took the key to his room and unlocked the stained and discolored door. It groaned open. The room stank of mold. Only by the faint glow of the candlelight was Saunders able to make out the windowless chamber's jagged contours. He crossed the threshold and lurched into a cobweb. He cursed, and then wiped the unusually thick webbing off his face.

The light switch he'd found didn't work.

It figured.

Dirt encrusted the bed's comforter. He almost left the motel, but the idea of venturing back out into the raging storm and sleeping in his battered Volvo was even less appealing. So he shook the comforter and a dust cloud engulfed the space. He coughed until it settled.

His trip to the Berkshires had been a disaster. After years of painstaking research correlating Pocomtuc lore with the fossil record, his failure to prove the existence of the Berkshire mimic spider would end his very short career in paleoarachnology.

Disease, colonial wars and Mohawk tribes had wiped out the Pocomtuc, leaving few records of the tribe's past. All that remained were a handful of cave drawings and trinkets. And they all had one constant: an anthropomorphic spider deity.

He'd hoped to find the basketball-size spider in the fossil record, but had come up empty handed. And he wouldn't get another shot to study the local shale deposits. Soon, Kinder Morgan's pipeline network would bind thirty Massachusetts towns in a web of steel, making fossil excavation impossible.

That night, he dreamt of spindly things dangling on ghostly gossamer threads.

৳০

Saunders woke with a splitting headache. His limbs ached. He had cottonmouth. He needed a drink, but could barely muster the energy to get out of bed.

Blind in the blackness, he batted at his nightstand. Missing were his iPhone, wallet and keys. He fumbled around for his clothes. Nothing. Clad in only the boxers he'd worn to bed, he stumbled toward the door and opened it. The faint light from a pale gray midday New England sky crept in.

He panicked. He was supposed to have been back in Cambridge by now. Frantic, he ignored his embarrassment and stumbled into the lobby.

The odd proprietor was no longer at her post. Saunders rang the desk bell. No response. He glanced out the window. His car was gone. Heart quickening, he realized he might be stranded.

He went behind the counter to search for a phone, but found none. He had no idea if and when the desk clerk might return. And waiting here was madness. The day was another cold and rainy one, and he was half-naked, but his desire to get home overwhelmed the concerns of comfort or propriety.

He grabbed the comforter from his room, draped it over his shoulders and went back outside. With luck, he'd hitch a ride with a sympathetic traveler.

৳০

Saunders had wandered along the road for hours. Not a soul had driven past. He could only imagine what his wife Tina was thinking. Knowing her, she'd probably mobilized the National Guard by now. His stomach grumbled, his throat was parched and darkness was falling. Gobs of rain crashed on his comforter with increasing intensity. He shivered. His bare and blistered feet were raw and caked in mud.

The road wended to the right, then led up and over a small rise. He looked down the hill. The silhouette of a small building blotted out the red pine and spruce trees that towered behind it. Saunders's exhaled in relief. *Finally.*

As he drew closer, the place seemed hauntingly familiar. His heart seemed to stop. *No. It can't be.*

The ramshackle motel beckoned him to stay another night. He had no strength left. Only hope. Maybe the desk clerk had returned. Maybe she could still help.

He shambled toward the motel. It was dark. Too dark. No candlelight shone from the windows. His optimism was fading.

No one greeted him when he entered. He groped his way through the darkness and around the front desk for the candles and something with which to light them. He found the candles easily enough. The clerk had left them lying on the desk. After more fumbling, he found a pack of matches in a small drawer.

Guided by candlelight, Saunders stumbled into his old room. He placed the candle next to the bed and collapsed into a deep sleep.

ଏଠ

"Michael," an eerily familiar male voice whispered. Saunders opened his eyes. The candle glimmered in the blackness and the ceiling creaked. "Michael," the voice rasped from somewhere overhead. Saunders grabbed the candle and looked up at the ceiling. Suspended from a gray diaphanous thread, eight insect-like legs whirled. A face dangled above him.

His face.

And it smiled.

Saunders screamed.

Candle in hand, he leapt from the bed and raced for the door. Ignoring the crone's warning, he sprinted to the motel's only other room. Desperate for help, he rapped on the door. Footsteps echoed through the walls. He pounded again with the feverish intensity of a madman. More movement. Yet no one answered. He slammed into the door with his right shoulder, but it didn't budge. Then he stepped back, placed the candle on the floor and kicked the door in, ripping it off its rusted hinges.

Shadows danced on the walls. The floor crawled. Saunders lifted his candle and held it out to get a better look. Spindly legs were piercing through a score of pale blue eggs. Dozens of spiders rushed toward him, his smiling face emblazoned on bulbous thoraxes.

He sprinted into the lobby, and stubbed his toe on the edge of the front desk. Pain stabbed up his leg. He gritted his teeth and ran for the exit, smearing the pale green linoleum with blood.

In a fit of terror, he rushed headlong into the road. Headlights blinded him. He cowered as a Peterbilt truck screeched to a halt.

Regaining his wits, he darted to the passenger's side of the semi. He swung open the door, climbed into the truck and said, "May I use your phone?"

The hooded driver handed Saunders a flip phone. Saunders called his wife.

"Hello," Tina said, in a tired voice.

"Tina, it's Michael. I need you to pick me up at a motel in the Berkshires. I'm in trouble."

There was a long pause. Then she said, "This isn't funny. Go prank call someone else. If you call again, I'll call the cops."

"But Tina, I…"

She hung up. He dialed again.

"I'm calling the police," she said.

"Wait. Please. Don't hang up. It's your husband, Michael."

"No, you're not. My husband's here with me. He came home last night." She hung up.

A swirl of emotions ranging from confusion to terror welled up in Saunders' gut. *Oh my God! I need to get home.*

Dozens of spiders emerged from the motel and scurried toward the truck. But the driver didn't seem to take notice.

"We need to leave! Now!" Saunders yelled. But the driver just sat there, ignoring him. Saunders grabbed the man's shoulder and shook him. The driver turned and Saunders came face to face with himself.

The doppelgänger smiled. Then his face leapt toward Saunders. The driver's clothing burst open in a riot of spiders.

Saunders screamed as mandibles beneath human-faced thoraxes gnawed on his skin, tiny legs tickling flesh.

As the man-spiders ravaged him, he cackled maniacally.

There you are, my magnificent little friends.

Saunders would die, but he wouldn't die a failure.

END

Afterword

I'm not entirely sure where the idea for "Twinwalkers" came from, but the story has obvious Lovecraftian influences. For instance, it involves an academic whose obsession with the fabled Berkshire mimic spider leads him to investigate things that humanity is better off not knowing. Doctor Saunders also never learns what is driving the creatures he is studying in the same way there tends to be unanswered questions in the typical Lovecraft story.

Lovecraft's stories also often have an isolated New England feel. Having lived in New England for three years and being married to a native New Englander, I tried to invoke that New England spirit in this story, working very hard to get the atmosphere just right all the way down to the caretaker's Massachusetts accent.

In my stories, I often intertwine elements of history with the supernatural. In this tale, the Pocomtuc were an actual Native American tribe that had settled in parts of Western Massachusetts and were ultimately wiped out by Mohawk tribes and diseases carried by European settlers like small pox. Other than that, very little is known about the Pocomtuc, which made it easier for me to invent speculative elements of their history such as their fictitious worship of an anthropomorphic spider deity.

Even the looming construction of the Kinder Morgan pipeline which drove Doctor Saunder's urgency to uncover evidence of the Berkshire mimic spider in the fossil record before it was gone was based on an actual natural gas pipeline project that Kinder Morgan had proposed building in parts of Massachusetts. While the company ultimately shelved the three billion dollar project in early 2016, it still served as a critical plot device to drive Doctor Saunder's hasty and ill-advised trip to the Berkshires.

This story was first published in December 2016 in the first issue of *Unnerving Magazine*. I hope you found this story both creepy and enjoyable.

Spirals and Starways

Detective Joey D'Alessio flashed his badge at the needle-scarred bag of bones using the rent-controlled building's doormat as a pillow. The bum just shrugged, so D'Alessio kicked him in the groin to give him some encouragement. D'Alessio was just annoyed that his first missing person case this year was in the Tenderloin, an area rife with criminality and reeking of human waste, marijuana and used condoms.

Today's edition of the *San Francisco Chronicle* had reported tremors in the Tenderloin and some whackos'd claimed they'd seen UFOs over the city. But D'Alessio knew better. If California was the land of fruits and nuts, San Francisco was its capital.

The detective shook his head. He missed his old Brooklyn stomping grounds where a cop could show a criminal what's what. But his autistic brother Marty needed him here. If D'Alessio hadn't screwed up after his parents' deaths, he'd be free to head back East. But now his brother was a ward of the state, and D'Alessio only got to see him when Jessica, Marty's social worker, gave him permission.

D'Alessio climbed a creaky staircase until he reached the second floor and found the missing man's room. After he knocked three times, a gaunt, stringy-haired blonde opened the door. Most civilians would've thought she was forty, but D'Alessio knew that was just in meth years.

He pulled out a notepad and a BIC pen. He took in the small studio apartment, noticing threadbare sheets on a torn mattress. Dishes were piled high in the sink and the stench of human filth threatened to suffocate him.

"Ma'am, I'm Detective Joseph D'Alessio and I'm here to investigate the disappearance of Reginald Saunders."

The woman nodded.

"Can you please tell me your name?"

When she opened her mouth to answer, D'Alessio saw a flash of rotten gray-green teeth. "Melissa Wilson."

"Okay, Melissa. Were you the one who reported Reggie missing?"

She nodded again.

"Can you describe him?"

She walked over to a refuse pile near the window, and pulled out a framed picture of an African-American male who D'Alessio estimated was well over six feet tall.

The detective smiled. "Even better. When did you last see him?"

Melissa lowered her eyes. D'Alessio waited impatiently, and then said, "Ma'am, I need an answer."

Then her stoicism shattered, and she began to sob. "I...I...saw him right here before he disappeared." She pointed toward the floor.

"It's okay," D'Alessio said as he tried to comfort the woman. "You're doing great. When did you last see him?"

"'Round 1:00 am. 'Bout the same time we had that mini-quake," she shuddered as a tear slithered down her wrinkled cheek. "One second he was here with me. The next, gone."

"I see," D'Alessio said as he scribbled a cartoon phallus in his notepad. "When you say 'disappear', what do you mean?"

"You know. Poof! Gone! Like magic."

"Ma'am, when's the last time you used crystal?"

The woman clammed up. D'Alessio knew better than to ask that question. "I'm sorry ma'am. I'm not here to investigate a drug charge. I'm here to find Reggie. I promise I won't turn you in."

Melissa nodded. "Well, we did some meth earlier last night, but I swear I'm telling the truth."

"Yeah, yeah, I'm sure you are, hon. Thanks for your cooperation." D'Alessio closed his notepad and made his way toward the door.

"Are you gonna find him?" she asked, eyes pregnant with hope.

"Ma'am, these things happen all the time. Most times, the guy turns up in a week or two. If we hear anything, we'll get back to you."

⁍

The next morning, D'Alessio stared at a blank screen on his desktop. A beer stein filled with steaming black coffee rested on today's *San Francisco Chronicle*. The paper had another article with more reports of strange lights and tremors in the Tenderloin.

D'Alessio hated filing missing person reports, especially when he had to admit the person was still missing. The phone rang, jolting D'Alessio out of his early morning stupor.

Lieutenant Carmichael's named flashed on the Avaya phone's display, so D'Alessio let the phone ring twice before picking it up. "What?"

"Joseph, this is Lieutenant Carmichael. I trust your week's going well."

D'Alessio sighed. "It's Detective D'Alessio to you, L-T. Can we dispense with all the BS? What do you want?"

Goddamn Californians. Always wasting words with passive aggressive bullshit. They all hated his guts. Everyone that is, except Detective Jesse Simmons. Simmons, he understood. The big, brawny black detective was from Oakland, but D'Alessio didn't hold that against him. Everyone else played like Joey was their best friend, but not Simmons. Simmons always gave him the straight dope.

Simmons chuckled and pointed at D'Alessio. D'Alessio gave him the finger. Simmons laughed.

There was a moment of hesitation on the phone, and then the Lieutenant said, "Now, now, detective, there's no reason to be so sensitive."

"Yeah, yeah. L-T. Whatchya want? I haven't had my coffee so I'm feeling a little frisky this morning." D'Alessio took a swig from his beer stein.

"Ah, well, ah, fine. I need you to investigate another disappearance in the Tenderloin."

D'Alessio spit his coffee all over his desk. "You've got to be fucking kidding me, L-T. The Tenderloin? Again? I went yesterday as a favor, but earlier this week, I almost shot someone because he threw feces at me. You send me in there again, you're asking for trouble."

"We need you because you have the highest clearance rate in the department. Another person is missing, and the circumstances are similar to the disappearance you investigated yesterday."

That got D'Alessio's attention.

"Let me guess: it happened at 1:00 am during a tremor?"

"Exactly."

D'Alessio was intrigued.

"Fine. I'll do it, but on one condition."

"Name it."

"I take Detective Simmons with me."

"Done."

80

D'Alessio and Simmons stood facing a stucco building covered with graffiti portraying a soldier wearing a gas mask with the phrase "If at first you don't succeed—call in an air strike" scrawled in unsteady lettering. The early morning fog was only starting to dissipate in the cold chill, while the pungent scent of freshly brewed coffee wafted in the air. Simmons was on his second menthol cigarette, while D'Alessio nursed his coffee.

Detective Simmons grinned and said, "You should've been with me last night, brotha. Me and the boys went to Broadway, and took the usual club tour.   A few bottles of Champagne later and it was off the hook. I took this one stripper home and tore into her."

"Well, that's why they call you, two-pump," Joey said.

"Huh?"

"Two-pump. You know, as in a two-pump chump. Once you stick it in, it's over."

"Aw hell no! Who calls me that?"

"Everyone in the department."

"Aw hell no, son. Ain't no two-pump here! More like the Viagra Niagra."

"The what?"

"The Viagra Niagra. You know, I can go for hours, but once it blows, it flows."

D'Alessio choked on his coffee.

"Now that you're done blowing smoke up my ass with tales of your Nubian sexual prowess, we can finally get to work."

Both men's expressions tensed. Simmons dubbed out his cigarette on the building and tossed the butt on the ground as the two made their way into yet another roach-filled rent controlled building. Once inside, they climbed three floors to get to the woman's apartment.

D'Alessio did a circuit around the room, noting every detail. He was unnerved that the studio apartment didn't reek of the sweet tang of marijuana leaf or have the paint-thinner-like odor of a meth lab. In fact, it was the opposite of what he'd expected. The kitchenette's countertops were spotless.

Books on the studio's two bookcases were arranged alphabetically by author, and the floor didn't have a single piece of lint.

"Speak to me, brotha crime whisperer," Simmons said.

D'Alessio rejoined his partner near the studio's entrance and then said, "This apartment's pretty damn clean for the Tenderloin. Some old broad probably lived here."

Simmons nodded. "The neighbors say it was a seventy-nine year old woman named Joan Finkelstein. Must have been one tough cookie."

"Yeah. By why's she missing? There's no sign of forced entry and the apartment's immaculate."

Simmons shrugged. "Well, doesn't seem like there's anything else we can do." Simmons offered D'Alessio a cigarette.

"C'mon man, you know I don't smoke."

"You might want to start. Looks like the L-T put you on this investigation to screw up your clearance rate."

D'Alessio hadn't considered that. "You're probably right. What the hell would I do without you?"

"For one, you wouldn't be in the department anymore. What's that little phrase you came up with that almost got you canned?"

"Happier than a fag at a big dick convention. And I didn't come up with it."

Simmons chortled. "I can't believe you said that shit in San Francisco. What the hell were you thinking?"

"I dunno, I could've just as easily said happier than a nympho at a porn convention."

"And then you told the L-T you wouldn't follow him to the Playboy Mansion. Where do you come up with this shit?"

"I guess I'm just special."

"You're special all right. Special ed."

D'Alessio glared at Simmons. Simmons backed away from D'Alessio, his palms facing outward. "Aw man, I'm sorry. I didn't mean anything by that."

Joey nodded and said, "I know. I'm just a little tense. I'm gonna go outside and get some air."

"All right. I'll catch you out there in about ten minutes." Simmons reached for his cigarettes as D'Alessio left the studio.

As D'Alessio descended the stairs, he shrugged off Simmons' comments. He knew Simmons didn't mean anything by them, but D'Alessio loved his brother and wanted to protect him. Then his thoughts returned to more professional matters, as he struggled to understand how two people who couldn't have been more different, disappeared under circumstances that seemed nearly identical.

An explosion threw D'Alessio to the ground floor and sucked the air out of him, as a wall of fire swept down the staircase. Driven by blind instinct, D'Alessio stumbled to his feet and bolted for the exit, rolling on the ground to douse the flames on his clothing once he emerged.

Simmons.

D'Alessio turned back and pushed himself back into the building's entrance, but the wave of heat was so intense, there was nothing he could do. He watched helplessly as the flames consumed every living soul left in the building, including the only man who'd besides Marty who ever understood D'Alessio.

He fell to his knees and wept.

ജ

Simmons's charred remains weren't even in the ground yet when the L-T called him to investigate a third disappearance two days later at the Hotel Mark Twain.

On his way to the hotel room, he bumped into a cop. "Watch where you're going," the man said in a high-pitched voice that belonged more to Alvin and the Chipmunks than it did to a grown man. D'Alessio just shook his head and moved on.

Another cop approached him. "You must be D'Alessio," he said in a high-pitched squeal. "Never mind our voices. Everyone who's been up here for more than a minute talks like this."

"Helium?" D'Alessio said, surprised his voice was several octaves higher.

The cop shrugged and said, "Do I look like a chemist to you?"

"Where are the witnesses?"

The cop pointed to his right. "Down at the end of the hall, to the left."

D'Alessio nodded and headed in that direction. A middle-aged brunette woman with two young daughters stood at the end of the hall, ringed by several investigators. She seemed frazzled. Her two daughters clung tenaciously to each side of her, one burying her face in the woman's leg.

D'Alessio caught wind of the conversation, "...not making this up. I was tossing and turning because the couple down the hall was carrying on quite a bit. You know, doing the stuff women and menfolk do together at night. All of the sudden, the floor started shaking. I looked at my alarm clock. It was 2:00 am. Exactly. Light flashed outside my window. Then nothing. I thought it was just thunder and lightning. We get that a lot in Alabama, but they tell me electrical storms are rare out here 'cause it's too dry," she said in a slow southern drawl, and in a voice unaffected by helium.

D'Alessio's flashed his badge. "Excuse me, ma'am, I'm Detective D'Alessio. You say this happened at 2:00 am?"

She nodded.

"And you saw a flash of light."

She nodded again.

"How'd you know the people at the end of the hall went missing then?"

"Well, as I said before, they'd been carrying on for quite a bit, then after the flash of light and trembling, bam! They were quiet as mice. It was so eerie that I called room service to check on them and then got dressed, walked down the hall and knocked on their door. Nothing. When the room service lady arrived, she knocked again. She tried a few more times, and then opened the door to find an empty room. Then we all started talking funny. You know, like when you suck the air out of a balloon. That's when I called the police and the next day y'all showed up."

D'Alessio scribbled down all the details into his notepad. He also wondered why the helium that appeared to be filling the room never quite dissipated. For Simmons' sake, D'Alessio wanted to solve this crime more than ever, but even with access to a reliable witness, he now had more questions than ever.

D'Alessio closed his notepad and said, "Thanks, ma'am, for your cooperation. We'll contact you if we have any further questions."

ಬ

Three days later, D'Alessio stood inside the Young-Ellis Food Center on Jones and Ellis. A massive structure resembling a silvery gray nautilus shell extended from the floor to the ceiling. It was one of the most beautiful structures he'd ever seen—like a sandcastle erected in such impossible complexity that it seemed to defy the laws of gravity.

Local residents had reported a flash of light and a small earthquake the night before at around 3:00 am. Today, three more people were missing.

The few witnesses D'Alessio had interviewed yielded little useful information, other than that the nautilus structure seemed to have appeared out of thin air overnight. At least D'Alessio had samples he could send to the crime lab for analysis.

As he made his way out of the small market, a mob of reporters surged against the police blocking off the crime scene.

"Detective D'Alessio," an anonymous female voice yelled from the crowd, "does the department have any leads on the recent spate of disappearances?"

D'Alessio shuddered. *How the hell did they know his name?* he thought. Then the answer came, *The L-T's trying to tie me to this investigation. To ruin me.* He longed for Simmons' counsel more than ever.

The besieged detective shoved his way through the crowd as reporters snapped his picture for the morning papers.

℘

It was late afternoon, and D'Alessio ran his fingers through his hair as he stared at the peg-studded map adorning the squad area's wall next to a whiteboard. Four pegs marked the location of each crime scene. A matrix was scrawled on the board with rows listing the addresses and with columns containing the number of missing persons, time, and days between each event. All three columns had the same mysterious sequence: one-one-two-three.

There's got to be a pattern, D'Alessio thought. D'Alessio was running out of options. He didn't have a perpetrator and there was no link connecting the missing persons.

A phone call broke D'Alessio's concentration. "Fuck!" he yelled as he slammed his fist on his desk before picking up the phone. "What?"

A female voice answered. "Joey, this is Jessica. I'm out front with Marty."

"Dammit! Jessica. Now's not a good time."

D'Alessio instantly regretted his words. He knew better than to treat Marty's social worker this way.

"I'm sorry, Joey, but this is the time we arranged for his weekly visit. We can always cancel it."

D'Alessio wanted to kick himself for forgetting the arrangement. He then said, "I'm sorry, Jessica. I didn't mean to snap at you like that. It's been a stressful few weeks. I'll be down in a minute"

D'Alessio opened his desk and pulled out a Twinkie from the box he'd kept there. He then headed down the steps and through the metal detectors near the entrance to meet Jessica and Marty in the main lobby.

A six-foot four man with a disheveled shock of black hair nearly bulled D'Alessio over when he saw him, "Joey! Want Twinkie!"

It took all of D'Alessio's strength to stay on his feet, and before his brother's crushing embrace knocked the wind out of him.

D'Alessio pushed his brother away, holding up the Twinkie. "Okay, Marty, calm down. Here's your Twinkie."

Marty snatched it from D'Alessio's hand, ripped off the cellophane, and inhaled it with a single bite. D'Alessio nodded at Jessica, and the diminutive brunette smiled back before turning to leave.

D'Alessio led his brother through the metal detectors and back up to the squad room. When D'Alessio and Marty entered the room, several detectives observed them with barely concealed smirks, and Lieutenant Carmichael was waiting at D'Alessio's desk.

The L-T looked at Marty with a scowl and then turned his head toward D'Alessio. "Are you ready to brief me on your investigation, detective?"

Of all the times Carmichael could ask for a briefing. "Can this wait, L-T?" D'Alessio gestured toward his brother. "I'm kinda occupied right now."

"No, it cannot wait, detective. I've got the chief asking me for daily updates on this case. The mayor's starting to get nervous as well. You can only tell him your best man is on the case for so long, before they start questioning your judgment. So, detective, you gonna clear this one soon? You know, before we start seeing this case in the national papers?"

So that's what this is about. D'Alessio decided to play along because what he actually wanted to do would've gotten him fired and possibly thrown in jail.

D'Alessio pulled out the chair behind his desk and motioned for Marty to sit down. At first, his brother just stared at D'Alessio, but when D'Alessio pulled another Twinkie out of his drawer, Marty sat enthusiastically.

Once Marty was in place, D'Alessio walked toward a map of the city hanging next to the whiteboard, "Okay. So what do we know? We've had disappearances here, here, here, and here," D'Alessio pointed to four multi-colored pegs on the map centered on the Tenderloin District. Then he moved over to the whiteboard, grabbed a marker and started scribbling. "We also know that the first two disappearances happened at 1:00 am one day apart. The second one at around 2:00 am, two days later, and the third, three days after that at around 3:00 am. Witnesses also reported tremors and flashes of light at the time of the disappearance. There's clearly a pattern here, but I'm at a loss as to what it is. All I've got is a sequence: one-one-two-three…"

Suddenly, Marty leapt up from his seat and began shouting, "One. One. Two. Three. Five. Eight. Thirteen. Twenty-one. Thirty-four…"

D'Alessio rushed over to his brother and tried to calm him by offering him another Twinkie. "It's okay, Marty." The detective looked over at the Lieutenant. "I don't know what it is that set him off. He's really good with numbers. Maybe it's this sequence."

Marty continued to rock back at forth, seemingly inconsolable. "I want pen! Give me pen! Joey get pen!"

"It's okay, Marty. It's okay."

The Lieutenant looked sternly at D'Alessio. "Give him the marker. It's erasable, so he can't screw anything up.

D'Alessio nodded in resignation, grabbed a marker from the whiteboard and handed it to his brother.

Marty beamed with a hearty smile and ran up to the map instead of the whiteboard.

"No! Marty! Don't!" D'Alessio yelled. But it was too late. His brother was already drawing a perfect spiral connecting each of the four locations, extending the spiral until his marker ran out of map.

"Put peg here! Put peg here! Five! Five! Five!" Marty pointed to a spot on his spiral.

"Five what, Marty? Days?"

Marty seemed confused. He was a genius with numbers, but he had always been incapable of contextualizing what the numbers meant. D'Alessio held up his hand with five fingers outstretched. "Five, Marty? Five?"

Then Marty nodded and launched into his sequence, "One. One. Two. Three. Five. Eight..."

"Okay, that's enough, Marty," D'Alessio said. "Lieutenant, do you know if there's anything special about that sequence?"

Carmichael shrugged.

"Aw hell, let's just Google it," D'Alessio said as he hopped over to his desk computer, typed in the digits up to eight and pressed Enter.

"I'll be damned. The sequence has a name—Fibonacci." D'Alessio beamed. "And Marty figured it out."

D'Alessio walked back over to his brother and hugged him. "Good boy, Marty. Good boy!"

The Lieutenant looked dubious. "So what? For all we know it's just be a random pattern. I can't go to the chief with this."

D'Alessio was apoplectic, "Are you kidding me? This is the best lead we've got. Not only has my brother broken the code, he's given you the location of the next disappearance. We need to get a surveillance team up there on Tuesday at 5:00 am."

"I'm sorry, detective, but I'm going to need a little bit more than the analysis of a code-cracking rain man before I commit departmental resources."

Before D'Alessio had a chance to think, he had Carmichael by the throat and jacked up against the wall. "You call my brother 'rain man' again, and I'll fucking end you, Carmichael."

D'Alessio had crossed the line and he knew it. His days in the department were now officially numbered.

ꙮ

Five days and one suspension later, D'Alessio sat alone in his beaten up Ford Taurus staking out the next suspected location, Hospitality House, on Turk and Leavenworth. He made sure to keep some distance between his car and the building. He didn't want to disappear himself. It was 4:30 a.m. and the fog hung over his car cold and heavy. Visibility was terrible and it was still dark.

D'Alessio reclined back in the driver's seat as he waited patiently with a pair of black binos, undeterred by the darkness. As he waited, he observed six hooded figures emerge from the fog from the vicinity of Turk and Leavenworth. The corner was an area well-known for drug dealing, and this early in the morning, it was more likely to happen when fewer people were around to witness it.

The figures headed straight for his car. One rapped on D'Alessio's window with a pipe. "Whatcha doin' here, man?" the stranger announced in a tone that sounded more like a challenge than a question.

For Christ's sake, not now, D'Alessio thought. He reached for his service weapon, and then remembered he no longer had his piece because of the suspension.

There was another, more forceful tap on the window. "Get out the car!"

D'Alessio looked around the inside of his Ford for anything he could use as a weapon.

"Get out the car!" a young voice yelled, punctuated by shattered glass. D'Alessio heard whoops and some laughter. Then his door opened. One of the men yanked him from his car and threw him onto the pavement.

"Give me your wallet," the tall youth wielding the pipe and wearing a skullcap and a brown leather jacket demanded.

D'Alessio got back on his feet and moved to within six inches of the kid's face. "Fuck you."

D'Alessio's jaw went slack and his ears rang all the way back down to the pavement after the teenager buffeted him with the pipe. A savage beating followed.

Tremors.

Several of his assailants lost their balance and fell to the ground. All six jumped back on their feet and fled back toward Turk and Leavenworth. But they didn't get very far.

As D'Alessio lifted his battered head to watch the fleeing thugs, there was a blinding flash of light. Then all but one were gone.

Screams.

The screams grew louder as people sleeping at the Hospitality House homeless shelter streamed out into the street.

The remaining youth, the ringleader with the pipe, stopped in his tracks. "Charlie! Antoine! Jackson! Scooter! Shan! Shit!"

He marched back down the street toward D'Alessio. "Whatchya do to my boys?" he yelled. "You gonna pay for what you did. I'm gonna tune you up, muthafucka."

D'Alessio struggled to get back on his feet, but the instant he did, the thug swung the pipe at D'Alessio's head. D'Alessio dodged, but the next blow connected with D'Alessio's left knee. He fell to the ground and raised his arms to plead with his attacker.

"Naw, naw. I'm gonna make you pay," his assailant taunted as he moved in for the kill. As soon as his attacker was within reach, D'Alessio grabbed his testicles and gave them a sharp, swift twist. The kid hit the ground hard, dropping his pipe.

D'Alessio picked it up, and limped passed his attacker and toward Hospitality House. People were still leaving the shelter in droves. D'Alessio grabbed one frail-looking man by the arm and said, "What happened in there?"

"Hell, man! I don't know. There was this earthquake and flash of light. Then this black shell thing just showed up out of nowhere, overturning our bunks."

"Where?"

The man pointed to shelter's entrance.

Once inside, D'Alessio found overturned mattresses strewn about the room from the path of another nautilus-like spiral structure fashioned from a semi-metallic black material.

D'Alessio took a sample and left.

ॐ

"You gonna tell me what this is about, Joey?" Jim Eddy, the station's lab tech asked. "And why we're meeting in an alley instead of the squad room to go over the test results?"

"Do you want me to make those parking tickets disappear or what?" D'Alessio said.

Jim rolled his eyes, and then nodded. "Fine. But I have to warn you. I ran three tests because I couldn't believe what I was seeing. The first sample you gave me, you know, the silvery-white stuff, was Lithium. Pure elemental Lithium. Never seen anything like it. You never find this stuff freely occurring in nature. It's usually found in ionic compounds. Where'd you find this stuff?"

"What about the other sample?"

Jim shook his head. "Boron. Pure boron. Again, you can't find this stuff naturally on Earth. It's usually found in compounds like borax."

D'Alessio sighed. "What do these two elements have in common?"

Jim shrugged. "Other than that they're both two extremely pure samples, I don't know. Are you gonna help get rid of my tickets now or what?"

"Do these elements have anything to do with Fibonacci?"

"What? As in the sequence?"

"Yeah, you know, one-one-two-three-five, et cetera?"

"D'Alessio, you surprise me more and more everyday. Come to think of it, Lithium's atomic number is three. Boron's is five. I'm surprised you didn't give me two samples of hydrogen and one of helium."

D'Alessio took a step back. "Wait. Did you say, 'helium.'"

"Yeah. Helium and hydrogen. Helium's got an atomic number of two and hydrogen, one."

"If you light a match in a room filled with hydrogen, will it explode?"

"Absolutely. Why?"

D'Alessio could no longer keep his findings to himself. With the loss of his buddy, Simmons, he desperately needed someone to trust. It would have to be Jim. "Jim, I'm sorry, but I was bullshitting you about those parking tickets. I've been suspended from the force."

Jim threw his hands in the air. "Goddammit, D'Alessio! I could lose my job over this."

"Calm down, man. I won't tell anybody, if you don't."

Jim just nodded. "At least tell me what's going on."

D'Alessio described the five crime scenes, the times they occurred, the number of days each was spaced apart, the number of victims, and how their locations traced along a Fibonacci spiral. He told him the strange nautilus configurations left behind, shaped by an element with an atomic number consistent with the Fibonacci sequence.

Jim scratched his head. "You see the Fibonacci sequence everywhere in nature at both the micro and macroscopic level—in ram's horns, in Nautilus shells, in the branching of trees, even in the formation of galaxies. Even Humans possess this symmetry. Take the shape of the human ear for instance.

"Jim, the more I investigate this case, the more I think I'm going nuts. I've got nothing other than the time, date, location, and number of victims in the next incident."

"You sure?"

"Well, I predicted the last one, or at least Marty did. That's how I was able to get that last sample before the cops arrived."

Jim seemed lost in thought. "Maybe someone or something is testing us. Trying to see if we're intelligent enough to decode the sequence."

D'Alessio chuckled. "You mean like aliens?"

When Jim's eyes met D'Alessio's, Jim wasn't laughing. "Think about it. All these events are happening at precisely choreographed dates and times based on Fibonacci sequences. Each event coincides with a tremor and a flash of light. The only thing left behind is a nautilus spiral composed of a pure elemental compound that doesn't occur naturally. Call me crazy, but it's the only theory I've got."

"If you're right, what do you think they want? How can we make them stop?"

"I haven't the faintest idea."

&

D'Alessio woke to the steady buzz of his four-year-old Nokia cell phone. Dazed, he glanced over at his alarm clock. Four a.m. Who the hell would call at four a.m.? D'Alessio considered ignoring the call, but today was the day—eight days after the last incident. Maybe he should answer. Then again, it wasn't his problem anymore.

Two more rings and he made his decision. "This better be important."

A frantic female voice responded, "Joey, it's Jessica. Marty's gone."

"What do you mean 'gone'?"

"He left his room last night."

"How's that even possible. Don't you guys have security monitoring who comes and goes?"

"Of course. But he didn't leave through the main entrance."

"What other way is there?"

"Through the window."

"You've got to be frick'in kidding me. He's on the fourth floor."

"Apparently, he fashioned a rope from his sheets and the sheets of other tenants, tenants who left with him."

"Let me guess: seven others."

"How'd you know that?"

"Call it a lucky guess. Meet me at the Golden Gate Theater in thirty minutes."

"Why?"

"You'll find your patients."

Thirty minutes later, D'Alessio was shivering at the corner of Taylor and Market. It was still twilight, but the sun's rays began to pulse faintly over the horizon.

Eight patients, including Marty were busy drawing spirals on the asphalt in diverse hues of colored chalk. They muttered almost incoherently in a numerical language that had only one word: eight.

D'Alessio found Marty entranced in this mystic ritual in the middle of the intersection. D'Alessio shook Marty, but his brother ignored him. D'Alessio grabbed his brother's arm and tried to pull him away, but Marty fought back.

Then D'Alessio saw Marty's eyes—white orbs, the iris tucked back into his skull. D'Alessio saw no malice in his brother's face, only a drive born of some unearthly purpose as Marty repeated "eight" over and over again.

D'Alessio relaxed his grip, unsure what to do. He'd learned the hard way that when Marty was intent on doing something, nothing could stop him.

Minutes later, Jessica arrived, her auburn hair topsy-turvy and her clothing wrinkled. Her bloodshot eyes widened as she took in the scene. "Joey, how on Earth did you know they'd be here?"

D'Alessio just shrugged. "You wouldn't believe me if I told you. But that doesn't matter now. We need to get them outta here now."

"I'm sorry, Joey, but that's not possible. Most of the center's staff won't be in until after 8:00 a.m. and I don't have enough space in my car to carry all these patients back. Plus, I can't leave any of them here without supervision from a properly credentialed mental health professional. Too much liability exposure."

"To hell with legal liability. We'll all be liable if a car runs over someone. Help me at least move them from the street and onto the sidewalk."

Jessica hesitated. "Fine."

D'Alessio again attempted to move Marty from the street, but Marty fought back, screeching in a high-pitched whine. D'Alessio relaxed his grip, as he watched Jessica cajole another patient to leave the intersection. The patient ignored her.

Jessica turned to D'Alessio. "It's useless. When they get this way, the only thing the staff can do is medicate them. All we can do now is call the police to block the intersection, and wait for the center's staff to arrive."

The last thing D'Alessio wanted was for his former colleagues to find him at a future crime scene. Even worse, he didn't want to see eight more people disappear. "Nah. That's not a good idea. Can you get those drugs now? We can medicate them and get them off the street and outta here now."

"Are you out of your mind. I could lose my job. I'm calling the police." She pulled out her iPhone.

D'Alessio grabbed her arm. "Please. Don't. Trust me on this."

Jessica's eyes seethed. "Take. Your hands. Off me."

D'Alessio released her arm and lifted his arms in the air to signal retreat. "I'm sorry. You go ahead and call the police, but I'm taking Marty with me."

"You can't do that. He's a ward of the state."

"Watch me."

D'Alessio walked over to his brother, put him in a headlock and squeezed until Marty passed out. Jessica screamed and slapped D'Alessio, but he ignored her. He lifted Marty's limp body over his shoulder and lumbered over to his Ford Taurus, while Jessica yelled, "You'll go to prison for this."

D'Alessio didn't care if it meant saving Marty's life.

∞

When Marty woke in D'Alessio's apartment two hours later, D'Alessio remembered why the state had declared the detective unfit to watch over his brother. Marty raced toward the door, frantic with an intensity that brought back D'Alessio's feelings of helplessness. In this state, D'Alessio knew it would be impossible to reason with Marty.

D'Alessio wrestled Marty to the ground. His brother struggled to regain his feet, drool slobbering from his mouth. "Calm down, Marty. Please!" D'Alessio pleaded.

D'Alessio struggled with his sibling until he choked his brother into unconsciousness again. Emotions of regret and loss nearly overwhelmed him. He fought back a torrent of tears, but submitted to the despair in the end. While his brother lay on the floor, D'Alessio sobbed as he hoisted his brother onto his couch and cocooned him in duct tape.

Then D'Alessio sat vigil over his brother on an old aluminum folding chair. When his brother awoke ten minutes later, he screamed, repeating "eight" over and over. D'Alessio wanted to cover his brother's mouth, but didn't have the heart to silence him. Yet D'Alessio could barely stand the screaming, until at last he just covered his ears and began screaming too.

Then, Marty stopped. His eyes rolled forward in their sockets and he looked at D'Alessio, confused.

D'Alessio checked the time on his cellphone. It was 8:01 a.m.

That evening, the only reason Marty's kidnapping wasn't on the front page of the *Chronicle* was because the sudden vanishings of seven autistic patients and one of their caretakers made for a better headline.

∞

Over the next five days, D'Alessio and Marty laid low. Their faces were now all over the newspapers, but D'Alessio figured no one cared much about two grown men lost in a city with much bigger problems. However, just to be cautious, they slept at local youth hostels during the day, and traveled only at night.

Marty seemed far calmer than he'd been in a long time. He stayed quiet and rarely caused a ruckus. His eyes showed a tinge of what D'Alessio sensed was regret. As day thirteen drew closer, Marty became more obsessed with his numbers and spirals.

One evening, at around midnight, as the two were walking toward Union Square Park, Marty began to fidget and then grabbed D'Alessio's hand. Marty then pointed forward. D'Alessio nodded and let his brother lead.

When they reached the center of the park, Marty pointed to the sky, drew a spiral in the air, and said, "Home."

D'Alessio couldn't begin to fathom why his brother made this request, but for the first time in his life he knew deep in his bones that Marty understood the cosmos better than D'Alessio ever would. At that moment, D'Alessio knew what he had to do.

ഔ

On a clear April day, D'Alessio led his brother to Union Square Park. The detective didn't know where they'd be going, but anywhere was better than here. Away from the petty politics and workplace intrigue. Away from the corruption and filth. A place where he'd have a future. And more importantly, a place where he hoped Marty would be understood.

The people around him breezed past him like the leaves of fall, seemingly oblivious to their role in Fibonacci's cycle.

D'Alessio checked his cellphone. In two minutes it would be 1300 hours. A tear rolled down D'Alessio's cheek, as he embraced Marty once more before oblivion.

One minute.

Marty began to shake, somehow in tune with something slightly out of phase with our reality, but more real to Marty than the strange world to which he never quite belonged.

The ground began to shake and a blinding light washed out the soft azure sky in a burst of photonic infinity, leaving a perfect spiral of elemental aluminum in its wake.

Marty was gone, along with twelve other strangers. Only D'Alessio remained. While he regretted being left behind, he hoped Marty went to a better place, a place that would appreciate Marty's mind.

For the first time in a long while, Joey D'Alessio smiled.

END

Afterword

"Spirals and Starways" is the first story in which Detective Joey D'Alessio appears, and it was the second story I sold to *Plasma Frequency Magazine*. It is also one of the five stories in this collection I would loosely classify as hard science fiction.

If it isn't already obvious, the Fibonacci sequence provided the main inspiration for this story. I planned to structure a narrative around the first several numbers in the sequence. I first tied each number to the atomic numbers of the elements on the periodic table. Then I overlaid a Fibonacci spiral onto a map of San Francisco and selected actual locations that intersected with points on the spiral. Lastly, I tied the timing of events in the story to the discrete numbers in a Fibonacci sequence.

All these connections may seem contrived, but that was the point of the story. While I never explicitly mentioned it, the unseen aliens in the story set up an elaborate and sophisticated riddle to detect signs of superior intelligence on Earth, and Marty, with the incidental help of Joey, rose to the occasion.

The story also very crudely attempts to explore the differences between what I perceive as the generally laid back and passive aggressive culture of the West Coast and the plainspoken and brutally direct style of the East Coast. D'Alessio is obviously a caricature of the latter.

I hope you found this story enjoyable if not thought provoking.

JOSÉ BAETAS

Tunguska

It wasn't every day that a man had to audition for his life. Stalin did not suffer fools, but it was how Stalin dealt with them that terrified Dr. Leonid Kulik. But a jolt of pain in Kulik's chest reminded him of far greater terrors and harsher masters.

Kulik had rehearsed his speech for hours as his train had barreled along the Trans-Siberian Railway. He'd labored to get every word right. But no matter how much he'd practiced, he couldn't imagine any sane person believing his story, let alone the General Secretary of the Central Committee of the Communist Party.

Shivering in his black woolen greatcoat and sheepskin *papaha*, a bespectacled Kulik huddled before Lenin's wooden mausoleum beneath the crenelated Kremlin Wall. A chill, howling wind whirled thick snowflakes around him while he waited in the dark for his tardy host.

Yuri Golikov approached Red Square from the Senatskaya Gate. His footsteps crunched on the icy snow. His unkempt greatcoat rippled in the cold gale. Golikov's off-kilter *ushanka*, ruddy cheeks and vodka-laced breath gave Kulik a good idea why the lanky Party official was late. Kulik rolled his eyes in silent protest.

Chiding Golikov for his unprofessionalism would be unwise. Kulik suspected the man was an OGPU agent. One could never be sure these days.

One wrong word or ill-considered phrase earned many a bullet in the head and a shallow, unmarked grave.

An unsteady Golikov guided Kulik past the Kremlin Necropolis and through the Senatskaya Tower Gate. From there, he directed Kulik toward the domed Senate Palace's private entrance. Once inside, Golikov ushered Kulik to the Catherine Hall rotunda.

A foul smelling cloud of mundungus hit Kulik's nostrils. He coughed and then entered the chamber. Tobacco smoke stinging his eyes, Kulik struggled to take in the dome-shaped hall's grandeur. Marble colonnades lined the chamber's edge at equal intervals. Between the columns, windows on the dome's far side offered a stunning view of the Senate Palace's inner courtyard. Sculptured bas-reliefs adorned the wall's remaining surfaces. A ring-shaped, polished marble conference table dominated the room's center. At the far end of the rotunda, Stalin puffed on a black iron pipe. He sat pouring over a swollen stack of documents, holding court over his cabal of senior Party and military officials.

Golikov nudged Kulik, rousing the mineralogist out of a scared stupor. Seeing Stalin in person felt so surreal that Kulik had lost his tongue. Stalin's pockmarked skin surprised Kulik, especially in contrast to the man's unblemished images on Soviet propaganda posters.

Stalin glanced up and raised an eyebrow. He removed his pipe. His stern gaze regarded Kulik as if he were gauging the man's worth. Or maybe Stalin was deciding whether to crush an insect. Kulik couldn't tell. But if Stalin only knew what Kulik was, the dictator would destroy him.

Stalin glowered at Golikov.

"Comrade Stalin, this is Dr. Leonid Kulik, chief curator of the Leningrad Museum's meteorite collection," Golikov said, his voice quavering.

Kulik shuddered every time he'd heard his city's new name. He worried he'd slip and call it Petrograd, infuriating Stalin. One had to be vigilant in Soviet Russia. It's been said that OGPU jackals like Vyacheslav Menzhinsky and Artur Artuzov created fictitious "resistance movements" to ensnare their political enemies. Here, in the heart of the Soviet police apparatus, Kulik was acutely aware of his own paranoia. But that paranoia was also a Russian's most vital survival instinct.

Stalin's rheumy eyes shifted from Golikov to Kulik. Kulik pushed his circular bifocals against the bridge of his nose, cleared his voice, and then spoke. "Comrade Stalin, it's an honor to meet you. Thank you for taking time out of your busy schedule to…"

Stalin held up his hand. "Too many words. Why are you here?"

Kulik nearly swallowed his tongue. Adrenaline flooded his system. "Comrade Stalin, I'm here to report the findings of my Tunguska expedition."

Stalin nodded. "Ah, yes. Now I remember. This is the Soviet Academy of Sciences-funded study, no?"

"It is."

"So where's my iron?"

"Excuse me, Comrade Stalin?" Kulik scratched his beard to avoid shaking.

Stalin's eyes widened. He raised his voice. "Iron. From the meteorite."

Now Kulik remembered. Stalin wasn't interested in scientific curiosities; only things that furthered the Revolution. "Unfortunately, we found no iron. But I think my discovery has far greater value for the Soviet people."

Stalin glared at Kulik and crossed his arms over his chest. "Who are you to tell me what holds more significance for the Soviet Union?" he said in an irritated tone.

"My apologies, Comrade Stalin," Kulik stammered. "What I meant to say is that once you hear more about what I found, you'll want to learn more."

Kulik's heart raced. Another adrenaline surge. This wasn't going well. Everything he'd so painstakingly rehearsed had come out all jumbled.

"What can be more important than organizing the proletariat against the capitalist forces gathering on our borders? What can be more ennobling than destroying the very powers that seek to extinguish the smoldering embers of class-consciousness? We are fifty to a hundred years behind the advanced nations. If we don't industrialize within a decade, they'll crush us. To industrialize, we need iron. It's one of the most critical components of our first Five-Year Plan. The aim of your expedition was to recover iron fragments from the Tunguska impact crater. I hope you're not here to report your failure."

Kulik winced. In his next breath he had to convince Stalin that the Tunguska discovery trumped salvaging iron deposits. Otherwise, it was the gulag or worse. "Comrade Stalin, within five months what I found at Tunguska could make the Soviet Union the most powerful nation on Earth."

An unnatural rush of contentment washed over Kulik. As if he'd just fallen in love. Dopamine. The answer pleased his hidden master.

Stalin thrust his pipe in his mouth and puffed. "Tell me more."

Kulik nodded. He barely suppressed a nervous sigh of relief. He took a deep breath and told Stalin his tale.

℘

Earlier this year, my survey team went into the Siberian hinterland to examine the effects of the 1908 Tunguska meteorite strike. We catalogued a swath of destruction covering thousands of *versts*. The impact's energy was so powerful, it had laid waste to over eighty million trees. Amid the destruction, I uncovered a strange artifact—one I believe is of extraterrestrial origin.

The Siberian taiga's rugged conditions forced me to abandon my 1921 expedition. But my second one this past April was more successful, though not without its own unique challenges.

The region's Tungus villagers were reluctant to discuss the 1908 event, much less lead us to the impact zone. Over the years, these superstitious and primitive people have accumulated a fair bit of lore about the site—lore that proved to have some basis in fact. For instance, the Tungus had an irrational fear of a cryptic tribe they called the Valley Men. Because of these superstitions, it was nearly impossible to hire a local guide.

The closer we got to the crater, we discovered increasing numbers of queer metallic shards composed of elements unclassifiable on Mendeleev's periodic table.

The Tungus peasants we encountered nearest the site were listless, pale, and sickly. If I'd believed in a God, I would have described them as soulless. Those some distance from the impact had reported an eerie green fog that drove men mad.

It was difficult to put much stock in these tales. Yet so many eyewitnesses reported the same phenomena that it was impossible to ignore the stories. Most believed the metallic fragments were cursed.

On the night of April thirtieth, I woke to screams. Gasping for air, my assistant, Sergey Malinovsky, rushed into my tent. "Petrukhin, Timoshenko and Shcherbakov haven't returned from the wilderness," he said. "Earlier tonight, they went to investigate odd sounds and electromagnetic phenomena. Others are reporting peculiar yelps and a faint, strobing green light."

A grim mood fell over the camp. Siberia's suffocating isolation, cold, and gloom only heightened the sense of despair.

In that part of the world even late spring is bleak. Mosquitos nipped at our skin, draining every ounce of blood from our bodies in the bog's chill damp. A cloud-covered sky blotted out the stars. For those accustomed to the warm glow of city lights, it's tough to fathom just how absolute darkness is in that forlorn and desolate place.

To calm my men, I dulled their nerves by issuing extra vodka rations. Then Malinovsky and I ventured toward the impact zone's epicenter. We took our rifles, lanterns, and two dogs to sniff out the scent of the missing men. As we closed in on the impact site, we crossed into a silent abyss where even the chirps of crickets and the hum of mosquitos were absent.

Our compass needles began spinning erratically, as if affected by a strange distortion of Earth's magnetic field.

As we descended deeper into the darkness, a ghostly trilling akin to the call of an American whippoorwill resonated in the blackness. Among the deathly silence, the eerie trills unnerved me. Nevertheless, I pressed on. After wandering several hundred meters, I stumbled onto Timoshenko's corpse. His skull had been pried open like a tin can. His brain was missing. The cuts on his cranium were precise, almost surgical. Several meters away, I found the bodies of Petrukhin and Shcherbakov. Their skullcaps had also been removed.

"We should turn back," Malinovsky said.

But as the expedition's leader, it was my duty to push forward. So we did.

Our dogs refused to go any further. So we dragged them by their leashes. They resisted. Malinovsky's dog savaged his hand. Frustrated, I handed my dog's leash to Malinovsky.

"Head back to the laager site," I said. "Resume the search tomorrow morning if I fail to return."

He was only too happy to oblige.

As I trekked forward, the emerald light pulsated with increasing frequency. The whippoorwills' trills and the unsettling yelping grew louder.

And I felt more alone than ever.

As I got closer to the source of that ghostly pulsing light, I unearthed much larger fragments of the strange metal. In some cases, chunks as large as human hands. The material had the texture and color of obsidian, but it was harder than tempered steel. Oddly, it also had unprecedented resilience. I could crumple it, but it would return to its original state within seconds. As a mineralogical specialist, I've seen nothing of its kind on Earth. I gathered samples until I felt nauseated.

It was becoming harder to breathe as a thick miasma, a kind of frothy green fog, increasingly permeated the wilderness like a toxic soup. My breathing became labored. I soon started coughing up bloody phlegm.

I hiked as far as I could, but the miasma's adverse impact on my health thwarted my efforts to push any deeper into the murky morass. So I turned and made my way back toward the laager site. When I passed the place where my comrades had fallen, their bodies were missing. I assumed Malinovsky and the others had retrieved the corpses and buried them.

But I was wrong.

The men were in a frenzy when I returned to the site. They were loading rifles, lighting lanterns, and donning their greatcoats. It was obvious they had no plan. The dogs were barking wildly, likely sensing their masters' unease.

When I tried to intercede, Malinovsky rested his hand on my shoulder and said, "The bodies are gone."

I knew there was nothing I could do to stop their ill-considered foray. But I could limit the damage. So I addressed the group, urging patience and calm. "Wait until morning," I pleaded.

My efforts failed.

When people are tired and afraid, they can be stubborn and irrational. If I couldn't convince them to wait, I could at least ensure they'd be safe. So against my better judgment, I accompanied them back toward the crater.

Twenty-one armed men ventured into the wilderness and into the blackest night I've ever known. Their lantern light flooded the darkness, scattered by the pervasive green fog.

Given my adverse reaction to the mist, I stayed a few meters behind the group. As they got closer to the site, the men ahead coughed and retched. Not long after, I felt sick again.

Exhausted and ill, I stopped to rest. The group pressed forward into the wispy miasma. The strange trilling echoed from beyond the toxic fog's swirling shroud.

A riot of commotion broke out about fifty meters ahead. A voice shouted, "Timoshenko!" A rifle shot cracked, reverberating in the night. With bloodcurdling screams, the crowd fled, stampeding pell-mell toward the laager site.

Malinovsky ran toward me. His face was twisted in a rictus of terror. He was wheezing. He grabbed my collar and pulled me close. He whispered, "The Valley Men are real and they're coming for us."

Earlier, I had discounted Tungus accounts of their ancestors rising from the earth. But every report on the Valley Men we'd examined had been consistent.

Malinovsky let go of my collar and fled. Others rushed past me. Soon, the only remaining light was from my lantern and the flickering green strobe.

The trills drew closer. Frozen from fear, I stared into the darkness. The steady crescendo of footfalls penetrated the silence. I say "steady" because they didn't sound like the shaky meandering of a man blindly fumbling in the fog. People walk in irregular patterns, especially in rugged terrain. This was different. These footsteps were as precise as a metronome.

Timoshenko emerged from the mist, his body riddled with wounds. His skullcap had been reattached to his cranium. When he saw me, he halted with military precision. His eyes stared through me. He handed me a black cube. It had a circular impression on its upper face. Paralyzed by dread, I could do nothing but accept the offering. Timoshenko headed to the impact zone, never to be seen or heard from again.

When I left Tunguska on the Trans-Siberian Railway, I placed the device in the train's brake van. An armed detail of ten decorated Red Army veterans guarded the van to ensure the device reached Leningrad.

On the third morning of my passage, I couldn't sleep. So I went to the brake van to check on the cube. I glanced at my chronometer the instant I entered the car. It was precisely 3:14 a.m. The guards stood rigidly along the center aisle in two ranks facing inward. Their eyes were transfixed on the floating obsidian cube. The artifact cast rippling green rays of light that connected each veteran's eyes like the nodes of a spider web.

The cube floated toward me. I watched, mesmerized and unsure what to do. The soldiers' eyes rolled back into their heads. The lights vanished. The cube descended to the brake van's corrugated iron floor. The men turned and faced me. Their eyes glowed a dull green. Two veterans marched forward in perfect cadence. One of them spoke. "Return. One year hence. We will be waiting." He frothed at the mouth and shook before collapsing.

The other man spoke. "Gather men of science and men of war. Bring experts on biology, physiology, and botany." Then he crumpled. And on it went, until all ten were dead. Then I blacked out.

When I awoke, I felt violated and unsettled. A notebook I had had in my possession at the time of the incident was filled with strange runes and mathematical equations I do not recall writing.

I ordered the brake van to be quarantined until the train's arrival in Leningrad. There, we ran several tests on the artifact and the shards we recovered from the impact site. Using the Townsend discharge process, we detected latent alpha decay, a clear sign of radioactivity. So we encased them in lead and sealed them in the Mineralogical Museum's vault.

„‟

After Kulik finished relating his tale, Stalin sat in silence as if weighing the options. The party officials were mute. Their dour and downcast faces betrayed an uneasiness that had become all too common in Soviet Russia. Many of them likely thought Stalin was testing their loyalty, forcing them to choose between treason on one hand and a madman who believed in extraterrestrials on the other. Given the OGPU's reputation, only a fool would bet against Stalin.

"Did you open the cube?" Stalin said.

"No. That's a decision for a head of state," Kulik replied.

Stalin chuckled. "You assumed right, Dr. Kulik. What do you intend to do with this artifact?"

"I'll keep it in Leningrad for further study," Kulik said. "I dare not bring the thing here. It's not worth the risk of endangering Moscow's citizens. Not all we found at Tunguska was a positive omen for the Soviet Union or the human race." Kulik's head throbbed with sudden pressure. He'd said too much. He fought through the pain. "There are forces in the universe far older and more advanced than our own."

Kulik let the last bit linger. He was counting on Stalin's paranoia. He needed to scare the man of steel into marshaling the state's resources to protect these secrets. If the rest of the world learned of Tunguska, there'd be chaos.

"What's this artifact's purpose?" Stalin said.

"I don't know. I think it's some kind of biological calculator. I believe it uses electromagnetic fields to control brain tissue and to transfer data like an analytical engine. I'll issue a full report once I have more time to fully examine it."

Stalin puffed on his pipe. "What did this?"

"I don't know, Comrade Stalin." Kulik lied, wanting to say more. But his fear of the thing inside him kept him silent.

Stalin nodded. "What else did the possessed guards say?"

"They provided instructions for what to bring to Tunguska in exchange for technology centuries beyond our own. Here's the list," Kulik said, placing a slip of paper on the table.

A colonel grabbed the document and handed it to Stalin. Stalin examined it. "What do you expect this future expedition to uncover?"

"I don't know," Kulik hedged, "But whatever's there, it's the most powerful thing on Earth."

Stalin raised his index finger. "One moment." The officials huddled around him. A mumbled exchange followed.

Minutes later, Stalin glared at Kulik. "Take your list to Marshal Tukhachevsky. He'll get you what you need. You'll lead a third mission to Tunguska on the appointed date and time. Until then, learn all you can about the device. Dismissed."

Kulik saluted Stalin. The mineralogist left the rotunda. A dark essence clouded his emotions.

He was no longer hopeful about the future. But a wave of exhilaration swept over him as the parasite rewarded him for his efforts in establishing a foothold on this world.

END

Afterword

The idea for "Tunguska" came from a discussion I had with Nick Mamatas in which he encouraged me to turn my short story, "Enemy Allies", into a novel. He told me that if I wrote an alternate history about the Russo-German front in World War II, I should have at least one scene with Hitler and another with Stalin. This story is that scene with Stalin, and it serves as the prologue for the novel based on my "Enemy Allies" short story.

To write this story, I spent a great deal of time researching the buildings in the Kremlin as well as 1920s Soviet history and the events surrounding Leonid Kulik's expeditions to the Tunguska impact zone.

While writing this story, the challenge I enjoyed most was trying to capture the tension inherent in Kulik having to give Stalin a message the dictator did not want to hear.

"Tunguska" was the second story I sold to *Kasma SF*, and it first appeared there in January 2016. I hope you enjoy it.

Chandler's Hollow

The demons come at night to eat souls," Lily said.

The child's dull jaundiced eyes, greasy blonde hair, and rotten teeth betrayed a neglect bordering on cruelty. She rocked on a rickety swing suspended from rusty chains. The chains dangled from a decayed wooden frame in the weed-infested backyard of an old, broken down log cabin. White oak, ash, and walnut trees swayed and creaked in the chill morning autumn breeze, shedding a riot of burgundy, gold, and russet leaves.

Something about Chandler's Hollow was off. It was as if the people here were out of time, belonging neither to the past, present, nor future.

"Have you told your mother?" Jenna said, scratching her head. Wisps of her curly brown hair fluttered to the earth.

"Momma sees them too. They sound like cadas in the night."

"Cadas? Do you mean cicadas?"

It was tough to understand Lily's accent. It sounded Amish, but different. More archaic.

"Yeah, cicadas. But they are bigger than you and me."

A stringy matron with straw-colored hair shambled out of the hovel and approached Jenna. The woman was pretty enough to win a Meth America pageant.

"Who's your friend?" the woman asked Lily.

"This is Miss Williams, momma."

Lily's mother rested her hand on her daughter's shoulder. "I'm Daisy. Is Lily telling you about the brood?"

"The brood? No, she was talking about demons," Jenna said.

"They are the same thing."

"What do you mean?"

"You've heard the stories. Our world is not what it seems. It changes. We feed this change by casting off what we are."

An odd response. Jenna dismissed it as backwoods banter. "How long have you lived here?"

"Long as I can remember. My mother passed this house to me. And her mother passed it to her," Daisy said.

"Is Lily's father around? I'd love to speak to him if he's available."

"Father? She has no father. I've never been with a man. One month my moon blood stopped. Nine months later, Lily was born. Same as my mother and her mother's mother."

Jenna stifled a laugh. She knew rural America had its share of yokels, but these folks were nuts. She decided not to press the issue. She needed the material for her article.

"Can you tell me anything about the cult house rumored to be out here?" Jenna said.

The two clammed up. It was as if Jenna had flipped a switch. One moment Lily and Daisy were lucid; the next, wallflowers.

"Can you at least tell me where to find it?"

Their eyes bored into Jenna's as though Daisy and Lily were one person. In unison, they said, "The shed will find you."

৪৩

Professor Wendell Winthrop Chilcott hunkered behind a beige oaken desk in an office teeming with walls of warped books. Wearing his velvet smoking jacket, pleated pants and bright burgundy bowtie, he was a fossil of a man. It was as if he were preserved in formaldehyde at the turn of the nineteenth century and only recently revived. His wispy white hair was combed over his glistening bald pate. The room reeked of mildew and mundungus.

"So, you're the reporter with an itch for seventeenth century deeds," he said, his fleshy jowls rippling like a rooster's wattles. He chomped on a corncob pipe.

"I am," Jenna said.

"Out of academic curiosity, what led you to the world's foremost historian on seventeenth century American legal history?" Chilcott said in a lilting American patrician accent reminiscent of William F. Buckley.

"Well, Professor Chilcott, I'm trying to understand the transfer of properties in Chandler's Hollow. After scanning sales histories on Zillow and Redfin, I've discovered a cluster of parcels that hasn't changed hands in at least ten years."

"What's that got to do with me?"

"I'll get to that, Professor."

"Well, you'd best make your point. I'm not getting any younger, and I have a class in thirty minutes."

"I searched both the New Castle and Delaware County Departments of Records. The only deeds for these plots stretch back to the mid-seventeenth century."

Chilcott nodded, smiling. He belched laughter. The fat on his bulbous midsection undulated in waves. "For whom do you work?" he said, raising an eyebrow.

Jenna flinched, then hesitated. If she told him the truth, he'd probably end the interview.

"You work for a tabloid, don't you?"

"Well, that depends on…"

He cut her off. "Oh, you most certainly work for one. I won't say another word until you agree not to quote me as a source in whatever cretinous rag you call a newspaper. I have a reputation to uphold."

"I promise."

Jenna's *New York Times* article had cast a long shadow. Securing a position at *The Weekly World Journal* had been her only option. Between her Harvard undergraduate degree and graduate studies at Columbia's School of Journalism, she'd amassed over a hundred and fifty thousand dollars in debt. In this economy, she was just happy to have a job.

Chilcott gazed at her. His fingers formed a wrinkled steeple. "It wasn't always called Chandler's Hollow, you know. German colonists first settled the area in the mid-seventeenth century. Outcast from the Swedish settlement of Fort Christina, they'd been among the first Europeans to set foot in the Delaware River Valley.

"To the colonists' chagrin, Lenape tribes had already populated the region. It didn't help that the Lenape had a matrilineal society where hereditary title passed from mothers to daughters. It was a cultural arrangement that baffled most Europeans. The only area the Lenape left unclaimed was Chandler's Hollow. They'd avoided it because they believed it was cursed."

"How do you know that?"

"Delaware's only cave is in Chandler's Hollow. In that cave, there are ten-thousand-year-old wall paintings advising people to avoid the area.

"Of course, the Germans ignored the Lenape warning, and built a ring of homes and mills. At the center of the hollow, the colonists erected a structure that conspiracy theorists call the 'shed' or the 'cult house', depending on which quack you interview. Many of these structures still stand today.

"After the community's establishment, no one heard anything from the colonists again. But over the years, people have reported sightings of oddly-dressed women on those properties, but never men." Chilcott crossed his arms against his chest, looking at Jenna expectantly.

"Can you elaborate on these sightings?" she said.

He glowered. "If you want to hear about that nonsense, you'd best meet with Doctor Eli Rosen while you're still at Princeton. He works in the Department of Astrophysical Sciences. One of the last quacks on campus who was associated with the Princeton Engineering Anomalies Research Laboratory, he fancies himself an Assistant Professor of Quantum Parapsychology."

"Quantum what?"

He rolled his eyes and then sneered. "Good day, Miss Williams."

☙

Disappointed she hadn't been able to connect with Rosen the day prior, Jenna entered Nick De Genova's office the next morning to give him an update on her story. It was an assignment that Jenna had only taken on reluctantly, but for some reason it now resonated with her.

"You had a visitor," he said in a thick Philly accent, frowning. He ran his ringed fingers through slick coal black hair that seemed unnatural for his age.

"Who?"

"Samuel Greenburg. He wants you to write a piece on him to, in his words, 'undo the damage you'd done by writing that *New York Times* article,'" he said, stroking a gaudy gold necklace floating on a puffy morass of gray chest hair.

"Okay," Jenna said, sulking.

Like many baby boomers, De Genova had stumbled into his position without much effort or talent when jobs were as plentiful as sand grains. But what De Genova lacked in intellect he more than made up for in reading people.

"What's wrong? This assignment too good for you?" he said, "I don't give a rat's ass about your fancy shmansy Ivy League degrees. You work for me, hon. You'll write what I say."

Jenna put her hand on his desk to avoid passing out. Sam Greenberg, media mogul extraordinaire. The same old arrogant bastard who'd gotten her fired from *The New York Times* for writing the truth.

"Okay," she said, grabbing a clump of hair she uprooted a bit too easily.

"Forget what you're working on now," De Genova said, "If we don't publish this piece, Greenburg's gonna buy our paper and fire us both."

"Fine," Jenna said, dejected. "I'll reach out to his assistant tomorrow to set up an interview. For now, I'd like to do more work on that 'cult house' piece."

"No. You'll interview him now. He's waiting outside."

ଚଠ

Clad in a navy blue suit, Egyptian cotton shirt, and a mauve power tie, Greenburg held court in his limo.

"You're late, Miss Williams," he said, scowling.

"If you expect me to be on time, try calling me before you schedule a meeting," she said. "Why am I here?"

"You're here because you want to keep your job."

Jenna clenched her jaw. She had to keep it together. She loathed Greenburg. But if she didn't cooperate, he'd spend millions on a worthless tabloid just for the satisfaction of firing her.

"How can I help you, Mr. Greenburg?" she said, fighting back an urge to empty her stomach.

He smiled. "Now that's a better attitude." He pulled out a highlighted copy of her *New York Times* article. "I wanted to spend our time correcting the many errors you made here."

For the next hour, the man droned on about his business principles, which, from Jenna's point of view, only made sense if one started out with extreme wealth.

Finishing, he said, "If there's one principle every American should understand, it's this: being poor is a choice."

Waking from a stupor induced by Greenburg's narcissism, Jenna said, "Wait, what?"

He groaned. "Haven't you been listening? I'll say it again because it's important. Being poor is a choice. People are poor because they choose to be."

It was easy for him to say. Some are born with silver spoons, but Greenburg was born with a sliver kitchen. Rather than call out his ignorance, Jenna held back her rage, managing a noncommittal, "I see."

Greenburg grabbed a tuft of her hair, and it came off without resistance. "Miss Williams, are you sick? Your hair's falling out."

She had been having a lot of hair and skin problems ever since her first trip to Chandler's Hollow, but she refused to give the man an inch. "No, I'm fine."

He smiled. Then he reached out and fondled her breasts.

She froze. It was so surreal she didn't know how to react. Then, she slapped him and made for the limo door.

He grinned. "I sure can't wait to read all the wonderful things you're going to say about me."

Jenna stormed out of the limo and slammed the door.

ॐ

At dusk, Jenna drove her rusty cherry 1998 Corolla along the potted roads leading to Chandler's Hollow. She parked her car in an empty field hidden behind a line of oak and maple trees. An icy wind whistled through their branches. Jenna pulled out a map she'd pieced together from her research and made her way toward the shed.

As she ventured deeper into the old growth forest, a faint metallic chirping echoed in the gloom. The sound crescendoed. She stopped. Dusk faded into darkness. The moon cast a pale glow on the dark woods.

Something rustled in a thicket ahead. She strained her eyes. Moonlight glinted off its slick black form. A cloaked thing lumbered toward her.

The chirping intensified. A man-thing darted from the trees. A whirling mass of tentacles, it was a mix of insect and cephalopod. The proboscis and antennae on its insect-like head quivered.

Mother! Its thoughts infested her mind.

It raced toward her. She screamed. Then it vanished, fading into the ether.

Flashlights!

"Who's there!" a woman shouted.

Jenna sprinted to her car. She fumbled with her keys. After unlocking the door, she rolled into the driver's seat. Shaking, she rotated the key in the ignition. The engine cranked, then puttered out. Engines roared to life in the murk.

She pumped fuel into the engine. Nothing. She turned her key again. "C'mon," she said, staving off panic. The engine cranked, then whimpered to a dull hum. She slammed her foot on the gas pedal. The car's wheels kicked up clumps of wet mud in their wake.

Lights behind washed out her vision. She struggled to see the road ahead. They drew closer. She accelerated. She glanced back. Two black Broncos with stadium lights.

One truck surged into the opposite lane. It roared past her. Cutting back into her lane, it boxed her in. She stomped on her brakes. Shadows poured out of the truck. She locked her doors.

A flashlight rapped on her window. She froze, terrified. Another rap. Then a metallic click.

"Wait! Don't shoot her," a woman yelled. "She is of the brood."

Jenna revved her engine and sped away, glad to be alive.

ॐ

Doctor Eli Rosen's patchy beard looked like a cluster bomb had exploded on his face and given birth to a staph infection. He was bald. He wore a plaid suit straight out of the seventies. It was so wrinkled it might as well have been laundered in a dishwasher. His office was a disorganized stew of coffee stains, stacked books, crimpled papers, and scrawled mathematical equations. There was no place for Jenna to sit. The room smelled of popcorn, sweat, mildew, and meat.

After Jenna recounted her tale, she said, "Dr. Rosen, I've been rude. I was so upset by what happened last night I never asked about your background."

Rosen smiled. "I'm an Assistant Professor of Quantum Parapsychology. Until 2007, Quantum Parapsychology was part of an interdisciplinary effort between the Princeton Engineering Anomalies Research Laboratory and the Department of Astrophysical Sciences. My research focuses on understanding parapsychological phenomena at the quantum level. I'm trying to reconcile quantum mechanical principles with gravitation theory at the quantum scale to learn more about the behavior of dark matter and dark energy."

"What's that got to do with the paranormal?" she said.

"My paranormal work centers on my theory that most supernatural activity can be explained by the interaction between matter and dark matter. Most reported extrasensory phenomena operate on higher dimensions than we're capable of perceiving. Humans sense the world in only four dimensions—height, width, depth, and time. Paranormal entities are nothing more than hyperdimensional beings composed of dark matter."

Confused, Jenna scratched her head, uprooting another patch of hair. "What does this have to do with the shed?"

Rosen hesitated. His eyes widened. Then he said, "Well, Miss Williams, I'm familiar with Chandler's Hollow lore. Most of it is bunk, but bunk based on real phenomena."

"How so?"

"Well, some of the lore describes the shed as a satanic cult house. But there's nothing in the historical record that lends credence to those stories. However, Chandler's Hollow apparition sightings stretch back over ten thousand years. Your story is just the most recent one."

"Well, what did I see out there?"

Rosen grabbed Jenna by the shoulders, and said, "Despite what you might think, you didn't see a ghost. It was something much worse."

She shuddered. "What do you mean?"

Rosen stroked his beard. "The being you saw occupied an adjacent dimension leaking into our own. For a brief time, that dimension resonated at the same frequency as ours."

Rosen's phone rang, rattling Jenna. Putting his hand over the receiver, he said, "I'm sorry, but I have to take this. Perhaps we can catch up later this week?"

She nodded. A swirl of emotions tugged at her ranging from morbid curiosity to sheer terror.

ༀ

After she left Princeton, Jenna didn't return to her desk until late afternoon. Seconds after she sat down, De Genova hovered over her cubicle like a Predator drone.

"Let me see the article," he said.

"Which one?" she said, feigning ignorance.

"The Greenburg piece," he said, frowning.

"Why the urgency? Why now? Why can't I get it to you later this week?"

"Because Greenburg keeps harassing me. And publishing that article is the only thing that'll shut him up."

"Fine. I'll get it to you first thing tomorrow morning."

De Genova wagged his finger at her. "Okay. But it had better be on my desk. First thing."

"Will do," she said. Apparently satisfied, he left her cubicle.

She took a deep breath. She fired up her laptop and opened a new file. Staring at a blank screen, she struggled to write something redeeming about a distinctly unredeemable man.

Jenna typed to get the words flowing. Then she stopped; then she started again. By eight p.m., she had only written a paragraph.

The phone rang.

She answered. The electronic screeching and wailing on the other end sounded like a fax mixed with a Tibetan chant without words. Yet, somehow, she knew she had to go to the shed.

She dialed Rosen.

"We need to go to the shed tonight," she said. "I can't explain how I know, but something's calling me there."

"I wish I could join you," Rosen said, "but I have a prior commitment this evening. And there's no way I can get out of it. Let's catch up tomorrow."

"Okay," she said, disappointed. "I'll call you with an update tomorrow."

℘

Jenna saw the shed for the first time amid a row of gnarled and sickly oak, ash, and maple trees. Their trunks twisted away from the ancient, dilapidated log cabin as if straining to avoid some unseen malady. The starry vastness of the evening sky cast a pale glow over the shed's dark edifice.

Nary a blade of grass grew within a hundred feet of the structure. Windows shaped like inverted crosses stamped the shed's timber flanks. A tiny human sentinel stood vigil before the shed's double doors.

Jenna crept forward. A rough semicircle of jagged things lay behind the shed. As she drew closer, the objects resolved to translucent forms of the strange being that had hunted her during her last visit. It was as though they had molted, shedding their chitinous exoskeletons. The solitary figure watched Jenna approach.

Lily!

Once Jenna was within earshot, Lily said, "I'm here to serve."

The shed's double doors burst open. Things, terrible things poured out. Their tentacles smothered the child, then ripped her apart in a riot of blood and viscera.

Jenna wanted to scream. But the sight also evoked far baser instincts of hunger, of violence, of longing.

The creatures and their carapaces evaporated.

℘

Jenna drove to work at sunrise. She'd been unable to sleep. Her mind raced, trying to process what she'd seen.

She called Dr. Rosen at seven thirty. He sounded groggy, but after she'd related her experience, his voice grew animated.

"Did Chilcott tell you about the cave paintings?" he said.

"Yes, but what's that got to do with what I saw?"

"Everything. Are you familiar with a cicada's lifecycle?"

"I'm sorry, Doctor Rosen, but what do ten-thousand-year-old cave paintings have to do with the lifecycle of a cicada?"

Rosen flashed a mischievous smile. "Why everything, Miss Williams."

"Explain."

"Well, to be more precise, your ten-thousand-year-old cave painting is actually ten thousand three hundred and thirty three."

Jenna raised an eyebrow. "You can't possibly know that."

"Sure I can. Uranium-thorium dating gets you to ten thousand three hundred years. The more precise number is ten thousand three hundred and thirty three because it's both a prime and an apocalyptic number."

"What's that got to do with cicada lifecycles?"

"Cicada broods emerge once every thirteen or seventeen years—both primes. When cicadas surface, they do so in overwhelming numbers. Their predators can't possibly eat enough of them to drive them to extinction. Etymologists believe cicadas' prime number lifecycles are an adaptation that prevents predators from synchronizing their own generations to divisors of the cicada emergence period."

"Okay," Jenna said, skeptical.

"Now, you're probably wondering what this has to do with what you encountered in Chandler's Hollow."

"Well, yeah."

"In brane theory, physicists conjecture that there's a multiverse of an infinite number of universes. These universes vibrate at different frequencies in higher dimensional space. Some resonate at the same periodicity but are slightly out of phase. You see, there's an adjacent universe that intersects our own at Chandler's Hollow. This nearby dimension is out of phase with our reality by ten thousand three hundred and thirty three years. My theory is that the shed acts as some sort of hyperdimensional tuning fork."

"Are you saying what I saw was real?"

Rosen nodded. "Yes. But the two realities aren't quite in phase yet, so what you saw probably seemed like a mirage. In the coming days, these sightings will become more anchored to our reality as we, in turn, become more anchored to theirs."

"So what does that mean?"

"Well, based on the cave paintings and the broader North American archaeological record, it doesn't bode well. When our world was last in phase with theirs, there was a mass extinction. Whatever inhabits that reality has a lifecycle whose cadence is resurgent every ten thousand three hundred and thirty three years. And whatever emerges from that realm when it is in superposition with our own eats large mammals."

Jenna felt a tap on her shoulder. Startled, she turned to see a grimacing De Genova. He pointed at the phone, motioning for her to hang up.

Disappointed, she said, "Doctor Rosen, can I call you back?"

"Sure," Rosen said.

She hung up the phone.

"Where's my goddamn story?" De Genova said, flaring his nostrils.

Her heart sank. In all of the excitement, she'd forgotten about her promise to get him the Greenburg article.

"I'm so sorry, Nick. Something really weird happened last night. So strange that I'd like to bring Marty with me next time to get some pictures," she said, alluding to the paper's one and only photographer.

"Really?" he said. "You blow off our single most important story, and then have the balls to demand more resources?"

"I know. I'm really sorry. I promise, I'll make it up to you."

"If Greenburg weren't so insistent that you write the article, I'd fire you on the spot. The good news is he wants to discuss the article with you tomorrow evening over dinner. So you still have time."

Jenna was both horrified and relieved. On the one hand, she had to suffer Greenburg again. On the other, she'd still have a job.

De Genova stared at her, his face registering concern. "By the way, you also might want a dermatologist to check out that rash on your face."

Self-conscious, she touched her face. It had the texture of sandpaper. "I will," she said, half-heartedly.

ॐ

Jenna fidgeted with her black velvet dress's straps at the entrance of The Excelsior, a high-end restaurant on Pennsylvania's Main Line. She hated dressing up for social occasions. Especially when the only outfit she could afford came from a thrift shop.

"There she is!" Greenburg said, gloating, as he entered the restaurant. His overstated white tuxedo definitely sent a message. She just wasn't sure it was the one he'd intended.

He eyed her up and down, giving her a creepy vibe. "You know, you really should have dressed better," he said. "People are gonna think you're my whore."

"That implies you only have one."

He glared at her. "Watch it. I'm trying to educate you. Successful people dress well."

Before Jenna could respond, the maître d' escorted them to a table against the restaurant's far wall. Jenna tried to sit against the wall, but Greenburg blocked her with his arm. "That's my seat."

It wasn't worth fighting over something so juvenile, so she let it go. "Why did you summon me?" she said.

"I want to make sure the article you write is fair and accurate."

"I already wrote a fair and accurate article in *The New York Times.*"

"You know nothing about good business, Miss Williams. Journalism is a world of gray, not black and white."

"No, Mr. Greenburg. Journalism aims for truth. My article was entirely factual."

He wagged his finger. "Your article was a character assassination filled with baseless allegations. You misquoted me in every respect."

Jenna guffawed. "Really? You weren't accused of sexual misconduct by at least ten of your former female employees?"

"Those were unproven allegations. When you're a successful billionaire, people constantly try to exploit your wealth."

"So you don't deny those allegations."

His face reddened. "That's not at all what I said. Are you really sure you went to Harvard?"

"I'm sure. Given your daddy's wealth and connections, why couldn't you get into Harvard? What's your excuse?"

He glowered at her and then said, "Being poor is a choice. And it's clear from your sinking career trajectory that you're an untalented shrew." He pulled out a cigar, lit it, and blew smoke in her face.

"How much money did you inherit from daddy?" she said, sneering. "You think you hit a homerun in life, without admitting you were born on third base."

Greenburg slammed his fist on the table. "I won't be lectured by some trailer park slut."

The restaurant's steady conversational hum died. Jenna didn't want to make a scene. She despised the man, but he had leverage. If this interview spiraled out of control, she'd lose her job. So she reached across the table and touched his hand. "Mr. Greenburg, I think we started on the wrong foot. Let's try again. How can I help you?"

"You'll show me a draft of your article before it's published."

"And if I do?"

"I'll publish it in all my syndicated newspapers, which have a combined reach greater than that of *The New York Times*. I'll also give you a job at one of my media companies."

"I see," Jenna said. She'd have a future, all for the low, low price of her integrity. "And if I don't write the article?"

He smiled. "As I said, being poor is a choice."

She nodded. "I'll show you a draft once I have one," she lied.

Greenburg raised his glass of Dom. Romane Conti. "Here's to an enjoyable evening."

∓

Jenna couldn't explain why she'd lured Greenburg to the shed. It was instinct. Lubricated by wine, she'd told him about her other story.

Capitalizing on his well-publicized urges, she'd suggested they go to Chandler's Hollow. Her logical mind had screamed, "No!" but something darker compelled her.

She stood with him before the shed. A strange energy in the air made her skin tingle. A waning gibbous moon's fading light seeped through the warped branches of mangled trees.

His rough, craggy hand grabbed her bottom. Hungry, Jenna didn't react.

"Ha, ha," he said, slurring his words. "This story is even less credible than your hit piece on me."

Like the moon above, her eyesight waned, her vision blurring into a honeycomb. Despite having a full stomach, an insatiable appetite raged inside her.

A field of carapaces shimmered around the shed.

"What kind of a sick joke is this?" Greenburg said in an indignant tone.

She became one of them. His eyes widened. Her geniculate antennae curled around his head. He stank of fear.

Greenburg ran.

She was human again. Dumbfounded, she tried to make sense of what had happened. Then she recalled Rosen's theory about two realities in superposition. What if two organisms could also coexist in a state of superposition?

The world changed again, transforming her into a ravenous thing, a thing that was neither here nor there, but existing simultaneously in both realms. Her brood burst forth from the shed, flooding the countryside like a locust swarm. Their hunger and their desire to propagate mirrored her own.

His scent fresh on her antennae, she chased Greenburg through the woods to his limo. Wheels squealing, it sped off.

She trundled forward, but her tentacles couldn't propel her fast enough to reach her quarry.

Lights.

A black Bronco surged past. Greenburg's limo screeched to a halt as a second Bronco blocked its path.

He scrambled out of his vehicle. A shot rang out. He fell. Two shadows descended on him. She slithered closer along the black sludge her new world had superimposed on the old. Her twin proboscises slavered for meat.

Daisy and a second woman held Greenburg against a Bronco. The scent of his bloodied shoulder only made Jenna hungrier.

"We live to serve the brood queen," they said.

Greenburg's eyes widened, and he sobbed. "Please. Don't let me die here. Please."

But in this new world, she was predator and he was prey.

Jenna devoured him.

Then she comforted her drones, promising to clone more human females to guard the gateway during the time between.

END

Afterword

"Chandler's Hollow" is my take on a local Delaware-Pennsylvania legend about a cult house near the Brandywine River. Growing up, I had heard several variations of this story. In most of them, the cult house had windows in the shape of inverted crosses and trees bowed away from the structure, presumably because it emanated evil. Onlookers who dared visit the site frequently reported being chased by a strange black Bronco with stadium lights.

To make this story my own, I took a kernel of the legend and melded it with multiverse brane theory, a mass extinction event occurring several thousand years ago, and some colonial history (some true, some reimagined).

"Chandler's Hollow" is the result.

It is also important to note that this is the first published story in which inter-dimensional traveler, Doctor Eli Rosen, appears. That said, it is not his "origin story." That distinction belongs to the next story in this volume, "Portal in Pasadena."

"Chandler's Hollow" first appeared in the March 2015 issue of *Perihelion Online Science Fiction*. I hope you found it entertaining.

Portal in Pasadena

When Rosen found Dr. Wiley's bleeding torso fused to the scramjet engine, he knew this was his kind of job. The flat and sleek rectangular apparatus rested on the cold concrete floor like a dead duck. In the murk, the engine's front-end converging inlet reminded Rosen of a duck's bill, only more stylish and aerodynamic.

NASA scientists had torn a rift in space-time, and they needed Dr. Eli Rosen for damage control.

The shadowy corridor stretched for miles deep beneath the Jet Propulsion Laboratory complex, but Rosen could sense that the breach was near, maybe a kilometer or so from the stairwell. A faint stench reminiscent of rotting meat and sulfur lingered in the stale air. Lieutenant Chip Mason, Rosen's Marine escort, emptied his stomach on the grimy gray floor. Lights flickered in the gloom.

Rosen's garish plaid suit looked like a pixelated rainbow had exploded on his clothing before he'd run it through a dishwasher. Like a leaking Soviet bioweapons facility, his patchy brown beard and wild whiskers spewed a petri dish of detritus ranging from cookie crumbs to errant toothpaste. His bald, shiny pate was the only clean part of his bulky mass.

Rosen shivered as he waited patiently for Mason to finish vomiting. "Is this ground zero?" he asked, exhaling a cool mist in the icy corridor.

The Marine wiped his mouth and shook his head. "No." He pointed farther down the corridor. "We think it's about a klick down."

Rosen scratched his head. "You think?"

Mason grimaced. "Don't know for sure. No one's ever returned from that part of the facility."

Rosen approached Dr. Wiley's remains, unfazed by the gruesome scene. He reached for the Pilot G-2 pen in his pant pocket—he refused to use any other brand—and lightly poked Dr. Wiley's eyelids, giddy as a child stripping the legs off an insect.

Wiley opened his eyes and screamed.

Rosen stumbled backward. Mason drew his nine-millimeter pistol and trained it on Wiley. The man's shrieks, both high-pitched and guttural, resonated in a chorus of voices.

Signaling Mason to lower his weapon, Rosen listened carefully. The voices seemed inhuman. A sharp pain spread from his eardrums to his skull.

Rosen reached into the inner pocket of his jacket, fumbling for his mobile phone. His Dunkin Donuts Perks Card fell from his pocket. *A fat lot of good that would do in California*, he thought.

Scrolling through the device's display, he pulled up a spectrum analyzer app and converted the audio signals in the corridor into their component frequencies.

As he expected, his screen showed normal activity between zero and four kilohertz with a magnitude of about sixty decibels. He hadn't anticipated a two hundred decibel spike at thirty kilohertz.

He grabbed Mason by the shoulders and yelled, "Run!"

Mason shot Rosen a confused expression. Blood began to trickle from the Marine's ears. Belatedly, he nodded and sprinted back toward the stairwell. Rosen wheezed behind Mason as the scientist lumbered to catch up.

ຮ

General Liu's desk had a blotter, a nameplate, and an antique hourglass. Otherwise, the desk was spotless.

The hourglass held Rosen's attention. He'd always been intrigued that the same non-Euclidian hyperbolic geometry that governed Minkowski space-time also shaped a timepiece humans had used for millennia. After all, an hourglass was nothing but a two-dimensional hyperbolic function rotated in the third dimension.

Liu frowned as he regarded Rosen. The General's light blue shirt was meticulously pressed; his hair, close-cropped; his physique, wiry and sleek.

"Ultrasonics," Rosen said as if the word explained everything. After much discussion, he'd convinced Mason not to report the encounter with Wiley. Otherwise, the military would have had them both committed. So Rosen wanted to say as little as possible.

"I'm going to need a bit more than that, Doctor," Liu said.

Rosen took a giant bite out of a powdered donut, spraying a prodigious mist of powder and crumbs all over his unkempt beard and loud polka dot tie.

"Ultrasonics," Rosen repeated, his mouth overflowing with donut chunks. He chewed and swallowed, then said, "The most likely scenario is that ultrasonics killed your people. And they wouldn't have known what hit them because their ears couldn't have detected frequencies that high."

Liu raised an eyebrow. "So what made you and Mason so special?"

"The fast Fourier transform."

"The what?"

"The fast Fourier transform," Rosen repeated, his animated gestures sprinkling more donut dust on Liu's desk.

"What the hell is a fast Fourier transform, Dr. Rosen?" Liu said in a stern tone.

Rosen smiled, sat back, and paused. He wanted Liu to think that he was carefully considering the General's words, when all Rosen was really doing was padding his billable hours.

"Well, General, a fast Fourier transform is an algorithm that converts discrete signals in the time domain to signals in the frequency domain," Rosen said before folding his powder-smeared arms across his chest as if his explanation had settled the matter.

"In English, please," Liu said. "Explain it to me as if I were a simpleton."

Rosen nodded, before assuming his best Captain Caveman impression. "Loud noise in phone. Humans no hear loudest noise. Noise so loud, noise burst eardrums. Sometimes noise so loud, noise kills. Loud noise no humans hear kill humans before humans know."

Liu's jaw tightened. The expression on his face wavered between that of a man who'd just seen someone gut his puppy and a harsh taskmaster who was finally getting his people moving in the right direction.

Rosen relished provoking Liu and then observing the outward signs of Liu's inner struggle as emotions and logic struggled for mastery of the General's mind.

"Understood," Liu said. "Tomorrow I'm sending you and Mason down there again with noise-canceling headphones. Adjust them to whatever specifications you need to survive." The General stood up and looked down at his watch. "The time is now thirteen hundred hours. Our meeting is over."

"But, but," Rosen said, playing for time. "We still need to discuss the details. I don't know if I can be ready that fast. I'll need to configure a low pass filter to screen out the ultrasonics. That could take some serious time," Rosen bluffed.

Liu smiled. "Take all the time you want, Dr. Rosen, as long as you're in the complex no later than oh-six hundred hours tomorrow."

Rosen harrumphed and left the General's office without saying goodbye.

ౠ

The Air Force must've been really desperate. Not only were the flyboys sending Marines to pick up their mess, but they'd also called in Rosen, an Assistant Professor of Quantum Parapsychology at Princeton. There, he'd worked as part of an interdisciplinary effort between the Princeton Engineering Anomalies Research Laboratory (PEARL) and the Department of Astrophysical Sciences. PEARL had had a reputation for groundbreaking paranormal research, but the university had shut it down in 2007, orphaning Rosen and giving him the odd distinction of being the only Assistant Professor in Princeton University's history whom the university hadn't asked to leave after failing to make tenure.

Serious people rarely paid Rosen any mind, unless of course, something threatened the very fabric of reality. Rosen had an odd sixth sense about him—the ability to solve problems that had bedeviled some of the world's best minds by applying some of the stranger aspects of leading-edge quantum theory, cosmology, and parapsychology.

Outfitted with noise-canceling headphones that enabled wireless communication between Rosen and Mason, the two made their way back through the shadowy corridor toward where they'd last encountered Dr. Wiley.

Mason scanned the area, keeping his nine millimeter close at hand. Eyes wide, he stopped mid-step and turned his head back toward Rosen. "You have got to be kidding me," he said, his voice coming in clear over Rosen's headset.

Wiley was gone.

Rosen searched the area around the scramjet engine for clues.

Blood trail.

Rosen normally took things in stride. Not this. His heart pounded. "You don't think he...do you?" Rosen said.

"What? Dragged his severed torso down the hall with nothing but his arms?" Mason replied, a look of incredulity marring his chiseled face.

"It's the only possible explanation. Ockham's razor," Rosen said, then scratched his beard, triggering an avalanche of donut crumbs.

"Huh?"

"Never mind," Rosen continued. "We might as well follow the trail and see where it leads."

Mason tensed, then nodded.

Rosen caught himself staring at the Marine's sidearm with envy. What the heck had he been thinking? Here he was, heading into a completely unknown and life-threatening situation, and he hadn't thought to ask for a gun.

"You go first," Rosen said. He gestured toward Mason's pistol to underscore his point. Mason nodded and forged ahead.

As the two continued down the murky corridor, the temperature gradually dropped.

"Something ain't right," Mason said.

"What do you mean?"

"We've gone about two hundred meters and other than Wiley's blood trail, we haven't found any signs of the others. Wouldn't that scream have killed them?"

Mason had a point, but Rosen didn't want to encourage the boy. "It's possible," Rosen said. "Let's go a little farther before we jump to any conclusions."

Mason marched down the corridor and around a bend. Rosen kept a safe distance. But in doing so, he lost sight of the Marine.

Something rustled ahead.

Gunshots!

Rosen rounded the corner. He found Mason standing several meters from Wiley's bloody husk. Smoke wafted from the Marine's nine millimeter. Wiley's chest was a ruin of broken bones and blood. Yet the mangled scientist still moved, gnawing on a disembodied human arm.

Rosen shuddered.

Mason aimed his pistol at Wiley as if ready to empty his rounds into the thing. Rosen grabbed Mason's arm, pulling the Marine away from the mutilated scientist.

"We need to think before we do something we can't take back," Rosen said.

After a delay, Mason nodded.

The two tiptoed toward Wiley, but the scientist paid them no mind as he devoured the limb.

"What do we do?" Mason said.

Rosen shrugged. "I guess we need to figure out if Wiley is still in there. I have an idea."

Pulling out his mobile device, Rosen activated his spectrum analyzer app and searched for his recording. Maybe if he played back the original signal, he'd find a means of communicating with Wiley.

"What the heck are you doing?" Mason said.

"An experiment," Rosen replied an instant before he played the recording.

Wiley jerked his head up. His mouth was caked with dried blood and chunks of flesh and sinew. Wiley's eyes rolled back into his head. His jaw widened to an unnatural angle. The room began to vibrate with Wiley's screams. Rosen could hear nothing.

Rosen stopped the playback and hit record.

The scientist raised his torso husk onto his bloody arms. Gnashing his teeth, he raced toward Rosen at inhuman speed. Mason traced Wiley's movement with his pistol, his finger on the trigger.

Wiley tackled Rosen. Stunned and supine, Rosen rolled onto his stomach. He crawled forward, fighting to get back on his feet. A stabbing pain pierced Rosen's right calf. Glancing back, Rosen watched in horror as Wiley tore a chunk out of his leg. Rosen kicked Wiley in the face and scrambled forward on all fours.

Mason fired three rounds into Wiley. They slowed the scientist down, but didn't stop him. Mason ran to Rosen. He flung the fat doctor over his shoulders in a fireman's carry, and retreated back toward the stairwell.

Rosen screamed.

ॐ

Reclining in his hospital bed, Rosen hammered away on a MacBook. The machine hummed as it churned through a series of complex algorithms. A bowl of Fruit Loops lay half-eaten on a tray at Rosen's side. His right calf was cocooned in an ACE bandage and nestled beneath the covers.

There was a knock at the door.

"Enter," Rosen said.

Wearing khaki pants and a blue collared shirt, Mason ambled into the room. "You okay, doc?" he said, sheepishly.

Rosen nodded, continuing to pound away at his keyboard.

"Whatcha working on?" Mason said.

"I'm trying to clean up the signal I recorded yesterday. I ran it through a high pass filter, but I still need to do some trimming. Too much distortion."

"Why on earth are you doing that?"

"I'm trying to decode the audio signal," Rosen said as if the answer should have been obvious to anyone but a chipmunk.

"Why bother? General Liu's ordering a strike team to clear out the breach site this afternoon."

Rosen abruptly stopped typing. He put his laptop at his side. He tore off the sheets covering him, exposing his prodigious and hairy girth. Rosen's faded tighty whities were the only thing that prevented Mason from being exposed to any further horror.

Shifting his bulk by ninety degrees, Rosen landed on his good leg like a drunken gymnast. The rolls on his belly jiggled like Jell-O.

"We can't let them do that," Rosen said.

"Not our call," Mason said. "Plus, you and me are in quarantine. They found some strange microorganism in your system. Docs say they can't get a read on it. Keeps changing shape or something."

"I'm sure it's nothing," Rosen lied. He took comfort that he didn't feel sick. Though the bite—the most likely source of whatever this strange infection was—still hurt like a mother. "Did they find the same thing in you?"

Mason shook his head. "No. I assume they're just being overly cautious."

"We still have no idea what's down there. The General shouldn't be doing anything until we know more."

Mason grimaced. "That thing tore a chunk out of your calf. I think he knows all he needs to know."

Rosen's face turned beet red. "Everything's always so black and white with you military types. Friend or foe. You're either with us or against us. What we do here could have far greater implications than we might realize. For all we know, Wiley could've been trying to communicate."

"He sure has a funny way of 'communicating'," Mason said, using finger quotes.

"We need to stall the General," Rosen said, ignoring Mason's joke. "And I know exactly what I have to do."

ᡐ

"You did what?" General Liu yelled from across his pristine desk.

"I called a press conference," Rosen said, sheepishly.

"You do realize you'll go to prison for this."

"For what?" Rosen said.

"For divulging information about a highly classified military project during an ongoing crisis."

"I did no such thing."

Liu ran his fingers over his scalp, fuming. "Why are you doing this, Doctor?"

"Because I'm saving you from yourself. You're about to take an irreversible action based on an insufficient number of data points."

"And what would you have me do?" Liu asked in an exasperated tone.

"Give me twenty-four hours to decipher Wiley's message," Rosen said.

"What message? All you've got are the ravings of a madman."

Rosen arched an eyebrow. "Give me twenty-four hours and I'll call off the press. Deal?"

The General put his arms across his chest and glared at Rosen for an uncomfortable thirty seconds. "Fine," he exhaled, "but only if you call off the press now."

Rosen paused to think. He'd lose his leverage if he called the press off now, but he didn't think the General would ever deceive him. After all, the man was a highly decorated military officer. Military officers took pride in their loyalty and integrity. Rosen decided the risk was an acceptable one.

Extending his hand, Rosen said, "Deal."

Liu turned his back on Rosen. "You have twenty-four hours, Doctor. At precisely 1500 hours, the strike will proceed no matter what."

Rosen hunkered down in his dingy makeshift closet office in one of JPL's older buildings. He wanted to douse himself in sugar and sit on an anthill for giving himself so little time. Three empty boxes of Krispy Kreme donuts towered over his coffee-stained desk in homage to his desperation.

He would've been the first to complain about unreasonable deadlines. But when he had the chance to set his own, he'd given himself just one day to decode the message—a message he believed was from a transdimensional being.

Rosen didn't even know where to begin. He tried converting the high frequency signal into an audible one. But when he played it back, he got nothing but an unintelligible whine. Then, he tried to translate the signal into a stream of images. But again, he could find no discernible pattern.

With ten hours left, Rosen was exhausted. He needed some sleep to think, but he had no time for it. Then, at his lowest moment, he had an insight—something on the edge of conscious thought that inspired him to prod further, to dig deeper.

What if the signal represented a series of numbers? He analyzed the data again and quickly began to see a pattern. There was a burst of signal, followed by a gap, then another signal—much like the pauses between letters in Morse Code.

Then Rosen had another insight: what if each number was part of a coordinate system? He tested his theory on the first two numbers. Sure enough, they corresponded exactly to JPL's longitude and latitude. After some false starts, he discovered that third digit represented the breach's radial distance from the earth's center.

Rosen smiled. After hours of trial and error, he was finally making progress. He surmised that the next sequence of numbers might lead him to the other side of the fissure. He reasoned that those coordinates would, in turn, lead to further insights and answers. But when he tried to convert the fourth number into a longitudinal coordinate, he hit a wall.

He racked his brain for a solution, but he had no idea where to begin. Then, like an ethereal tidal wave, an energy surge swept over him and a flood of images assailed his mind.

He saw two human specters moving backward in time toward the Big Bang just before a black hole swallowed the earth. He watched in horror as an adjacent dimension's harmonic frequency resonated with that of our own reality, threatening human extinction. An infinity of parallel possibilities unfolded in his cerebral cortex, pounding him with a stream of horrifying calamities too upsetting to describe.

And he'd lived through them all.

For an instant, it had all become clear. Time had flattened. From the godlike perspective of a fifth spatial dimension, Rosen experienced eternity. Time was simultaneous. Past and future were as one.

The experience was both overwhelming and exhausting. An instant of clarity followed by an accelerating process of forgetting. But he had no time for reflection. His fading awareness urged him to act.

He knew how to decipher the signal. He also knew exactly what he needed to do.

Because he'd been the one who'd sent it.

଼ଅ

Waking from his fever dream, Rosen glanced at the analog clock on his wall.

And panicked.

The clock read a quarter past three.

The raid was on.

Rosen raced from his cramped office to the building where scientists had torn a rift in space-time. Within minutes, he was dripping with sweat and gasping for air. His sprint decayed into a brisk waddle. Yet he pressed on.

He stopped abruptly at the building's entrance only to stumble into a wall of stern-looking and armed Marines.

"I'm sorry, sir, but access to this site is restricted," said a looming Marine with chevrons on his collar.

Already winded from his exertion, Rosen began to hyperventilate. Then, in his mind's eye, time flattened, and he saw his future.

Rosen projectile vomited all over the Marine's uniform. "What the fuck?" the Marine swore, brushing Rosen's puke off his chest. Using the distraction, Rosen zipped past the Marine and into the facility.

He jiggled down the stairwell as fast as he could.

"Stop or I'll shoot!" the Marine yelled. Rosen kept running. A loud crack sounded. A bullet zipped past his ear. Smoke and chunks of mortar exploded from the bullet's impact.

In seconds, Rosen was on the ground floor, out of the stairway, and out of the Marine's line of sight. Rosen lumbered through the corridor, toward ground zero.

"Stop!" the Marine shouted. Rosen's pursuer was closing in. But Rosen didn't look back. He had to get to the vortex before it was too late.

"Stop or I'll fire again!" the Marine hollered.

Rosen glanced over his shoulder. The Marine stood with his rifle aimed at Rosen. Rosen could've used one of those premonitions about now, but none were coming. If the Marine took a shot now, Rosen was confident the Marine would hit his mark. So Rosen turned and surrendered.

"Please, I have a critical message for the strike team. You have to let me go," Rosen pleaded.

"Negative. I have strict orders to shoot anyone who attempts to pass through my perimeter. If you don't start walking toward me now, I'll put you down."

Rosen hesitated.

"You have three seconds," the Marine said. "Three. Two..."

The rumble of heavy automatic weapons fire ahead drowned out the Marine's warning. Rosen made a break for the corridor. The full force of the round hit him before he heard the gunshot. He watched in slow motion as bits of his chest cavity sprayed the wall with bone and blood. The force of the impact knocked him to the floor.

Dizzy from shock, Rosen glanced at his chest. His sternum was shattered, and a ruin of ribs barely covered his still-beating heart. He was no physician, but he was certain that the shot should've killed him.

His assailant's footsteps quickened. The battle ahead climaxed in a cacophony of screams and explosions.

Then silence.

Rosen stumbled back to his feet. The Marine drew closer. His face registered a mix between confusion and fear. Rosen turned and darted past the scramjet engine and toward the bend in the corridor. More shots rang out from behind, but he forged ahead.

Rosen slipped on something slick. He got up. Pausing, he took in his surroundings. The wreckage of dismembered bodies cluttered the corridor.

Something skittered in the darkness. Intermittent sparks from torn electrical wires flashed with sporadic illumination. Whatever was out there was coming closer.

The Marine arrived on Rosen's heels. "Jesus Christ!" he howled.

With preternatural speed, the torso of a shredded skeleton surged forward and past Rosen. Wiley leapt at the Marine. The thing ripped off the man's face with pitted teeth.

For an instant, Rosen wondered why it hadn't attacked him, but deep down he knew. The infection had made him immune. He and Wiley now had a strange kinship. Yet somehow, Rosen had been able to maintain his sentience.

Rosen trudged through the bloody remains of the strike team and toward a faint blue light that shimmered in the blackness. Along the way, he passed the torn remains of the original project team. His body pulsed with energy, the power of the rift super-charging the air around him.

For the brief instant that time had flattened, he knew he had to infect Wiley so Wiley could then infect him. Otherwise, he'd risk breaking the causality loop that kept him from being stranded in this soon-to-be-annihilated universe. The signal was the infection's siren song. And he understood why he'd always had the ability to see so easily what others could not.

Once the hyperdimensional parasite had infected him, he would always be infected. He had always been infected.

Eternity was now.

Rosen strode toward the pulsating light, absorbing its rippling energy. Like Icarus, NASA's scientists had flown too close to the sun. Their boundless curiosity had met with folly. By tearing a rift in space-time, they would annihilate two realities, including their own.

But the parasite would allow him to transcend both.

Rosen stepped through the rift so he could return to when the scientists had sundered space-time with their antigravity generator.

While he'd not survive in this universe, in non-Euclidian space there were infinitely many realities to explore. Rosen smiled with the hope that wherever he went next, he'd find powdered donuts.

END

Afterword

"Portal in Pasadena" was inspired by a trip I took to NASA's Jet Propulsion Laboratory with my daughter, who received an assignment as a Scholastic News Kid Reporter to interview screenwriter Jonathan Nolan and theoretical physicist Kip Thorne about the film *Interstellar*. As part of the trip, the Jet Propulsion Laboratory staff graciously organized a guided tour of the installation. There, we got to see the Mars Exploration Rover Command Center and the Low Density Supersonic Decelerator as well as many other projects NASA was managing. That said, there were plenty of other places on the installation that were off limits to outsiders. This story is about one of them.

While this story is not the first in which Doctor Eli Rosen appears, it is, in a sense, his origin story. In it, he is infected by a hyperdimensional parasite and can briefly perceive all time and space simultaneously—a fact highlighted by an in-story reference to another Rosen tale: "Quantum Shadows." The story also explains why Rosen seems to have a knack for investigating unexplained phenomena for the U.S. government.

Another important aspect of this story is that while it is technically not a hard science fiction story, it has hard science fictional elements, particularly regarding the theory and practical applications of fast Fourier transforms in converting signals in the time domain into signals in the frequency domain.

I originally submitted "Portal in Pasadena" to *Outposts of Beyond*, but the editor felt it was more of a horror than a science fiction story. So he bought it instead for *Disturbed Digest* in 2016, and it appeared in that magazine in September 2017.

My personal opinion is that this story is more science fiction than horror, but I'll let you be the judge of that.

ULIA KOLTYRINA

Quantum Shadows

I knew the pale lady was real the first night she appeared at the foot of my bed and whispered, "You were warned in two weeks, but you will ignore me yesterday, Silas," her raspy voice so much like crumbling parchment carried on an astral wind. It was 3:14 a.m. when her coal-black eyes pierced mine, but she was too far away for me to see the contours of her semi-translucent face. Her diaphanous form cast no reflection in my nightstand mirror, and she wore a flowing white gown, her raven hair swirling in some ethereal breeze. The moonlight reflected off her alabaster skin with an eerie eldritch glow.

I felt a crushing weight on my chest, pinning me to the bed and paralyzing me. I labored to exhale cold wisps of white breath that became shallower as she leached heat from my body.

I was cold, so very cold, feeling less substantial the longer she remained in my presence. I struggled to lift my arms, but they failed me. It felt as though I were imprisoned in a block of translucent cement. Unable to move, I closed my eyes, comforting myself with the hope that this night caller would lose interest and fade away.

I took three more breaths, and then opened my eyes to find her still there, a silent sentinel holding vigil over my paralyzed body. When my eyes locked on hers, her lips creased ever so slightly at the edge in what seemed like a knowing smirk.

A desperate and primal panic overwhelmed me. I wanted to flee with every fiber of my being, but my mind had no control over my body. Only my eyes could move, shifting in their sockets, searching for a rifle that wasn't there. The only option left was to ignore the apparition and shut my eyes, yearning for sleep to overcome my terror.

&

Later that morning, I awoke with my clock radio broadcasting an NPR piece about a black hole's accretion disk appearing on the edge of Alpha Centauri. Gwen would've loved it. The featured astrophysicists spoke excitedly about their finding, their voices betraying what sounded like barely suppressed panic. Before Gwen, I'd never listened to NPR, but she'd insisted. Over time it kinda grew on me, especially during the war. Listening to it reminded me of her.

I turned off the radio and lay in the old apartment exhausted and drained of energy. My memory of the pale lady was faint and receding into a willowy whisper of a dream, an electric field dissipating with distance.

I glanced at my alarm clock. It was already eight a.m. and I had to be at the warehouse in thirty minutes. There was no way I could make it in time, and frankly, I was too tired to spend the entire day on my feet, so I called in sick.

Ever since my medical discharge, it was hard to find a sense of purpose. And it was tough to earn a decent wage when your skill set included operating a fifty-caliber machine gun. When I'd returned from Afghanistan for the last time, everyone thanked me for my service, but few offered me a job.

After I hung up the phone, I saw Gwen's missed call.

No voicemail. Figures. Before we broke up last week, Gwen had lived in this place for five years, while I was stationed at Fort Drum. Between deployments, I'd spent every spare weekend and day of leave here. After I'd supported her through four stressful years of physics at Stanford and then five years of grad school at Princeton, she'd dropped me like a hot potato. On one level, I couldn't blame her. After I'd left the Army, I'd moved in with her, but had difficulty keeping a steady job.

It sucked. I really missed her. She'd been my rock during my frequent deployments. She'd written me a letter every week like a metronome. I never knew if I'd live or die from one day to the next, but I could always count on that letter. But ever since I'd left the service, she'd grown more distant. What really irked me was that it wasn't like her to call me out of the blue like this—unless she needed something. I wouldn't be surprised. She could be a cold and calculating bitch.

I committed to not returning her call, but then I wondered, maybe it was important. Maybe she really needed my help.

So I steeled myself, rehearsed my greeting, and then pushed the number "one" on speed dial.

"Hello?" Gwen answered, her voice projecting professionalism and confidence.

"Ah…Gwen…ah," I hesitated. "I see you called me last night?"

"Who is this?" she said in a tone that sounded like a challenge.

Why didn't she recognize my voice? Now I was worried. Had I really meant that little to her?

"Exactly how many men did you call last night?" I said before I realized how defensive I must've sounded.

She hung up.

I fumed and fretted for a few minutes, and then sucked up my pride and called her again.

"Hello?" she answered.

"Gwen, this is Si. I had a quick question for you."

"Oh, hello, Silas. Did you just call?"

I wavered and then said, "Well…ah…yes, but…I…"

"That was really rude of you, you know."

"Well…yes…but, well…did you call me last night?"

"Oh, *that's* what this is about?"

"Well, yeah. I was just returning your call."

"I was calling to let you know that NPR was going to air my interview this morning. But it's too late now. You already missed it."

I had mixed feelings about her response. On one hand, I was disappointed she wasn't in some sort of trouble. After all, I wouldn't have the opportunity to save her. On the other hand, I was relieved she wasn't in danger. But ultimately, her calling me just to brag pissed me off.

I tried to stay calm. "Actually, I caught the tail end of it. Something about a black hole near Alpha Centauri."

She huffed. "Oh, you heard the quack portion of the segment, and it wasn't a black hole. It was a black hole's accretion disk." She never passed up on an opportunity to lord her mental superiority over me, but her voice still held a hint of what I sensed was her passion for astrophysics, a passion that made me fall in love with her so many years ago.

"Damned radio astronomers think they can see things others can't," she said, nearly betraying a subtle trace of her carefully suppressed Appalachian twang. "You do realize that if a black hole were that close to Earth, it wouldn't be long before it swallowed us up."

"So that's why those guys were so excited," I said.

"Yup."

"Is there anything else you wanted to tell me, Gwen?"

"No. Were you expecting something else?"

Dejected, I said, "Ah…no. I hope all's well."

"Things are going great!" she said. "But I really need to get going, Silas. Cheers!" She hung up the phone, and now I felt worse than I had before I'd spoken with her.

ℰℭ

"The reckoning came one week from now and last week you will do nothing to stop it," the apparition said.

I woke up at 3:14 a.m., paralyzed. I felt her presence before she emerged from the edge of my peripheral vision. She didn't so much move as drift, a dim pulsing glimmer in the night, and she moved faster than my eyes could track.

In seconds, she was kneeling on my chest restricting my airflow. Because her face was closer to mine than it had been in my last encounter, I could see her features more clearly.

No. It wasn't possible. How could Gwen be haunting me when she wasn't dead?

ℰℭ

"Mr. Webb, I'd be happy to exorcize your apartment as a precaution, but your problem doesn't seem like a supernatural one. It's more likely a medical issue," Father Barlow said over the phone. "It sounds more like sleep paralysis, which is fairly common."

As a Baptist, I was frustrated by his response. I'd gotten to the point where I was crazy enough to invite a Catholic priest to my home to exorcize it, and he'd dismissed my concerns. "But, Father, these events feel very real for me."

"Son, I don't deny you really believe you saw a spirit. All I'm saying is that you should seek medical help, especially given your time in the service, before you try more radical solutions. That's all."

I struggled to keep my composure. I knew Father Barlow was just trying to help, but not everyone who's served has PTSD. "Thanks for your help, Father."

The instant I hung up the phone, it rang again, and I instinctively reached for a phantom rifle.

Gwen.

℘

With some reservations, I'd agreed to accompany Gwen to her departmental cocktail party. She'd even apologized for the flippant way she'd handled my phone call. We'd decided to meet at Professor Wong's crowded home so we wouldn't have to be alone together and face the associated discomfort and awkwardness. I knew I reminded her too much of the life she'd wanted to forget back in Pocahontas County, West Virginia, and I probably worried more than she did that I'd embarrass her if I said too much.

I was almost certain Gwen was using me, but I also hoped there was a chance we might get back together. Hell, we grew up together. I would spend my weekday evenings at football practice, while she'd pass every spare hour she wasn't in school or with me pestering astronomers at the National Radio Astronomy Observatory in Green Bank, studying remnant signals from the Big Bang. But really, I just needed someone to talk to. My parents were both dead and I didn't have any siblings or close friends. I'd devoted nine long years of my life to this woman, and I had nothing to show for it.

When I arrived at the professor's home, a massive Georgian house situated on a cul-de-sac in an exclusive part of Princeton Township, I viewed the colossal structure as the ultimate testament to ivory-tower arrogance. It didn't surprise me one bit that Gwen would keep company with these people. It was also obvious to me I didn't belong here among them.

The instant I walked into the foyer, I realized I was woefully underdressed in my blazer and khakis. Everyone else wore a tux or cocktail dress. While one gentleman was kind enough to introduce himself, he seemed to lose interest the moment he learned I didn't have a doctorate.

Gwen was late to the party, so I became a wallflower to avoid any further humiliation. That's when I saw an eclectic-looking bald man, whose patchy beard looked like a bacteria culture had exploded on his face. His plaid suit was loud and wrinkled.

I immediately introduced myself. "The name's Si Webb."

The man beamed and shook my hand. "Dr. Eli Rosen, Assistant Professor of Quantum Parapsychology."

"Quantum what?"

"Quantum Parapsychology. Until 2007, it was part of an interdisciplinary effort between the Princeton Engineering Anomalies Research Laboratory and the Department of Astrophysical Sciences. My research focuses on understanding parapsychological phenomena at the quantum level. More specifically, I'm trying to reconcile the principles of quantum mechanics with the theory of gravitation at the quantum scale in order to learn more about the behavior of dark matter and dark energy," an animated Dr. Rosen explained.

"What the heck does that have to do with the paranormal?" I said.

Dr. Rosen's eyes widened and he smiled. He then wagged his index finger at me. "You're the only person who's ever asked me about that part of my research. Most academic types are too embarrassed to talk about it because they've concluded I'm a nutjob."

"Well, I have a bit of a vested interest in your response," I said.

Dr. Rosen grabbed my shoulder and ushered me outside, past throngs of arriving guests. Once we were alone, he said, "You're having night terrors, aren't you?"

I was shocked. "How on earth…?"

He cut me off. "You started seeing the phantoms about a week ago. Right?"

I nodded.

"These encounters, they happen at precisely 3:14 in the morning?"

"Yes. How'd you know that?"

Dr. Rosen looked around him and then, in a hushed voice, said, "I see them too."

"Do you have a theory?" I asked.

"Perhaps. The work I do on the paranormal centers on my theory that most supernatural activity can be explained by the interaction between matter and dark matter. Most reported extrasensory phenomena operate on higher dimensions than we're capable of observing. You see, humans are evolved to perceive the world in only four dimensions—height, width, depth, and time. Paranormal entities are nothing more than hyperdimensional beings composed of dark matter."

"That's a fascinating theory, but why are we seeing these things at a precise moment in time?"

"Well, that topic's a little sensitive. I think it's related to…"

"There you are, Silas!" Gwen shouted from across Professor Wong's front lawn. "I've been trying to find you all night."

I waved at Gwen. "Gwen, come on over here. I'd like you to meet my friend, Dr. Rosen."

Gwen hesitated for a moment and then trudged across the lawn. She extended her hand to Dr. Rosen. "It's a pleasure to meet you, doctor."

Dr. Rosen shook Gwen's hand and said, "Likewise, Gwen."

Gwen raised her chin ever so slightly and said, "Actually, it's Gwendolyn. Or Dr. Cochran, if you prefer."

Dr. Rosen just smiled and said, "Oh, I'm sorry. In that case, just call me, Eli."

To avoid any further awkwardness, I shook Dr. Rosen's hand and said, "It was truly a pleasure to meet you, doc. Do you have a card or something?"

He smiled and handed me his card. "I'm looking forward to continuing our discussion."

For the rest of the evening, I was never far from Gwen. While she seemed to impress most of the other guests, I'd like to say that I masterfully played my part as her accessory and didn't embarrass her...much.

It felt like Gwen was starting to warm back up to me, almost as if we were a couple again.

At the end of the evening, I hugged Gwen and she thanked me for being a good sport. While we didn't set up plans for a future date, I felt hopeful for the first time in a long while, even if I was terrified to fall asleep.

࠾

Two weeks after my initial encounter with Gwen's shade, a second specter emerged from the shadows. As he hovered toward my bed, his features materialized from the cold darkness—square jaw, dimpled chin, blue eyes, and dark hair. It wasn't until I saw the thin scar on his forehead that my mind processed and confirmed what my instincts sensed the instant I saw him: he was a twisted simulacrum of me.

"If you miss the call two weeks ago, you died two days from now," he whispered in a voice like grinding gravel.

Weakness overcame me while he and Gwen's specter watched and smiled.

࠾

I called Dr. Rosen the instant I woke. "Dr. Rosen, it happened again, only this time, I saw myself."

"When we last spoke, we never had a chance to discuss any details. Do you have any mirrors in your bedroom close to where these spirits appear? More specifically, do they tend to appear between a set of mirrors?"

"Well, I do have one mirror at the foot of my bed, but that's all," I said.

"Interesting. When I searched the Internet for similar incidents within the last two weeks, every single night phantom account has a specter appearing between two mirrors."

"What the hell's that supposed to mean, doc?"

"I'm not sure, but I suspect it's got something to do with photons and dark matter."

"Go on."

"Well, we can't actually see dark matter. The only reason we know it exists is because of its impact on gravity. I believe these hyperdimensional apparitions marshal enough gravitational energy that they can manifest images of themselves by bending the light around them.

"Since mirrors reflect light in our realm of matter and energy, they serve as conduits of dark matter and dark energy in the phantom realm, portals to higher dimensional realities."

My head was spinning, but Dr. Rosen still hadn't answered the most burning question. "But why now?"

The line went silent for several seconds. "Well, I can't talk about it, but let's say there's a major cosmic event that may be coming to a head in two days which could warp space-time. It's my belief that these shadow entities are somehow trapped in our dimension as a consequence."

"But it hasn't happened yet," I said.

"For them, it already has."

"Who do you see in your night terrors, Dr. Rosen?"

The doctor hesitated again, but I could hear his tremulous breaths. Then he answered, "I see myself, and he speaks to me about future events as if he's already experienced them."

☙

Gwen called me in tears. She wouldn't tell me why she was crying, but she begged me to meet her in person. So I went to a local bar and found her huddled at a corner table, sipping a strawberry margarita. Her cheeks were glistening with tears.

I would've ordered a drink first, but something seemed very wrong, so I went directly to her table. I'd never seen Gwen so upset before. She was normally as tough as a linebacker, but the woman I saw today was a physical and emotional wreck.

"What's wrong, Gwen?"

"I'm so sorry, Si. For everything. We never should've broken up. I was selfish. I focused too much on my career when I should've spent more time with the only person in the world who truly loved me."

I smiled in an involuntary bout of *schadenfreude*. For an instant, I felt vindicated and self-righteous, but what Gwen said next changed everything.

"Tomorrow, the world will end."

☙

Gwen had explained that only a handful of scientists knew the truth, but they'd decided to keep it secret. Yet Gwen's apocalyptic pronouncement had the odd effect of reigniting our passion, if only for a day. Nothing mattered anymore. The day-to-day dictates of life no longer commanded us. So on the evening of the apocalypse we made love at the old apartment for one last time.

As I embraced Gwen after our lovemaking, I stared at the mirror on my nightstand, waiting for the black hole to swallow our reality. Then I wondered: what if I could make my time with her last forever?

I checked my alarm clock. It was 3:10 a.m. I shook Gwen awake.

She groaned. Her bloodshot eyes cracked open. "What is it, Si?"

"What time is it supposed to happen?"

"3:14 a.m." she said.

"How will it feel?"

"I doubt it'll feel like anything. One instant we'll be here, and in another, gone. Wiped from existence."

"Do you have a small mirror or compact in your purse?"

She raised her right eyebrow. "Why? And what's that got to do with anything?"

I looked in her eyes and said, "At this point does it really matter? C'mon. Indulge me."

She grabbed her purse from the floor, rifling through it until she handed me a small pink compact.

I glanced at the alarm clock: 3:12 a.m. I turned my head back toward Gwen, embraced her, and kissed her for what I thought would be the last time.

At 3:13 a.m., I opened Gwen's compact and placed it behind us, facing the mirror on my nightstand. Both mirrors shone with an infinity of shadowy images.

A minute later, the world ended at light-speed as space and time merged into infinity. But we had not, did not, and will not end. We reversed course against the grains of time. We will warn ourselves until two weeks ago when humanity will discover the singularity, and we will thrive until the Big Bang gave birth to the stars.

END

Afterword

"Quantum Shadows" is based on my interpretation of a friend's dream in which his ex-girlfriend would appear at night and suck the life from him. After doing further research, it turns out that many people experience a similar form of sleep paralysis where they wake up in the middle of the night, sense a menacing supernatural presence, and are unable to move. Oftentimes, that presence immobilizes them by sitting on their chest, making sleep paralysis a terrifying experience.

While my friend's dream and the concept of sleep paralysis inspired this story, I wanted to make it my own. So I combined the paranormal ambience of a parasitic ghost story with the stranger elements of cosmology and quantum mechanics. To achieve this eerie effect, I experimented with mismatching verb tenses and temporal adverbs like "yesterday" and "tomorrow" to distort the reader's conception of space and time.

Another important thing to note about this story is that while this is not the first Doctor Eli Rosen story that has appeared in print—that distinction belongs to "Chandler's Hollow", which appears earlier in this volume—it is the first story in which I introduced the character.

I sold "Quantum Shadows" to *Stupefying Stories* in 2014, and it appeared in print in October 2016.

I hope you find this story both chilling and thought-provoking.

THE DECISION

Sean Patrick Hazlett

catleonardart.com

CAT LEONARD

The Decision

For years, business leaders from Mars to the Kuiper Belt have been asking me to outline my principles on leadership, especially as they relate to the 2259 Terran Crisis. When the editor of the *New Harvard Business Review* first approached me for this article, I was reluctant to open old wounds. The Decision was a tough and controversial one. I ultimately agreed to pen this piece because our society is still in desperate need of good leaders. This article outlines the principles that guided my actions during the nineteen-year period leading up to the Decision.

⁝

1. Perception Is Reality

The hardest lesson I've ever learned began with an intricate deception. In 2240, Mars Colony was on the verge of rebellion. Earth Protectorate, or E.P., had required every Terran between the ages of eighteen and sixty to take a battery of tests on spatial reasoning, emotional intelligence, physical fitness, analytical ability, and psychological stability.

None of us knew why. We just did what we had to do. Like any young person aspiring to greatness, I strove to do my best. I scored high enough on the tests to get a one-way ticket to the Red Planet. Yet, my friend Lily, who by all rights was much more intelligent and accomplished than I, did not. It was only much later that I discovered why.

At the time, Mars Colony had crippling labor shortages in all areas from habitat management to waste disposal. Even worse, the corrupt corporate syndicate running Mars was not operating at peak efficiency. Rather than scuttle the operation as a sunk cost, the E.P. had caved in to Martian demands by sending the colony more labor.

The *burons* at E.P.'s New York headquarters showered the successful candidates with praise. The E.P. Secretary General himself met with a group of the twenty most promising management candidates, including me. To this day, I remember his words: "You all have a solemn responsibility to restore order on Mars. In doing so, you will be performing a patriotic duty for Earth."

I never bought his appeal to selfless service, but one thing he said caught my attention: "This is a once-in-a-lifetime opportunity to bring order to a world on the brink of chaos. You will be remembered as Mars's founding mothers and fathers."

Despite his being a career *buron*, the Secretary General was the best salesman I've ever encountered. He could have sold leprosy to a fashion model. His smooth talk and gregarious style, coupled with an expensive suit replete with diamond cufflinks, belied an underlying gravitas impossible to ignore. I was in awe of him.

Soon I began to see opportunities for shaping Mars's future that I hadn't considered before. I imagined myself as a power broker bridging Terran and Martian society. What Rockefeller was for oil, and Carnegie for steel, I would be for interplanetary commerce. These thoughts of a bold future invigorated me.

It wasn't until I signed up for a lifetime contract and sat inside a space elevator festooned to a floating anchor station in the southwest Pacific that I'd begun to suspect I'd made a terrible mistake. The elevator, with its multi-decked promenades, had one uniformed officer for every ten passengers. It was an unusual level of security for an off-world excursion.

Despite my unease, I sat in my assigned seat on the space elevator's twelfth level, heady with dreams of a future on the red frontier. A brutish Asian man with a shiny bald crown and goatee shattered my lingering delusions of grandeur.

He grabbed my shoulder and demanded I stand. I stood up, expecting him to shuffle past me and take a seat nearest the wall. To my chagrin, he sat in my assigned seat. When I told him so, he pawed at my breasts and then forced me to the floor. If one of the uniformed officers hadn't rendered him unconscious with a shock lance, I might not have lived to tell this tale.

While I lay on the steel grated floor, I looked up at the officer and asked him why I'd been assaulted. He just shook his head and said, "With this many convicts heading to Mars, we expect outbreaks of violence."

Dumbfounded, I said, "Convicts? I'm not a convict."

The officer just smiled and said, "No. Not yet at least."

It was at that moment when I had an inkling that the E.P. viewed my leadership style with fear and suspicion. It was also the first time I began to understand why the Protectorate sent us to Mars.

While I'll get to that soon, the early part of my journey to Mars taught me that perception is everything. So much so, that an E.P. *buron*'s cheap charm persuaded me to travel tens of millions of miles from a comfortable home on Earth to a hardscrabble, desperate world on the brink of rebellion. In business, form is function. You can be the most skilled musician in the solar system, but if you cannot deliver a great show, you are nothing.

ॐ

2. Make Strategic Relationships to Further Your Interests

As an attractive young woman surrounded by violent felons, I had to build a coalition to survive. To do so, I had to find a locus of power and cultivate its source.

Before the officer who'd rescued me left the scene, I gripped his arm and said, "Who was that?" I pointed to the man who'd assaulted me.

"Hyun Park," he said.

I stared at the officer for ten long seconds. His looks were striking in a primal sort of way. "What's your name?" I batted my eyelashes and smiled.

"Sergey Vatutin."

"Well, Sergey, thank you for saving me. You mind keeping a gal company?"

That night, we slept together. From then on, he was mine. After we left the protective tether of the space elevator and embarked on our voyage, I got to know every officer on the freighter. I learned and memorized every security protocol.

Early in the journey, I met another handsome officer named Robert Howard. The man also happened to be Sergey's rival. So I started bedding him too. I kept this volatile secret from both men so that I could later use it to my advantage.

Twenty years ago, many business gurus would have criticized my methods and called me a whore. Of course, most of these theorists perished after the Decision.

A great leader must focus on making many strategic relationships to achieve her ends. She must leverage the assets she has available to her. Surrounded by violent convicts with overwhelming physical advantages, I used sex as my weapon.

৪০

3. Leverage Your Informational Advantage

In business, as in war, having more information than your rivals is a competitive advantage. A few choice words whispered in a sympathetic ear can make all the difference.

Hyun Park was still a threat, so I'd been keeping tabs on his whereabouts and schedule. In the afternoon, he went to the gym like clockwork. Using this information and my knowledge about the timing of key operations on the ship, I planned to neutralize Park.

Wearing my tightest skinsuit, I scheduled my workout to coincide with Mr. Park's. I double-booked dates with both Sergey and Robert, offsetting them by only five minutes. I also brought an aerosol can containing trace amounts of cyanide.

Park was bench-pressing over three hundred pounds when I arrived. I strolled by his station and sprayed him in the face. He squinted and coughed, nearly dropping the bar on his neck.

I got on the treadmill with my back facing him. I acted as if nothing had happened. He grumbled and coughed. A meaty hand gripped my shoulder. He spun me around and forced me to the ground. I slammed my head against the rubber surface. A white flash flooded my vision. Then pain. He punched me in the jaw. I bit my tongue and tasted blood. He punched me in the stomach. He coughed again. His manhood stiffened.

I panicked. I prayed that Sergey and Robert arrived on time. Park tore my skinsuit. His calloused hands bruised my skin as he held me down.

I screamed.

Seconds later, Sergey ripped Park off me. He threw my attacker to the floor. Straddling Park, Sergey walloped the brute with his fists until the man's face was a bloody pulp.

Just as I thought the fight was over, Park forced Sergey's arm into his chest, and then rolled on top of Sergey, pinning him. Park pummeled Sergey until my lover was unconscious.

I had to escape, but I couldn't compel myself to leave. The raw savagery of it all awoke something inside me. Something primal. Something beautiful. Park beat Sergey until his face was a riot of blood and bone. He hit Sergey until Park heaved with exhaustion. Sergey stopped breathing. Park raised his head and scowled at me. He slowly rose and stalked me like a tiger.

I played the part, whimpering like a scared sow. I backed away from his advance. But I wasn't frightened. Everything was going according to plan. Either Robert would kill him or the cyanide would.

Moments later, Robert entered in the room. Unlike Sergey, he was still on duty and armed with a shock lance. His eyes widened as he took in the scene. He raised his weapon and fired. Park jolted as electric current spiked through his body.

Robert seemed distraught, as if uncertain what to do.

"He tried to rape me," I said, pointing to Park. I hoped Robert would execute the *coup de grace*.

Robert nodded. He had a vacant look in his eyes.

He needed more motivation. I seized his wrists. "He. Tried. To. Rape. Me. He killed Sergey. What are you gonna do about it?"

Like most sheep, Robert lacked the will to do what was necessary. Fortunately, Park died several days later "from his wounds and trauma."

While my plan hadn't worked perfectly, it had gone well enough. My relationships had paid off as did my surveillance of Park.

છ

4. Delegate, Delegate, Delegate

No woman is an island. She needs a good team to actualize her vision. A strong leader knows when to apply the lash or the drug to influence her subordinates.

But what if a leader has no followers? I had none when I began my journey, but hundreds by the time I arrived on Mars.

Given that my capacity for violence was not as well honed as many of the convicts on board, I leveraged my intellect and charm to build a coalition around my vision.

A good leader doesn't work. She convinces others to work for her. She either inspires them with her vision or terrifies them with her ability to mete out violence. In my experience, the latter is more effective than the former.

On long interplanetary voyages, cabin fever takes on a whole new meaning. Crammed into tight quarters, people crave a release. This desire often explodes into violence. I found a way to channel this angst to achieve a higher purpose.

It started with Karl Gustav, an unstable German chemist. I'd accessed the crew files and learned he didn't have the same aggressive tendencies many others did. He was a manic-depressive, and in his manic phase he was an alchemical genius. Gustav had an encyclopedic knowledge of synthesizing exotic drug cocktails from common ship chemicals. He also had a knack for innovation. Under my guidance, he whipped up an addictive stimulant we called "Nitro" and a soporific we called "Bliss." In the right concentrations, I could speed a man up so he could kill and then slow him down enough to put him in a coma.

In just five weeks, I had a critical mass of addicts. After that, I could make anything happen.

At first, my inaugural business venture was the ideal solution to on-ship violence. So security turned a blind eye to my operation. By the time the authorities realized what I had really been up to, it was too late. No one could as much move to another module without my say so.

ℂ

5. Boredom Is the Bugbear of Modern Business

Stagnation is death.

Once I had consolidated my power base, things grew quiet. Too quiet. My people were becoming lazy and complacent.

I was concerned that they'd lose their edge before they landed on Martian soil and faced the rebels. So I ran some experiments. It was crucial that I understood how my people would behave under extreme stress.

About ten percent of the population consumed more resources than they contributed. This group, which I selected for my experiment, included the sick, the crippled, the mentally weak, and the incompetent.

I then selected another five percent of passengers at random. I had ship security sequester this fifteen percent in a sealed section of the ship. I cut off their access to drugs and food. But I did allow for ample access to water.

Within two weeks, the subjects had exhausted the food stores they'd smuggled into the section. In another two weeks, the weakest began to perish. Mere hours after the first death, the survivors ate the remains. A week later, the strong corralled the weak, setting up a makeshift human abattoir.

In one bold stroke, I had culled the ship's weakest members. Once the initial three hundred subjects had whittled themselves down to fifty, I ended the experiment.

I then commissioned a second one.

I wanted to know how the fifty survivors, after having experienced severe depravation, would react to having too many resources. When they reemerged from their isolation, I gave them three months of rations all at once. Another twenty died after their stomachs burst.

I promoted the thirty survivors to lead the other seventeen hundred passengers. I was pleased to see my new cadre impose these Darwinian conditions on everyone else. Once they'd purged and purified the overall population to an elite one thousand, I ordered an end to the culling. While we could have used more winnowing, we still needed manpower to take control of Mars.

By keeping my passengers engaged, I prevented them from succumbing to the fatal ennui associated with long interplanetary passages. And for that, my new organization had been honed to a razor's edge.

ॐ

6. Dwelling on the Past Is a Prelude to Failure

The mutiny took me by surprise. I had forged my crew into a core of strong-willed and efficient leaders. When Robert put a knife to my throat, my mind raced through every action I'd taken during the voyage. What could I have done better? What had I done wrong?

Robert, having survived the culling, was a harder man now. But he still put too much trust in others. I cried and cried. I told him that I loved him, that I had done everything for him. I professed that I wanted nothing more than to raise a family with him on Mars.

After we made love, he identified his co-conspirators. I kissed him, thanked him, and then stabbed him in the throat.

My loyal followers rounded up the mutineers. Each day, I fed these traitors their own body parts until they died of blood loss.

After that, no one dared oppose me.

ॐ

7. Emotions Cloud Judgment

After the mutiny, I intercepted an E.P. transmission to one of the dead traitors. I had always believed that the E.P. had discarded us, but what I uncovered in the transmission was far more insidious. And it made me furious. Our exile was part of a plot to install sociopaths into critical management positions on the Martian Colony. According to the intercept, the E.P. leadership believed this act would sow enough chaos and discord on Mars to end the rebellion.

They couldn't have been more wrong.

They were right about our impact on the rebellion. It took me about two years to stamp it out. The E.P. may have considered us sociopaths, but we were more than that. We were wolves among sheep—iron-willed warriors united by the perfidy of our exile.

When I arrived on Mars, I leveraged my narcotics network to addict the population to "Nitro" and "Bliss" and a number of other nasty new formulations. But addicting the Martian colonists one person at a time was too slow. So I laced the water and food supply, and steadily increased the dosage over time.

Then one day, I cut it off.

After the population had exhausted itself in an orgy of violence, I unleashed my shock troops to restore order and seize power.

Many of my detractors have argued that my actions were callous and will cast a long shadow on future generations. They claim that my adulteration of the water supply harmed the brain development of young children and the unborn.

While it is true that my actions may have harmed a few children, it was a small price to pay. Inaction would have been worse.

Had I let my emotions cloud my judgment, we'd still be slaves to a hostile blue world. But I didn't. And for that, we are now free.

৪০

8. Improvisation Trumps Long-term Planning

Many historians think I had a master plan, and had faithfully followed it for years.

They could not be more wrong.

Long-term planning can be an asset, but it can also stifle creativity. Sometimes taking action based on raw instinct can be more effective than ten five-year plans. Improvisation works. It clarifies. It is bold and decisive. It cuts through to the heart of a problem in a way that years of detailed analysis cannot.

In 2256, the E.P. had been gathering an armada in response to my refusal to enforce a series of tax increases. The effort was unprecedented, involving the coordination of seventy nations and at a cost roughly three times the then-China's GDP. At the same time, the E.P. demanded our immediate and unconditional surrender.

I agreed with E.P.'s terms pending the arrival of its fleet. In the interim, I rigged all twenty of the Martian biodomes with nuclear tripwires.

If I couldn't control Mars, no one would.

By sheer luck, I found a solution that would spare me from having to make such a suicidal decision. *Persephone*, a near Earth object, would pass to within ten thousand kilometers of Earth before the armada arrived on Mars. It would not get close enough to threaten Earth.

Unless someone gave it a little nudge.

The idea was so controversial, only a small cabal knew about it. I compartmentalized parts of the effort so that none of my scientists knew how their individual projects fit into the overall picture.

Everyone was told we'd be harvesting more resources from asteroids to reduce our dependence on Earth.

The roboticists were to design autonomous drones capable of latching themselves to asteroid fragments and towing them to precise locations for mineral extraction.

The exoatmospheric nuclear demolition engineers were to design precision nuclear warheads capable of fragmenting large asteroids in very specific ways to prevent these pieces from striking nearby planetary objects.

The propulsion engineers had to design a craft capable of landing on an asteroid traveling at five miles per second. The craft would then have to land a robotic and nuclear payload precisely on a hostile microgravity environment where temperatures could range from minus one hundred ninety degrees to plus one hundred seventy degrees Fahrenheit.

My flexible decision-making caused a bit of a stir among many of my scientists and engineers. But any time one opposed me, I replaced him or her with someone more compliant.

My team ultimately completed its task, and we launched the mission with much pride and fanfare.

∽

9. Frame Your Interests Persuasively

The Terrans never knew what hit them. At the last minute, I triggered the shaped nuclear charges on the asteroids to blow before the E.P. could deploy its planetary countermeasures.

Because I'd compartmentalized the effort, no one knew of my final plans. Based on their questions, many of my senior project managers suspected I might use the asteroid to blackmail Earth. I doubt any of them had imagined I'd use it to destroy our home world.

During trying times, a leader will often have nervous employees who second-guess every decision. A great leader must use her powers of persuasion to frame her interests so they align with those of her subordinates.

Throughout the crisis, I managed their hopes and fears to get the best out of them, while concealing my true aims.

Some believe that the more certainty a leader has, the easier it is to persuade others. I disagree. It is easier to persuade others when things are uncertain.

When we first outfitted the asteroid with nuclear charges, I used the margin of error associated with the near-Earth asteroid's flight path to my advantage. I told my people it was unlikely the asteroid would hit Earth, but it was still possible.

Playing on my scientists' and engineers' love of analytical arguments, I framed the issue as a question of risk versus cost. While the risk of the asteroid hitting Earth was low, if it did, the results would've been catastrophic. By outfitting the asteroid, we could divert it if necessary and thereby earn the E.P.'s goodwill. My rationale unified our effort. It gave people a sense of purpose.

This changed when the margin of error steadily decreased as *Persephone* drew closer to Earth. When it became extremely unlikely it would hit our home world, people began to question my motives. So I "came clean." I told them what they wanted to hear. I argued that having the capability to destroy Earth would be a useful lever in our ongoing dispute. Most accepted my logic. But if they'd dug a little deeper, they would have found my argument lacking. All Earth had to do was delay negotiations until the asteroid passed and I lost my leverage. In other words, they'd have to engage in an existential game of chicken. But no one had considered the unthinkable. No one thought I might actually annihilate the cradle of civilization.

Nobody except me.

❧

10. Apologies Are for Indecisive Leaders

Some still blame me for the Decision. They claim it was unnecessary. And they are outraged I show no signs of remorse.

Those people have no understanding of what leadership is. Apologies are for the weak. I did what I did because Earth forced me to. I had no choice. If I hadn't destroyed Earth, Earth would have destroyed me.

A leader acts alone. She must make decisions alone, and she alone must live with the consequences. A leader never apologizes for making hard decisions.

A leader only does what's right.

END

Afterword

"The Decision" considers what might happen if Earth infiltrated a group of highly intelligent sociopaths into key leadership positions on Mars to sow chaos on the rebellious colony. Of course, this plot ultimately results in Earth's destruction as one sociopath turns on her home world to further her quest for power.

The story's philosophical hook is to explore how a successful sociopath might reconcile her horrific decisions in the guise of a dispassionate *New Harvard Business Review* article on leadership where each "lesson" is actually an allusion to a specific sociopathic behavior. The meta-theme of the story is how disturbingly similar her voice is to leaders in many segments of our society today.

I would classify this story as experimental or non-traditional since it adopts the voice of a sociopath in the guise of a cold and detached business article on leadership. I also consider it a hard science fiction story with its descriptions of space elevators and orbital mechanics.

"The Decision" first appeared in *Sci Phi Journal* in July 2016. I hope that it made you think and that you found it to be a disturbing story.

JOSÉ BAETAS

Pinned

Acold December wind howled as Sergeant Willis Johnson's platoon shivered in the Mojave Desert's darkness. Most seemed too scared to acknowledge an obvious truth: Johnson would be dead by morning.

Wedged between two seventy-ton Abrams tanks, Johnson gazed upon the grim faces of the fifteen men flanking him. The vehicles were all that kept his innards from spilling onto the asphalt.

Pinned.

"Hang in there, Sergeant. We called your wife. She'll be here with your children soon," Lieutenant Roberts said in a tone booming with what Johnson took for a newly minted West Pointer's false bravado. Roberts clearly didn't know what the hell he was doing, but neither would Johnson if he found himself comforting a man so near death.

Gravity slowly sucked the vitality from Johnson's body, his blood pooling into his lower extremities. He'd only have a moment to say goodbye to Zoe and his two children. Then the soldiers would separate the tanks, and with them his bottom half from his torso. Dizzy from blood loss, Johnson struggled to compose his last words, but the disembodied voice in his head wouldn't let him.

"I'm sorry to bother you with this, but the investigating officer, Lieutenant Martinez, just arrived, and needs to ask you a few questions,"

Roberts said in a stilted "reassuring" tone like a nurse before she jabs you with something sharp and painful.

Johnson smiled. Even if he hadn't been so light-headed, no one would believe his story.

The crowd made way for Martinez as he approached. Dark rings circled the lieutenant's sunken eyes.

Martinez averted Johnson's gaze, instead rifling through his paperwork. Johnson couldn't blame Martinez for his reaction. The lieutenant likely needed time to process his horror. Moments later, Martinez looked up at Johnson and said, "S-S-Sergeant Johnson. Ah…can you tell me how this happened?"

Johnson opened his mouth to speak, but instead of finding his voice, choked up blood.

Martinez's face paled. Johnson imagined it matched his own deathly pallor. Watching Johnson gurgle, Martinez seemed locked in a moment of indecision. Warm blood slithered down Johnson's throat.

Shattering the stubborn silence, Roberts said, "Private Saunders, grab a rag and wipe up that blood." He hesitated, and then added an awkward, "For Mrs. Johnson."

Saunders, a hulking blonde Nebraskan, pulled a rag from his coveralls and wiped Johnson's throat from chest to mouth.

Again, Johnson tried to answer Martinez. He took a deep breath and said, "Earlier tonight, I was working on my tank. I heard the engine on Charlie One Four fire up. I just assumed Sergeant San Felipe was driving his tank to the wash rack, but it sounded like it was coming closer. I remember the smell of it most, the stench of rubber with a hint of jet fuel. Ain't nothing in the world smells like that but an M1."

"How'd you get pinned?" Martinez asked.

"Next thing I know, I turn 'round and it's coming right at me. Like it wants to kill me. Before I could move, the tank jammed me up against my own Abrams. It hurt something awful, then nothing. I couldn't feel nothing."

"Who was driving the tank?"

Johnson tried to answer, but only sputtered blood.

He tried again. "Sir, you wouldn't believe me."

"Try me."

"Nobody. Ain't nobody was driving that tank."

"Johnson," Roberts interrupted, "this is an official Fifteen Six investigation. You owe it to the Army to identify your killer."

"I meant what I said, sir. No one was in the driver's hole."

Roberts glared at Johnson. Then he turned to Martinez and said, "When the MPs get here, make sure they get prints from the other tank."

Martinez's brow furrowed. "I think I got it under control, butter bar."

Several soldiers snickered. Roberts's hostile glare stifled their laughter.

Martinez continued. "I need everyone to step back. Don't touch anything." He waited for the men to establish some distance, and then said, "Did anyone else see what happened?"

The men either shrugged or shook their heads. Martinez turned back to Johnson. "If nobody was driving the tank, how, in your estimation, did it get here?"

Oh what the hell. I'll be dead in an hour.

"It started in Nineveh."

"Nina what?"

"Nineveh. Modern day Mosul. Iraq"

"What's that got to do with anything? Focus, sergeant," Roberts said, making Johnson want to do anything but focus.

"Goddammit! You're not listening," Johnson gasped and then coughed up more phlegm and blood. "It was dusk when they attacked. An RPG knocked out the main gun on my Stryker. Then the mortars started exploding all around me. That's when I saw the mace, bronze studs embedded in bone, glistening in the twilight."

"The what?"

"The mace. It'd been buried under the surface for God knows how long. The instant I saw it, the shelling stopped. It got all quiet like. Scared the piss outta me.

"Next thing I know, I'm carrying this thing across the Old Bridge over the Tigris River and toward Nineveh's ruins."

Seemingly undeterred by the gore, Roberts grabbed Johnson by the collar, "Get your shit together, man! You don't have much time left."

Johnson didn't appreciate being reminded of his imminent demise. He glared at Roberts for thirty uncomfortable seconds and then said, "You done, sir?"

Roberts went ballistic. Martinez cut him off. "Roberts, you're interfering with my investigation. One more outburst and I'm including you in my report."

Roberts fumed, but kept his mouth shut.

Martinez shifted his attention back to Johnson. "Go on."

"That's when I heard the whisperers in the darkness. I saw shadow men whose eyes glowed red. Massive feral dogs with glowing red eyes followed in their wake. You know, the kind over there that rip heads off German shepherds. You've heard the stories."

Several soldiers nodded.

"Okay Sergeant. That'll be enough. Thank you for your cooperation. My sympathies go out to you and your family." Martinez turned and walked away.

A foul wind blew in from the desert, reeking of rot and sulfur. Its noxious miasma swept through the motorpool like cancer. Martinez put his hand over his stomach, frowned, then dropped his clipboard. Roberts bent over and vomited. More soldiers emptied their stomachs.

A solitary coyote's howl pierced the tomblike silence. The yips and yelps of a pack followed. Their yowls drew closer.

"What the hell's happening?" Roberts said, his voice unsteady.

"Lieutenant Martinez, come closer," Johnson pleaded, each word weakened by wheezing.

Martinez regarded the dying man, hesitated, then approached. Johnson put his hand on Martinez's shoulder and whispered, "It's coming. Send my wife, Zoe, back home when she gets here. Tell her to bring the artifact." Johnson paused to catch his breath, and then said, "Tell her not to bring the children."

"The artifact?" Martinez said, his face contorted in confusion.

"Yes. Please. She'll know."

Martinez nodded. "I'll call her now."

Johnson shook his head. Through labored breaths, he murmured, "Won't work."

Pulling out his mobile phone, Martinez said, "What's her number?"

Johnson gave him Zoe's digits, knowing it was pointless. Martinez dialed and waited. He clenched his jaw. "I...I can't get a damn signal."

The dying man nodded. He didn't have much energy left to talk. His head buzzed, black patches occluded his vision.

"I'll stop her in the parking lot," Martinez said. "She should be here soon." He spun on his heels and left the motorpool toward the howling gloom.

‚Äπ‚àû

Fifteen minutes after Martinez had returned, Zoe arrived, carrying a meter-long object wrapped in burlap. Despite his warning, Johnson's two doe-eyed children were in tow. When Zoe saw Johnson, she screamed. The children huddled around her, their eyes wide with terror. Johnson's three-year-old son Tyler wailed. His nine-year daughter, Hannah, stared blankly at Johnson as if beholding an illusion.

Zoe handed the bundle to Martinez, ran past the stunned soldiers and cradled Johnson's head in her arms, sobbing. "Not you too!" she shrieked. "Why? Why!?!"

Johnson regretted smuggling the artifact into the States, but Specialist Lewis had goaded him into it. They'd hidden the ancient weapon in their tank's ammunition ready rack before the vehicle shipped home. Now Lewis was dead. Torn apart by wild animals, they'd claimed. But Johnson knew it had been something far worse.

"Mace," Johnson muttered. "Bring. It."

Martinez laid the bundle before Johnson. The dying man unwrapped it with great effort. When his fingers touched the beautifully wrought weapon of carved bone studded with bronze spikes, the foul wind blew again. Dozens of glowing red eyes closed in from the murky perimeter.

Coyotes bayed. Out of the abyss two coyotes struck, ripping Saunders's guts out. He screamed. Other soldiers panicked, scrambling onto the tanks despite the fact that the Abrams carried no ammunition.

A surge of power rippled through Johnson's body. His pain faded. The voice in his head became stronger, more assertive. *Tell them.*

"Gather the men around the weapon. Sharur will protect us," Johnson said, his voice amplified by an eerie metallic ring.

Martinez's mouth gaped open. "Sharur? What are you talking about?"

"The weapon," Johnson said without pain. "It will protect us from Asag." Johnson could see terror and confusion on Martinez's face. The dying man had only seconds to impart his knowledge. "Please. Listen carefully. We were not the first, nor will we be the last. Those who came before left behind items to protect us, to keep the dark entities that lurk in spectral dimensions from passing into ours."

"You're making no sense," Martinez said.

The coyotes tore into Specialist Kim's calves, yanking him off one of the tanks. The wiry New Yorker fought back against his mangy attackers, but their onslaught wore him down until he lay prostrate on the bloodstained asphalt.

More coyotes circled, slavering, their demonic eyes aglow with an unnatural intelligence. Roberts swung a mattock at the mad canines. "Quick, men!" he yelled. "Grab anything you can find and brain these bastards."

Martinez seemed lost in the chaos around him. Johnson was losing the man's attention. "Listen!" Johnson yelled, his voice magnified by the ancient weapon. "Take Sharur. Kill them," Johnson pointed at the coyotes. "The shards of Asag's spirit can only possess lower life forms. Destroy them, and you may still have time."

"What then?" Martinez said. A coyote lunged at Roberts's throat, narrowly missing the West Pointer. The junior lieutenant drove his mattock into its skull.

"Then, you need to return Sharur to Nineveh," Johnson continued, "closer to its power source. If you don't, more people will die until Asag takes possession of the weapon."

"What happens then?"

"I don't know."

Another coyote tore a chunk out of Roberts's Achilles tendon. He swore and swung the mattock wildly, before a second coyote tackled him and ripped out his throat.

Martinez grabbed the mace. Johnson felt light-headed as its power and influence left his broken body. He gagged and then vomited froth-corrupted blood.

Taking control of the weapon, Martinez exuded an aura of power. He strode into the pack of American jackals, wielding the mace. Each successive strike atomized its target, leaving a spark of lightning and wisp of smoke in its wake.

Johnson's family huddled around him and watched as Martinez dispatched Asag's hosts. Darkness began to overtake Johnson. His vision faded, then oblivion.

છ

A sting of white light jolted Johnson from the abyss. "He's still alive!" a male voice announced. It was still dark and cold, but Johnson's family and the eleven surviving members of his platoon provided some warmth. Martinez was gone, but so were the coyotes.

"What happened?" Johnson said, forcing his words out as he struggled for oxygen.

A tear rolled down Zoe's cheek. "You were right, Willis. The mace saved us all. Lieutenant Martinez is finding a way to get it back to Iraq."

Johnson smiled. Zoe hugged him. Hannah climbed on the tank and kissed him on the cheek. "I love you, dad," she said with a stoicism that made her father proud.

"Take. Care. Of Mom," he stammered.

She nodded, her moist eyes betraying her sorrow.

Johnson grinned at Tyler. The boy cowered, burying his face into Zoe's side. "I love…you, Ty-ler." Johnson choked up more blood. He jerked his head at Sergeant San Felipe, signaling the end.

With sad eyes, San Felipe nodded.

Two soldiers climbed into the drivers' holes of both tanks and started the engines.

"Say your last goodbye," San Felipe said as he escorted Zoe and her children away from the tanks.

"I love you," Johnson said. He shuddered as a warm tear trickled down his face. The tanks separated. The last sound he ever heard was the dead thump of his disembodied legs hitting the pavement.

Vision fading, Tyler's glowing eyes were the last thing Johnson ever saw.

END

Afterword

Prior to reporting to Fort Knox for the Armor Officer Basic Course (AOBC) as a newly-minted second lieutenant in November 1998, former tankers and cavalrymen had warned me of soldiers getting grievous injuries after making careless mistakes when operating the infamous seventy-ton M1A1 Abrams tank. They would regale me with stories of soldiers losing arms when they failed to remove a tank round from the ammunition storage compartment quickly enough before the automated blast door sealed shut or people losing fingers because they failed to remove their wedding rings before climbing onto a tank.

When I first reported to AOBC, our instructors never ceased warning us about the dangers of operating the M1A1. For instance, our non-commissioned officer (NCO) instructors would tackle any oblivious second lieutenant who unwittingly ventured under a tank's main gun—the logic being that if the gunner decided to lower the main gun at that precise moment, it would crush the lieutenant's skull. We even had an incident during tank gunnery in which a lieutenant nearly suffocated when his tank's halon firefighting system malfunctioned.

As part of this tank "lore", I heard a story about a soldier who got pinned between two tanks at the torso. The other soldiers knew that the instant they separated the tanks, the pinned man's torso would be severed from his waist and legs. Consequently, while the dying man's blood slowly drained from his face, the Army rushed to bring his wife and children to him so he could see them one last time and say goodbye. I can't remember if this incident was rumored to have occurred in Germany or at Fort Knox, but everyone in the Armor branch seemed to be familiar with it. I've never been able to confirm if the story was true, but it obviously served as the inspiration for "Pinned."

I based this story's firefight on an actual one that happened in 2004 during the Battle of Mosul near ancient Nineveh where there was extensive fighting between U.S. forces and insurgents over control of key bridges spanning the Tigris River.

Similarly, Sharur and Asag come straight from Sumerian mythology. Sharur is an enchanted mace belonging to the god, Ninurta, that is used to defeat the primordial demon, Asag. Of course, I added some of my own fantastical elements to these mythological components to make the story my own.

This story first appeared in *Kasma SF* in December 2016. I hope you found it interesting.

The White

We cooked Emily first.

I sawed off Emily's arm and put it on the spit. Sandy and Ted stormed off in protest, unable to partake in my grim ritual. I didn't know how she'd died – it could've been exposure or starvation – but we needed food, and she was all we had.

Our world was slowly dying. The last of us had hunkered up in the Sierras living on whatever we could scavenge. The White had herded us from San Francisco all the way up to this godforsaken wilderness.

Some say civilization and anarchy are only seven meals apart. I disagree. Add wind and rain to the mix and that number drops to three.

The wind whistled and wailed through the redwoods towering above our camp – silent sentinels that bore witness to our rapid devolution. Here long before our progenitors, they'd stand long after the last embers of humanity cooled into oblivion.

The smell of sizzling meat wafted toward the edge of the campfire. With heads hung low, Ted and Sandy shambled back to the fire, their eyes avoiding mine. Sandy's stomach grumbled and saliva slavered from Ted's mouth as they beheld my barbarism. They stank of shame.

I took the first bite, implicitly granting them permission to partake in my savagery. Once they had a taste, their hesitance gave way to baser instincts, and they gnawed on Emily's charred flesh with disturbing alacrity.

I didn't mourn the loss of my innocence, but I didn't embrace it either. It was just something I'd gotten used to, like eating steak. Few empathize with the cattle we slaughter to eat, so consuming human flesh wasn't much more of an ethical leap. And ethics don't matter if you're dead.

ॐ

I awoke in darkness.

An intense headache and warm blood trickling from my ears alerted me to the banshee's hypersonic wail. I rustled out of my sleeping bag and stumbled to my feet. Frantic and with bleary eyes, I searched the blackness for our night visitor.

She emerged from the night into the fading firelight. Covered in a cloak of the glistening White, her mouth gaped as if to scream. She squirmed and struggled, the White suffocating her like latex.

Ted and Sandy were both fast asleep. I glared at Ted. The bastard was supposed to be on watch. His snores only pissed me off more.

Milky-white tendrils slithered toward us from the banshee's marble-white toes, framing a fractal pattern over red pine needles. It stretched and reached for Ted's sleeping form.

In half a second, I shook Sandy awake. She flailed as if awakened from a nightmare.

"What's the hurry?" she said, groggy. Then she saw the banshee and screamed.

Ted wasn't so lucky.

Before I could wake him and pull him away, a tendril had clawed a beachhead onto his fingers and began to swirl up his arm.

By instinct, I grabbed my hacksaw and started cutting into Ted's arm at the shoulder. He woke, shrieking.

Sometimes removing an infected limb could prevent a widespread infection.

Sometimes.

I sawed as fast as I could, but the White continued its inexorable climb up Ted's arm, reaching as far as his elbow. Ted howled. The tendrils on the forest floor hastened toward me. The apparition stood fast while the White spread its snaking pestilence.

Two-thirds of the way through Ted's bone, the White had slithered to within an inch of my hacksaw. I looked into Ted's wide eyes and shook my head.

"No! Please, don't give up! Please!" he screamed.

I pulled away, but Ted wouldn't quit. "Give me the saw," he rasped. "Hurry!"

Ted stumbled to his feet and ambled toward me as the White continued its steadfast march up his arm. Sandy stared at Ted, as if paralyzed. I grabbed her arm and pulled her with me as we fled into the forest.

The last time I ever saw Ted, he tried to yank the remaining bone strand out of its shoulder socket.

ॐ

The snow came early this season.

Alabaster snowflakes drifted down from a gray sky. Their fleeting beauty gave way to a sinking sense of dread. Snow would be the ultimate camouflage for the shrouded predators that stalked us. If we didn't find shelter soon, we'd have little warning when the White came calling.

Bone thin and exhausted, I herded Sandy up an isolated mountainside dense with redwoods. On the verge of death, she was becoming a liability. But she was all I had left. If she died, I'd have to face the White alone.

So we climbed and climbed, hoping to find a better vantage point, a place we could spy any settlements that might have food.

I wasn't optimistic.

When we reached the summit, we came upon a pile of human remains nestled in a redwood grove. Upon closer examination, the bodies showed uneven patterns of decomposition, as if something had stripped only the flesh from the bone.

I cast Sandy a knowing look. Her expression mirrored my own.

Guilt.

Then I smiled.

We weren't the only people out here.

Sandy screamed.

A white wall of banshees flowed up the mountainside, their calm and steady advance colder than the swirling snow.

Collapsing, Sandy wept. Everyone had her limit.

I grabbed her arm and dragged her through the snow. She resisted, wailing and thrashing her arms.

The banshees crept forward.

"Get up!" I yelled. "Stop feeling sorry for yourself!"

She cried, "Just let me die."

My head ached. The silent hypersonic wail of the banshees rattled my skull.

"Move!" I screamed, kicking Sandy's back.

I turned to look back down the path. *Should I leave her and save myself? Was life worth living alone?*

The banshees had crested the mountainside. The snow-dusted surface rippled with activity as their tendrils snaked toward us.

At that moment, I made my decision.

Ripping a rotting femur from the bone pile, I swung blindly at the banshees. If I was gonna die, I'd die fighting.

Expecting to hit human bone beneath the veil of white, I discovered something else. It was a sensation not unlike bursting a bubble or feeling your ears pop in an airplane.

A pile of ash stood where a banshee had once been.

The others closed in. Their pace quickened.

Swinging the femur, I cleared a path of ash through the White wave. The rest was a blur. When it was over, I was panting and sweating from the effort, despite the near freezing temperatures. My next thoughts turned to Sandy. In the chaos, I'd lost track of her. I searched around me, frantic.

Gone.

I panicked.

Had the White claimed her? Was she now one of the ash heaps surrounding me?

The prospect of loneliness was crushing. I crumbled and sobbed. Anguish overwhelmed me.

Then, something warm touched my cheek.

Sandy.

ॐ

At sunrise we happened across a fortified lodge. Nestled in a narrow draw between two hillsides and surrounded by a white palisade, the structure was more fortress than cabin. White smoke billowed from its chimney.

My stomach grumbled at the sight. For my entire life, I had been conditioned to mistake shelter for food and warmth. But shelter is also where people are. And where there are people, the White waits.

No one knows where the White came from. By the time scientists had identified the threat and the military had mobilized, most major cities had become bustling hives of infestation. Everyone had either been infected or had fled from the major urban centers.

Sandy and I crouched behind a thick redwood. "What do ya wanna do?" she asked, brushing her scraggily blonde hair behind her ear.

"Don't know." I nodded toward the cabin. "I'd bet top dollar there's food in there."

She rolled her eyes. "Yeah, looks ripe for the taking," she said in a voice dripping with sarcasm. "There are probably people in there as hungry as us."

I nodded. "You think they know that bone kills them?"

Pointing at the white palisade, she said, "What do you think?"

I shuddered at her implication. "I don't like this at all. Not one bit."

"Me neither," said Sandy, "but what else is there to do?"

She had a point. Starvation was more likely to kill us than a banshee would. Other than tree bark, we hadn't eaten anything in two weeks, and we weren't strong enough to travel much farther.

Nope. The answer was clear: our path to survival led through that cabin.

"Here goes nothing," I said, stepping out into the open and toward the palisade.

"What the hell are you doing?" Sandy whispered. "Get back here. We need a plan!"

Ignoring her plea, I walked into the open at a slow, even pace with my hands raised, palms facing outward. Too fast might startle the inhabitants. Too slow might give them the impression I was up to no good. Calm and steady wins trust and arouses the least suspicion. Or so I told myself.

Several paces later, Sandy followed.

Behind the palisade, a door creaked open. Then a gate opened in the bone palisade. A rail thin man crept forward, rifle in hand.

Under her breath, Sandy murmured, "This feels off."

The starveling stared at Sandy. His eyes lingered on her scrawny body for ten seconds longer than most civilized people would've considered proper.

"Ahem," I said to break the uncomfortable silence.

He glared at me. "We haven't seen any folks in weeks. Can't offer much in the way of food, but you're welcome to stay the night."

The man's lips quivered. He wiped frozen spittle off his chin. His eyes betrayed his charitable sentiment. None of it felt right, but if we stayed out in the open, we risked infection.

I glanced at Sandy. She hesitated, then nodded.

"Thank you for your kindness," I said. I gestured toward the bone palisade. "So you figured it out too?"

The man smiled. "Yup. Banshees can't touch dead things. Turns 'em to ash. Banshee ash turns 'em to ash too."

"Hadn't heard that," I said. "Have you shared this with any other survivors?"

Shaking his head, the man said, "Last of the propane ran out weeks ago. And even if we had any, then what? Charge up a cell phone? Tried that. None of them cell towers works no more."

I shrugged. Maybe we'd already had enough good news for one week. "How about heading to San Francisco and spreading the word?"

"Nah. Too late. Too many banshees 'tween us and them."

Two more men passed through the gate. One was as skeletal as the first. The other was a plump bald man with a ragged beard. The man with the rifle tilted his head at the other skinny man, "This here's Vern." He inclined his head toward the fat one. "And this is Eli. He can tell ya what's what. He's super smart like. Genius and such. My name's Chuck, but my friends call me Pork Chop."

I walked closer, extending my hand. "Name's Garrity. Tim Garrity." I gestured for Sandy to come forward. "This here's Sandy Morgan."

Pork Chop stared at Sandy and licked his lips. It felt all wrong, but we had no choice. We needed to hole up here until we could convince these folks to make a move toward San Francisco where there'd be more food.

"Should we head in?" I said, breaking the uncomfortable silence.

Pork Chop blinked and nodded as if I'd just roused him out of a wet daydream. He turned toward the cabin and waved the group through the palisade gate. Sandy hesitated. I gave her a look that said I'd have her back. She nodded, overcoming whatever reservations she may have had and passed through the gate ahead of me. Once we were within the palisade's protection, Pork Chop closed and barred the gate, and then led us into the cabin.

The structure was one of those redwood log cabins common in the Sierras. Scarlet curtains covered a window next to the entrance. The warmth of a fire burning in the hearth quickly calmed my nerves. Few people realize how good they have it until they don't.

The three men took seats around a square oak table dominating the center of the room. Their backs faced us and the curtains. Pork Chop motioned for us to sit on the opposite side of the table. Three candles flickered on the table, providing the cabin's only other ambient light.

Sitting, I wondered how this Eli fellow had been able to keep on so much weight when food was so scarce. While Vern and Pork Chop made me nervous as hell, for some strange reason, the plump one put me at ease. It was the oddest damn thing.

I had to keep 'em occupied while I figured out what to do. For all I knew, these men were gonna slit my throat in my sleep and then have their way with Sandy.

Trying not to stare too much at the candlelight, I said, "If you know what kills the White, you probably have an idea of what the hell they are. Where they come from."

Pork Chop nodded and said, "Eli here's got a pretty good theory. It'll blow off your nut sack hairs. Hear 'em out. Hell, if someone told me two months ago 'bout the White, I'd a told 'em to go fuck theyselves."

"I suppose anything's better than nothing," I said, "tell us what you know, Eli."

Eli shrugged and then stroked his bushy and disheveled beard. "We are experiencing something I call multiversal shearing. Brane theory posits that we inhabit one universe amid an infinity of universes. Our reality is a bubble in space-time floating among many other such bubbles."

This guy was crazier than a cuckoo on a counterclockwise clock in an upside down elevator. I held up my hand. "What the hell does this mumbo jumbo have anything to do with the White, and what makes you qualified to talk about it?"

Eli nodded. "If I told you where I came from, you wouldn't believe me. All you need to know is that I used to be an Assistant Professor of Quantum Parapsychology at Princeton. Doesn't matter. It's probably the last thing you'll ever know anyway."

Pork Chop glared at Eli for a short, barely perceptible moment.

"Go on," I said. The longer he droned on, the more time I'd have to formulate a plan to take control of the cabin.

"When two realities grind against each other, it causes a gravity quake in five dimensions. Sometimes invasive trans-dimensional species like the White are drawn to these seismic forces. They're akin to a sort of fungal kudzu, infesting our world until assimilating every last living organism."

I'd had it. These guys were clearly drinking too much of Eli's Kool-Aid.

Exasperated, I stood up. "How can you all believe this guy's bullshit? He's crazier than a football bat."

Pork Chop rose, mirroring my behavior. "Only reason we made it this far is 'cause of Eli. He's been right at every turn."

I held out my arms to calm Pork Chop.

Inclining his head toward Vern, Pork Chop said, "Let's quit with the bullshit and get 'er done."

Pork Chop raised his rifle. I leapt across the table, tackling him to the floor and scattering the candles. I struggled for control of the weapon. Vern hollered. There was a metallic click. Grappling Pork Chop, I rolled to my right. A shot rang out. Pork Chop wheezed. Warm blood drenched my torso.

Vern stood still, his face creased with worry. Sandy reached for his rifle. A struggle ensured.

I wrested the rifle from Pork Chop's dead hands and took a shot at Vern from the hip. My bullet landed with a scream.

Sandy!

"No!" Eli yelled. "Stop! I can see it clearly now. Stop! This is the end!"

Unharmed, Vern turned and took aim. I fired another round before he got the drop on me. The blast knocked Vern backward. He wheezed as air escaped from a collapsed lung. I pointed my rifle at Eli. He shrugged. His face didn't register a single shred of fear. I smelled burning.

"My God!" Sandy gurgled. "The curtains! Fire!"

Arterial blood spurted out of the bullet wound I'd put in her neck like a fountain synchronized to her decaying heartbeat. I glanced over my shoulder. The flames had spread from the curtains to the wall. I looked back at Eli.

"I warned you," said Eli, "This is the end."

"You don't seem too concerned about," I replied.

"For me, it's but one end among many. For you, there is only this. I'm sorry it had to end this way for you and your girl."

"What the hell does that mean?"

The fire was raging. Smoke was filling the room, obscuring my vision. Coughing, I said to Sandy, "I'm sorry. There's nothing I can do. I have to go."

She nodded weakly. The smoke was thick. So thick, I lost sight of Eli. With pangs of guilt and regret, I abandoned Sandy, making my way toward the exit, the fire not far behind.

ℬ

Hundreds of shrouded white forms encircled the burning cabin, pressing in. I ripped two femurs off the smoking palisade and strode toward the wall of banshees.

There was nowhere to go but forward. So I raced down the mountainside, sullen and snow-blind, swinging the bones like a machete through swarms of white wailing banshees. I prayed I'd find someone, anyone, who could help me wrest civilization back from the brink.

END

Afterword

"The White" was inspired by a cross-country trip I took from the Mojave Desert to Massachusetts in 2003. On my way there, I passed through Tennessee, where I was struck by how thoroughly kudzu, an invasive plant that can grow up to a foot a day, had infested the region, swallowing up entire trees with its leafy vines. What if, I thought over a decade later, a hyperdimensional species swallowed up humanity the same way that kudzu had covered up those trees?

While I think the milky-white banshees are a nice touch, what makes the story effective, in my opinion, is the atmosphere of distrust that lingers in the shadows between the two separate bands of survivors who have nothing to eat but each other. Even the first line of the story—"We cooked Emily first"—nicely foreshadows the cannibalistic conflict to come. It's also a not-so-subtle homage to the first line of Jeff Carlson's novel *Plague Year*, which opens with: "They ate Jorgensen first."

This story also involves an older, more jaded Doctor Eli Rosen, long after he was infected by the hyperdimensional parasite in "Portal in Pasadena" and acquired the ability to perceive all space and time simultaneously for brief interludes. This tale hints at Rosen's ability to see snapshots of the future, but never outright states it since he vanishes before the protagonist has a chance to ask Rosen any further questions.

I hope you enjoyed this piece.

Necromancer

0300 Hours, 25 October 1904, Hill 203, Port Arthur, Manchuria

The menacing peaks of 203- and 210-Meter Hills loomed on the horizon. Hordes of Imperial Russian troops had dug in for a protracted siege. The wind howled, masking the anxious nattering of frightened Japanese farm boys. The acrid stench of *shimose* powder wafted through the air. The whistle to advance sounded. A wave of bayonets glinted in the moonlight, rippling like millet grains in deepest Manchurian summer.

The wet thing beneath Captain Tanaka Hideki's hobnailed boot burst open like a melon. He glanced down to see a wreck of blood, bone fragments, and brains from a severed head.

Major Ogasawara Akira led the way through a slit trench. He stumbled over splintered plywood, disembodied limbs, and steaming coiled viscera. Sporadic small arms fire echoed around them. Tanaka kept his head low, using whatever cover he could find.

The major knelt behind a stack of torn sandbags. He inclined his head toward Tanaka. "General Nogi intends to present this hill to the Emperor for his birthday. I expect to do the same with Zinchenko's head." He paused, then said, "Tanaka-kun, never forget why Unit 108 exists. Only we sense the unseen. And only we store supernatural energy like batteries."

He faced the hill and stood up. In half a heartbeat, Maxim machine gun fire ripped the major in two, peppering Tanaka with chunks of flesh and bone.

Tanaka dove to the ground. Confidence shaken, he panicked. He wiped his smeared bifocals, struggling to see amid the chaos.

He fought to find his center. The one person in a hundred *li* who knew how to unearth the undead necromancer was gone. Now Tanaka was responsible for the mission. He hadn't the faintest idea where to begin.

୬

2030 Hours, 29 November 1904, Hill 203, Port Arthur, Manchuria

Over the past month, Tanaka had begun to recognize the portents: discordant wind chimes in windless nights, rat packs scurrying through corpse piles, and wild dogs with glowing red eyes.

The signs' increasing frequency troubled Tanaka. It was as if the necromancer were feeding off the dead, becoming more potent with each passing day. For reasons he couldn't explain, Tanaka was certain the necromancer was on Hill 203.

Despair's stifling burden grew heavier on Tanaka as more bodies piled in the trenches. Yesterday, three battalions from Japan's First Division and the First Kobe Brigade had failed to seize the Hill 203-210 saddle.

In mid-November, Third Army troops entrenched near Hill 203's base had received a much-needed manpower boost with the Seventh Division's arrival. But Tanaka wasn't convinced these reinforcements were a positive development. Their deaths would only fuel Zinchenko's power.

Tanaka followed advancing troops up the hill. Along his path, he ran into his old friend, Captain Sato. The battalion translator was interrogating a shivering Russian officer. The prisoner wore a non-standard *tulup* coat and shaggy *papaha* on his head. His bushy beard framed empty light blue eyes.

Seeing Tanaka, Sato's scarred, soot-encrusted face broke into a wide grin.

Tanaka shook Sato's hand. "I was hoping for a favor, old friend."

"Anything you need."

"I have questions for your prisoner. If you don't mind translating, I'd appreciate it."

Sato slapped Tanaka on the back. "Of course!"

The officers faced the Russian.

"Sato-san, who is this man?" Tanaka said.

"Captain Malinovsky."

"Ask him where Colonel Vladimir Zinchenko is."

Sato translated. Malinovsky's eyes widened and blood drained from his face. But he said nothing. Sato slapped him. Malinovsky stuttered a response.

Sato turned to Tanaka and said, "He claims Zinchenko's dead."

"Tell him I know the colonel's dead, but I also know he's still fighting. Where is he?"

Sato gaped at Tanaka as if his friend had just eaten a rock. Tanaka jerked his head toward Malinovsky. "Go on, Sato-san. Tell him."

Sato shrugged, then spoke to Malinovsky.

Malinovsky rocked back and forth, mumbling. A crow flew out of nowhere and latched onto Malinovsky's face, pecking out his eyes. The Russian wailed.

Sato leapt to his feet.

In a one deft peck, the crow severed Malinovsky's carotid artery. Blood sprayed from his neck, pooling into a steaming puddle that slowly froze. With Malinovsky's last gasp, the bird dropped to the ground, dead.

Moments later, Malinovsky's body stirred. He jerked his head up. His face contorted in a sneering rictus. In perfect Japanese, he squealed, "I'm freeeeee!"

Sato retched.

Tanaka reined in his fear. "Who are you?"

Eyes bulging, Malinovsky's corpse cackled and said, "I am of the ruins beyond, an eater of souls. You are of those who can see, and I am freeee!"

"Where's Zinchenko?"

"Release meeee!"

The corpse flailed. With preternatural strength, it freed itself from its bonds and lunged at Tanaka. Tanaka unsheathed his *Murata-to* saber. In one swift cut, he decapitated the corpse. But the headless thing thrashed toward him.

Tanaka swung again, lopping off its arm. The thing stumbled toward a shocked and motionless Sato. With its remaining arm, the corpse felt around for its head. Grasping it by the hair, the corpse flung it at Sato. The head connected with Sato's leg. Malinovsky's mouth tore a chunk out of Sato's calf. Sato shrieked and then fell.

Tanaka hacked until he'd completely dismembered the squirming cadaver. Tanaka turned to Sato and said, "You all right?"

Sato nodded, his face moist with frozen tears.

Tanaka tossed a spade to Sato. "Let's bury the remains."

ৡ

0230 Hours, 30 November 1904, Hill 203, Port Arthur, Manchuria

Tanaka waded through piles of dead to reach the front. The steady pitter-patter of Maxim machine guns had tapered off. Russian arc lamp searchlights cast swaying conical rays down the hillside.

Tanaka's trench was nearly one hundred meters below the trenches the Japanese planned to assault. Soldiers formed in dense ranks. They advanced in quiet section rushes of fifty yards each.

A ray of light exposed the ranks. Machine gun fire ripped through the men. Bodies buckled around Tanaka. Officers raised their sabers and ordered their men to storm the Russian battlements.

A barbed wire fence blocked the approach. Soldiers in the advance party crawled toward the entanglements with wire cutters.

A blue, electric surge singed the first man who touched the barrier. His limp body shook violently. The scent of seared flesh drifted through the air.

The soldiers passed a long bamboo pole up the line and toward the obstacle. The man nearest the barrier lit a fuse at the pole's tip. He pushed it through the barbed wire. Seconds later, a smoldering hole rent an opening in the fence.

The men resumed their advance. Along with the others, Tanaka rushed into the Russian-controlled trenches. The enemy was so close that the fighting devolved into a brutal hand-to-hand affair.

One tall, shaggy-capped Russian lunged his bayonet at Tanaka. Tanaka parried the blow. He thrust his bayonet into the Russian's gut. The man screamed, then slumped. More Japanese soldiers streamed past Tanaka.

A teeming mass of Japanese troops swelled toward Hill 203's summit, leaving a trail of corpses in their wake.

In the firelight of a broken battlefield, Tanaka watched with pride as his fellow soldiers raised the *Kyokujitsu-ki*, Japan's rising sun flag, on Hill 203's crest.

The faint sound of discordant chimes dashed that feeling. Hundreds of crows descended upon the dead, stacked like meat in a gutter.

No. It can't be.

Tanaka had to do the unthinkable. "Retreat!" he yelled. A nearby soldier scowled.

The dead began to rise. They shambled down the hill. Soldiers fired their rifles to little effect. Troops near the apex panicked in a headlong rush down the hill.

Tanaka retreated to a chokepoint in the trenches, where an overhead earthwork protected a dozen other Japanese soldiers who'd gathered there.

Tanaka raised his saber. "Rally on me! Find a blade. Sever the legs, then the head. Then move on to the next one."

He formed two ranks of six men each. The front rank held their sabers unsteadily. The second rank aimed their six-point-five-millimeter *Arisaka* rifles at the ambling corpses' legs.

The second rank fired a volley, forcing the attackers backward. The swordsmen wheeled forward, slicing off the cadavers' legs. The soldiers then repeated the tactic.

A ruin of squirming torso husks accumulated in blood puddles. But the dead kept coming. The spirits inside them taunted the men. "We are many. You cannot stop us. Our brethren will wear your flesh."

Legless carcasses propelled themselves forward with their arms. More corpses lumbered toward Tanaka's strongpoint. Soon the infernal things were nipping at the defenders' feet. Tanaka grabbed a rifleman and said, "Quick! Run to the nearest artillery battery. Have them drop shells five meters ahead of our position!"

A man howled. The dead pulled a soldier beneath their sputtering flesh mound and tore him apart. Tanaka watched, aghast.

He had hoped the artillery would buy him time, but it didn't start soon enough. If he didn't withdraw now, he'd be overrun. So he ordered his riflemen to retreat. The swordsmen fought a rearguard action. The dead dragged another man into their ravenous heap. Using the distraction, Tanaka sent his remaining swordsmen to the lower trenches.

The dead continued to advance until a hail of artillery and Hotchkiss machine gun fire obliterated them. Yet another day had passed with the Russians controlling Hill 203's heights.

ॐ

1430 Hours, 30 November 1904, Hill 203, Port Arthur, Manchuria

Tanaka craved sleep, but he had to warn the newly arrived Seventh Division commander about the supernatural threat. Tanaka had advised the general to pre-plot artillery targets along the upper trenches to stem any future incursions from the dead. On Tanaka's advisement, the men dug tiger pits lined with sharp wooden stakes along the main axis of advance. They also rigged grenades and laid modified naval mines along the trenches. They'd marked the mines with flags so soldiers wouldn't accidentally detonate them in their next advance.

Nothing stirred on the hill save hungry rats feasting on the dead's charred remains. After a brief but vigorous firefight, three Japanese battalions pushed forward through clouds of smoke masking the battlefield until they reoccupied the trenches just beneath the summits of Hills 203 and 210. Tanaka saw a company—about a hundred and fifty men—storm the slope near Hill 210's zenith.

Ten minutes later, dozens of Japanese flooded down the hill and into the lower trenches. Their eyes were wide with terror.

Tanaka grabbed a fleeing soldier by the suspenders. "What happened?"

Tears gushed down the man's blackened face. "I may be a coward, but how does one face what's already dead?"

"Go on."

"We were about to take the hill, but our dead rose up and ambushed us."

Tanaka approached a nearby lieutenant and said, "Order fires on the pre-registered targets, now!"

The lieutenant nodded and relayed the order. Tanaka shifted his attention back to the soldier. "Did you see any crows?"

The man shot Tanaka a confused expression and shook his head. "No, but I saw a lot of rats."

Tanaka ran his fingers through his hair, frustrated. He worried he couldn't prevent the infestation from spreading. So long as there were scavengers, there'd be demons cloaked in human skin. He'd have to try a different approach.

Minutes later, the eleven-inch Krupp howitzers pounded the abandoned trenches, shredding the undead assailants. The ground thundered. Columns of Japanese soldiers rallied and advanced up the hill again. Yet by morning, the Russians still held Hill 203.

ໃ

1000 Hours, 2 December 1904, Hill 203, Port Arthur, Manchuria

Batteries charged by supernatural energy.

Ogasawara's words haunted Tanaka. But they'd also given him an idea so reckless he could scarcely believe General Nogi had sanctioned Tanaka's plan.

Tanaka strode past pieces of minced humanity. He waved a white flag that rippled in the frigid wind. Both sides had agreed on a temporary armistice to bury their dead.

The first Russians Tanaka encountered were little more than frightened boys. Bundled in tan woolen greatcoats, the soldiers wore *bashlik* hoods capped with *papahas*. The *papahas* extended from their eyebrows to the sky in a riot of black fur and sheepskin.

Two Russians flanked Tanaka. They gripped his upper arms as they escorted him up Hill 203. Near the summit, they handed him to a colonel who motioned for Tanaka to surrender his rifle and saber. Tanaka gave up his rifle but refused to relinquish his sword. The colonel looked back up the hill and shouted something in Russian.

A lanky soldier jogged down the hill and, in Russian-accented Japanese, said, "Why you here?"

"I've come to see Colonel Zinchenko."

The translator winced. "Your request is, how you say, unusual. But before I leave you with Colonel Gordunov, you must give sword."

Tanaka shook his head. "I already surrendered my firearm. But as a matter of honor, I will not cede my saber. I promise to keep it sheathed so long as no one harms me."

The translator said something to Gordunov, then looked at Tanaka and said, "Very well. Colonel Zinchenko's expecting you. Colonel Gordunov will take you there."

Gordunov led Tanaka through the upper trenches until they reached a tunnel chiseled into the hillside. The colonel lit a lantern near the entrance. He motioned for Tanaka to follow him into the darkness.

The icy tunnel emptied into a spacious cavern. Arches composed of pearly gray spheres stretched across the ceiling like ribs on a carcass. In the cavern's heart, a man's silhouette loomed.

Gordunov pointed at the shadowy figure. He handed Tanaka the lantern, and then left. Tanaka slinked into the cavern. As he approached Zinchenko, Tanaka saw a bald man with a bushy gray beard that extended to the middle of his shirtless chest. Boils dotted his leathery skin. As Tanaka drew closer, what he first took for boils, he recognized as eyes—sickly, jaundiced eyes—each boring into Tanaka's soul with unsettling malice.

Before Tanaka could speak, he heard distant squealing, scraping, and scratching. He raised his lantern toward the tunnel's entrance. An undulating mass of squirming rodents swelled toward him, a river of red eyes in the murk.

Tanaka jumped away from the entrance to avoid drowning in greasy vermin sludge. The rats flowed past Tanaka and into the cavern, surrounding the necromancer in a ring of tails and fur.

"So a suitable vessel has finally come to us," Zinchenko said, a chorus of voices echoing off the cavern's arches. Tanaka unsheathed his saber.

Zinchenko cackled and said, "We are the undying. Neither earth nor fire can touch us. We hunger for souls. Submit and embrace oblivion."

The closer Tanaka got to Zinchenko, the more his gut roiled. The pain became so intense that Tanaka had to stop before collapsing.

"Claim him!" the necromancer said. He pointed at the captain. The rats swarmed Tanaka, covering him in a coat of living fur. Their weight forced him to the ground.

Tanaka felt one bite, then another. The tortured memories of a pre-human civilization gnashed at his soul. The entities infecting him were so alien and of such infinite variety he could scarcely describe them. Some sailed on the winds of an auburn sky, four membranous wings extending from translucent insect-like thoraxes. Others slithered out of a primordial goo, more fin than body and covered with horns. Tanaka could sense their desires. Despite their diversity, their aim was single-minded: replace their rotting host with Tanaka's fresh body.

Tanaka fought to contain them, denying them control over his will. But the more he resisted, the more he slipped within their thrall.

Then he remembered. He was a battery. His purpose wasn't to resist; it was to endure. So he let go. He opened himself up to a legion of dark intelligences.

After the vermin infected Tanaka, they dropped dead. Tanaka crawled out of the rat pile. The entities inside him panicked. Their thoughts howled. Tanaka still had control. They struggled to escape. Their telepathic voices cajoled and pleaded with Tanaka to set them free.

You'll be free soon, Tanaka promised.

He glanced down at his chest. Jaundiced eyes coated his skin. Ignoring the horror of his metamorphosis, Tanaka ambled toward Zinchenko's prostrate corpse. It was no longer covered with eyes. Tanaka raised his saber with one arm and touched Zinchenko's remains with the other, and said, "I release you," in an echo of tortured voices.

The demons cursed at Tanaka. Their roiling energies surged into Zinchenko. A new eye marked the passage of each spirit on the necromancer's rotting flesh.

After Tanaka emptied his well of souls, Zinchenko tried to stand. Tanaka decapitated the rising necromancer, and then chopped the corpse to bits. He then used the lantern's fire to reduce the necromancer's remains to ash.

❧

1900 Hours, 3 January 1905, Hill 203, Port Arthur, Manchuria

Tanaka entered General Nogi's field tent. He saluted the Third Army commander and recited Unit 108's motto. "One, nothing, everything."

Nogi returned the salute. "Tanaka-kun, excellent work with Zinchenko. You're a true servant of Japan."

"Thank you, sir," Tanaka said, "Congratulations on the Russian surrender of Port Arthur."

Nogi shrugged. "Your success was instrumental in capturing Hill 203. It allowed us to sink most of Russia's Pacific fleet with our land-based howitzers. Yet we still lost fourteen thousand brave Japanese on that Hill of Souls, including my second son."

Nogi wiped away a tear. "As per Unit 108 protocol, I'm classifying your actions at Hill 203 at a level above Top Secret. The world must never know what lurks in that hill. I trust you'll do your duty?"

Tanaka nodded.

"Good. I'm giving you a respite from Unit 108-specific missions. I have a more conventional operation in mind. You're to liaise with *Hung-hu-tze* bandits up north to scout Russian forces along the Southern Manchurian Railway. See Colonel Ito for more details."

Tanaka saluted the general. "I won't let you down, sir."

"You never have, Tanaka-kun. You never have."

END

Afterword

"Necromancer" first appeared as "Hill of Souls" *Outposts of Beyond.*

It takes place during the Siege of Port Arthur, a bloody land battle in the Russo-Japanese War that lasted from August 1904 to January 1905. It is also the first historical fantasy story I've ever written.

The story focuses on a Japanese soldier named Captain Tanaka Hideki who is a member of an occult organization known only to Japan's senior leadership as Unit 108. His mission is to track down a possessed Russian necromancer who lays in wait on the strategic terrain feature known only as Hill 203.

To craft the story and build the world, I spent a great deal of time researching the events, personalities, and weapons of this historical siege that turned out to be an eerie foreshadowing of the First World War's attrition warfare.

I hope you enjoy the story as much as I enjoyed writing and researching it.

Mukden

Manchuria's biting winds chilled Captain Tanaka Hideki to the soul, but the child-sized frozen corpses piled like cordwood bothered him more. As a father, he shuddered to imagine what it'd be like to see his own three-year old son, Yoshi, among the dead. While the cold blunted most of the odor, Tanaka could still smell the lingering stench of human filth. "Who did this?" he said, struggling to keep down his last meal.

"Not who, what," Fu Shih said, wiping ice flakes off his salt and pepper beard. The *Hung-hu-tze* bandit leader pointed to one child's belly, flaps of skin peeled back like an inverted starfish. "Whatever did this, it ain't human."

Tanaka had heard accounts of similar mutilations all along the Russian-controlled Southern Manchuria Railway. It was as if a blight radiated from the tracks—a festering sore of modernity marring Manchuria's pristine landscape. For Tanaka, the atrocities also evoked an unsettling feeling of déjà vu.

Ever since the Boxer Rebellion, a Russian occupation force of several hundred thousand had hunkered down along the Russian Empire's Manchurian rail line stretching from Harbin to Mukden all the way down the Liaodong Peninsula to its terminus at Port Arthur. Despite assurances they'd eventually leave, the Russians had been steadily cementing their foothold in

Manchuria for nearly half a decade. The Japanese military had landed in Manchuria to force the issue and liberate their Chinese brethren from the yoke of European colonialism.

Tanaka adjusted his bifocals and reluctantly took a closer look at the body. He'd had enough of death, and had hoped to avoid it out here and away from the bulk of the fighting. He'd already seen more than enough killing at Port Arthur's siege to last a lifetime.

On closer inspection, Tanaka noticed that the child's viscera were gone. Whatever had been responsible, it hadn't spared a single villager. The peculiar wounds reminded Tanaka of his mother's superstitions about keeping his navel covered when he was a child.

As a reward for destroying the Port Arthur necromancer, General Nogi had assigned Tanaka a more conventional mission to help Tanaka recover from the psychological and spiritual damage he'd suffered. Yet, no matter where Tanaka traveled, he seemed to cast a pall of death all around him. So much so, that he felt himself becoming more attuned to the otherworldly with one foot firmly planted in the realm of the dead. Before Tanaka returned to the highly secretive Unit 108, he'd need to seek out a Shinto priest for cleansing lest his exposure to so much defilement infest other Japanese soldiers.

"What kind of an animal does this?" Tanaka asked in fluent Mandarin.

Fu shrugged as though unmoved by the atrocities. "Not an animal. Something else. Not natural. Not good. I seen something like this before near a Cossack camp."

The hair on Tanaka's neck stood on end. "What do you mean 'not natural'?"

Fu laughed. "No wild beast did this. Something else. Probably sorcery."

Ever since his experience at Hill 203 in Port Arthur, Tanaka had learned not to be so easily dismissive of such claims, but he'd also realized that he shouldn't trust everything these rustics said. Sometimes they'd make things up just to test him. Oftentimes, they'd repeat a litany of age-old superstitions. But if Tanaka was to work with them, he had to play along. "Explain."

"Death magic. Rumor has it a Cossack regiment's creeping around these parts. Some say these ghost faces got a necromancer."

Tanaka shuddered. He'd encountered one of these dead sorcerers at Port Arthur, and had no desire to face another out here, alone in the wilderness. Yet something about Fu's claim didn't seem quite right. It didn't fit the lore. Tanaka shook his head. "I don't believe it. Even if it were true, what purpose would this serve the Russians?"

"Necromancers use children's souls to grant Russian warriors extra lives," Fu answered in what Tanaka sensed was with the utmost seriousness.

Tanaka worried that investigating these murders would divert him from his primary mission. Mapping the Imperial Russian Army's location would be difficult enough for veteran Japanese cavalry, but convincing Chinese bandits to do anything in this cold Manchurian waste was akin to herding hungry spiders. Anytime they'd encounter a small Russian unit, the *Hung-hu-tze* wanted to raid it for booty and blood, motivated by revenge for the Blagoveshchensk massacre. Five years earlier, the Russians had driven thousands of Chinese men, women, and children into the Amur River, drowning them in cold blood.

Part of Tanaka wanted to let them loose, but as the long-range eyes and ears of General Nogi Maresuke's Third Army, he could ill afford such distractions, especially with thousands of Japanese lives at stake. But ignoring such savagery was also unacceptable, and Tanaka was convinced he'd lose face with the bandits if he let it go unchecked.

"Fine," Tanaka decided. "We'll track these Cossacks. But as soon as we deal with them, we'll return to scouting Russian positions."

ॐ

"Feed us," the gaunt hag said, her voice more rasp than whisper. She wore a white, torn dulcimer gown that swayed with her wispy and frayed gray hair in the windless air. A warm campfire glowed behind Tanaka, where the *Hung-hu-tze* carried on, drinking cheap, pilfered vodka.

Tanaka could hardly see the pale lady in the darkness, her hazy form shimmering in the moonless night. He approached her tentatively, his hand on his cartridge pouch, gathering a pinch of rice. Tanaka drew closer, the night growing colder.

He offered the crone his rice, trying to convince himself his actions were born out of kindness. He partly believed it. But deep down, he knew that winning peasant hearts and minds was more important to him and the Japanese military effort. Spurred by acts of Japanese benevolence, and a Russian occupation notorious for its butchery, Chinese peasants had become a treasure trove of intelligence, enabling the Japanese to stay one step ahead of their lumbering but numerically superior European foe.

"Feed us," she groaned in guttural tones akin to crumbling parchment.

Tanaka refused to move any further forward. And why should he? He was offering this poor, starving woman a meal, and she couldn't walk fifty meters to retrieve it?

"If you want a free meal, come get it," he said.

Before Tanaka could blink, the alabaster woman had bridged the gap between them, her eyes pure white and her teeth, a riot of rotting ivory spikes. Tanaka felt paralyzed. As an officer accustomed to commanding troops, Tanaka hated losing control, and now, he was helpless.

"Feed us!" she growled just before a gust of frigid wind dissolved her haggard form.

⌀

Tanaka woke in the morning twilight, blistery-eyed and drained of energy. His inner thighs ached from a long day of riding. A layer of frost covered his wool blanket, and the sweat from his feet had hardened to ice inside his hobnailed boots.

"So you saw the night hag," a seemingly unimpressed Fu said by the campfire's dying embers. "You're lucky you ain't dead."

"You saw her too?" Tanaka said, half-surprised Fu didn't mock him.

"Course not."

"How'd you know I saw her?"

"I can tell. The dark rings under your eyes. Your face is paler than usual. I've heard 'bout others seen her in these parts. 'Specially during these times."

"What do you mean?"

"The pale ladies come 'round when people die. War, famine, disease. They come callin'."

Fu seemed to know a lot about something he hadn't seen. Tanaka began to feel uneasy, as if Fu were hiding something.

"Have you ever met someone who's seen these women?" Tanaka asked.

"Aye," Fu said and then winked at Tanaka.

"What happened to them?"

"You'll see," Fu said, smirking as he walked away from the campfire and toward his horse.

Tanaka knew that was the best he was going to get from Fu, so Tanaka didn't push him any further. Instead, Tanaka put on his khaki military tunic, goatskin jerkin, greatcoat, and pistol belt. When he reached for his

Murata-to saber, it wasn't where he'd left it the day prior. But he was certain he hadn't misplaced it. Someone had to have taken it.

Tanaka panicked. An officer losing his sword, even a lower quality, mass-produced one, would bring dishonor to him, his family, and his unit.

Not wanting to draw attention to the missing weapon, Tanaka wandered over to Fu while Fu was busy saddling his mount. Tanaka stopped and cleared his voice.

Fu ignored him.

"My saber's missing," Tanaka whispered, "Have you seen it?"

Fu glanced at Tanaka, smiled, and said, "How should I know? I'm not your saber's keeper." He returned to his business, then stopped and looked back at Tanaka as if Fu were about to tell a joke. "Besides, ain't it a great dishonor to lose your weapon? Wouldn't you have to commit *seppuku*? Oh wait, you can't. You don't have a blade," he said, then snickered.

The captain mustered every ounce of discipline he had to avoid unholstering his pistol and shooting the bandit on the spot. "Well if you see it, return it to me. Immediately."

"Ha ha! Brave little Japanese samurai warrior! I shall indeed," Fu said an instant before he mounted his horse and headed off toward his band. As Fu rode away, Tanaka noticed a scabbard tucked beneath Fu's saddle.

"Stop!" Tanaka yelled, but Fu ignored him.

Tanaka pulled out his pistol and discharged a round into the air. If not for the rider's skill, Fu's horse would've thrown the man from its back. After regaining control of his mount, Fu rode back toward Tanaka.

"Are you crazy, you four-eyed Japanese dog?"

Tanaka stood his ground. "Return my weapon."

"Are you dense? I already told you I don't know where it is, little man."

"Liar. It's tucked beneath your saddle." Tanaka made his accusation loud enough for Fu's men to overhear.

"That's not your saber. I captured it in a raid," Fu said.

"Prove it."

Fu laughed. "How am I 'sposed to do that? All you Japanese devils carry the same sword."

"That's not true. Do you have a man who can read numbers?"

Fu glanced at his men. A large, porcine bandit named Chen nodded. Fu turned back toward Tanaka. "Aye."

Now Tanaka had him. "Every sword has a stamped serial number near the blade's base. I'll present Chen with the appropriate markings. If those markings match the stamp on the saber, I trust you'll do the honorable thing and return it to me. And I'll consider it a simple misunderstanding."

Fu's furrowed brow and intense glare reminded Tanaka of a cornered rat's eyes. Fu glanced back at Chen and said, "Do it." Fu tossed the scabbard onto the ground. Tanaka marched toward the saber. When he arrived, he pulled a small diary and graphite pencil out of his pocket, and scribbled down the serial number.

Chen picked up the scabbard, unsheathed the sword and inspected the stamp. Tanaka tore a sheet out of his diary and handed it to Chen. Chen read the number and then glanced at Fu as if seeking guidance.

Fu nodded.

Chen sheathed the saber and handed it to Tanaka. Tanaka waited for an apology, but Fu just spun his horse around and galloped away. Nothing left to say, Tanaka walked over to his horse, mounted it, and headed toward the band for another day of riding. Now, Tanaka was worried. Nothing good could come of Fu's losing face in front of his countrymen.

෨ඏ

Fu shook Tanaka awake. "Dress quickly!" Fu said, his face glowing in the lantern light, "Cossacks!"

Spurred by the chance to be rid of another necromancer and to resume his mission, Tanaka willed himself out of his fur-lined sleeping bag, dressed, and prepared his horse. He noticed that Fu's bandits were already awake, alert, and on horseback.

Tanaka rode over to the others, seeking out Fu. "Where are they?"

Fu pointed ahead. "In a ravine about two *li* that way. About fifteen men."

"Why don't I see firelight?"

Fu didn't hesitate. "Because like the Japanese, the Cossacks are very disciplined."

Now Tanaka knew Fu was bullshitting. According to his pre-war briefings, the term "disciplined Cossack" was an oxymoron. But for the time being, Tanaka deferred to Fu so as not to inflame an already shaky relationship. "What's the plan?"

Fu grinned. "You'll wait here until my bandits kill the Cossacks. We'll leave the necromancer for you, so you can stab him with your mighty sword," he said, his voice oozing with sarcasm. "We'll signal you with this." Fu held up a metallic whistle suspended from a hemp lanyard around his neck.

Tanaka nodded. Fu and his men trotted into the darkness, while Tanaka waited, shivering.

Shots rang out, followed by screams, then a whistle.

Tanaka led his horse at a canter toward the encampment, now illuminated with fire. As Tanaka spurred his mount into a full gallop, he noticed the wind had stilled.

Several cadaverous hags blocked his path, their gazes mesmerizing him. "Feed us," they said, their voices a chorus of discordant melodies. In seconds, his horse was on top of, then through them—their ethereal forms disintegrating into oblivion.

Disoriented, Tanaka followed the light of the raging blaze. He rounded a small spur leading into a deep ravine. There, he watched as Fu's men looted bloody corpses.

Fu was soaking up the fire's warmth while sitting astride a squirming man-sized burlap sack wrapped in cords of hemp. "Ah, there you are, Tanaka. I've bound the necromancer. Why don't you take out your fancy sword and stab him like you stab your mother with your tiny prick."

Tanaka bore the insult with grace, but his patience with Fu was running thin. He dismounted his horse, unsheathed his blade, and confronted Fu. "How do you know it's a necromancer?"

"Boy, I been doing this longer'n you been yanking your twig. Trust me. It's him."

Tanaka didn't sense an inhuman presence inside the man, so he stared at Fu, uncertain what to do, and then said, "Let me see his face."

"Stupid, fish-fucker. If I show you his eyes, he could hypnotize you. Just cut off his head. Kill 'em any other way, and a demon can jump into his body. And then you got real problems."

"Please," the necromancer pleaded in fluent Japanese, "Let me go!"

Tanaka hesitated.

"He's just messin' with ya. He smells fish and rice, so he talks Japanese to trick ya. Kill 'em quick so he doesn't cast any spells on us."

Tanaka opened the sack, locking eyes with a fellow Japanese soldier.

Fu grabbed the man by his hair, dragging him away from Tanaka. With his other hand, Fu covered the Japanese soldiers' eyes. "What the fuck ya doing, tiny man? That sack needed to be sealed, else that necromancer's soul escapes and could possess you, me, or anyone else within a tenth of a *li*. Do it now!"

Then to Tanaka's horror, he spotted a bandit tossing the *Kyokujitsu-ki*, Japan's rising sun flag, into the flames. Fu watched Tanaka. The bandit leader's eyes gleamed. His left hand gripped the hilt of his knife. The blade rested on the captive's neck. The soldier stared wide-eyed at Tanaka. In one swift motion, the bandit leader slit the captive's throat.

"You son of a bitch!" Tanaka said, "You set me up. I almost killed one of my own countrymen. Why?"

Fu blew his whistle and the band surrounded Tanaka. Then Fu said, "Because you're cursed."

Tanaka felt a blow to the head.

&

Tanaka woke beneath a stack of corpses. Frozen blood caked his woolen undergarments in burgundy patches. He was so cold he could barely bend his fingers. He wormed his way out of the pile. The sky was gray, but the light was bright enough that Tanaka judged the sun, hidden above the clouds, was at its apex.

Surrounded by the dead, Tanaka felt utterly and irredeemably defiled. No Shinto priest could purify him now. If he'd had his saber or pistol, he would've ended his life.

Then the women appeared. Their razor-sharp teeth marred already twisted faces. Their features contorted in angry rictuses. Their black and gray hair, scattered topsy-turvy on rotting skulls, had the roughshod quality of burlap. They reminded Tanaka of the *shikome* from ancient myth, *Izanami*'s fell servants of the underworld.

"Feed us," they said, pointing west in perfect synchronicity, black, curled nails extending from their index fingers. An instant later, lightning sundered the horizon, punctuated by thunder. The women's white marble eyes penetrated his thoughts, knowing him for who he truly was. Then one touched him.

Choking in blackness, Tanaka felt death's void flood into his empty soul, its filth putrefying his frozen form. Then a surge of dark energy animated his cold limbs, breathing a perversion of life into them, instilling a strange otherworldly sense of purpose that Tanaka couldn't put into words.

In seconds, Tanaka was on his feet, looting a Japanese corpse for its khaki winter uniform under the ghostly hags' chilling glares.

"Feed us," they said, before vanishing.

So Tanaka wandered west, meandering through the furrowed rows of a fallow millet field. Soon, he came across of copse of ash trees, where bodies swayed from a makeshift gallows on barren branches. When Tanaka got closer, he discovered the ripped and bloodied corpses of Cossacks hanging over the mangled meat of horse carcasses strewn about the lifeless landscape. From the Cossacks' wounds, Tanaka figured someone had either shot them in the back or had cut their throats. And he was certain that someone had been Fu.

Fu's bandits had stripped nearly everything useful from the Cossacks' corpses, save the belongings of one dead, scarlet bearded man. Tanaka removed the man's greatcoat and shaggy *papaha*, hoping it would help Tanaka pass for a Russian.

All Tanaka needed now was a weapon. But if he couldn't find one, he'd happily kill Fu with his bare hands. Tanaka didn't care much more for life. The dead had so violated him that his spirit reeked of filth. The only thing that drove him now was his honor, and he would die to preserve it.

As he reached the edge of the millet field, Tanaka ascended a slow rise until he came across railroad tracks littered with human bodies and horse carcasses. Both man and beast had their abdomens splayed open like inverted starfish.

Fu's bandits.

Tanaka despaired. Unable to avenge his honor, he searched their remains for his saber and pistol. He found both on Fu's desecrated corpse.

The lightning and strange wounds suddenly reminded Tanaka of the folklore tied to his mother's superstitions. Legend had it that a *raiju* favored the comfort of a child's belly. During electrical storms, it would seek refuge there. To uncover its companion, a *raijin* would strike children with exposed navels using lightning to drive out the *raiju*.

But if either demon existed, the folklore had understated their cruelty given the grievous wounds Tanaka had witnessed here. Then he remembered the story of the goddess *Izanami*. She'd sent both *raijin* and *shikome* to capture her husband, *Izanagi*, after he'd abandoned her rotting form in *Yomi*, the death realm. When *Izanagi* had escaped his wife's minions, *Izanami* had vowed to claim a thousand lives a day in revenge. In response, *Izanagi* had promised he'd breathe life into fifteen hundred more.

৪১

Tanaka liberated a pale mare from a nearby village. He'd offered to trade a farmer for the horse, but the man had refused, so Tanaka had taken it by force. He regretted such harsh measures, but he'd needed to salvage his reconnaissance mission.

Before Tanaka had left the village, several peasants had reported large concentrations of Imperial Russian troops in the vicinity of Mukden. So Tanaka rode west beyond the railway. Through dark gray clouds, a faint glow traced the sun's descent below the horizon, ushering in twilight, and with it, a deeper cold. Foreshadowing rain, the clouds released giant flakes of snow instead.

Along the way, Tanaka happened upon a second village. Expecting to find light and heat from warm hearths, he found a raging conflagration in its place. Thatched huts burned, and the smell of cooked meat made Tanaka's stomach grumble.

As Tanaka ventured away from the fiery homes and into the darkness, he smelled vodka mixed with borsch.

Cossacks!

A shot rang out. A bullet grazed Tanaka's arm. Tanaka's mare whinnied. Its forelegs rose, bucking Tanaka. The captain landed hard. The fall knocked the wind out of his lungs.

Russian voices chattered in the murk.

Tanaka scrambled to find cover. But the men, armed with torches and bayonet-tipped Mosin-Nagant rifles, easily found him. Underneath the cover of shaggy black sheepskin *papahas*, the Cossacks' curly moustaches accentuated their grimy yellow teeth, a pack of jackals encircling for the kill.

One brute held Tanaka down, while another beat him bloody. Tanaka felt the sharp pain of a broken nose and smashed cheek. The men pounded on Tanaka until blood streamed down his neck, freezing in place. He shuddered as the Cossacks dragged his shattered body toward two crossed railroad ties lying on the snowy ground. They forced Tanaka onto the contraption, his limbs tracing an "X".

A Cossack grinned, pulled out a hammer and finger-length spike, and nailed Tanaka's palms and feet to the railroad ties. Each time a nail pierced his flesh, intense stabs of pain coursed through Tanaka's limbs.

Just when Tanaka couldn't endure any more suffering, the yelping Cossacks hoisted the structure up, propping it against a small hut. Supported only by the nails driven into his hands and feet, Tanaka struggled to breathe.

The men mocked Tanaka and chortled as he cried. Yet, Tanaka accepted his fate. Better to die in the cold Manchurian wilderness than to live and dishonor his family. Tanaka lowered his head and prepared to die.

"Feed us."

The ghostly hags glided through the cackling Cossacks with an eerie preternatural grace, their shredded gossamer gowns dancing in the darkness.

No matter how much the hags twisted and whirled, the Cossacks paid them no mind. The men just laughed and drank themselves into a stupor.

The old crones smiled, their needle-fine teeth glinting in the moonlight. Tanaka heard a faint beat in the gloom, crescendoing until it was so intense, it stirred the Cossacks from their torpor.

Boom-dada-boom-dada-boom-boom-boom!

The Cossacks loaded their bolt-action rifles. Several ventured toward the drumbeat.

Then the pale hags pointed toward its source. A lightning bolt struck the ground, punctuated by thunder. For a split second, Tanaka saw something lurking beneath the lightning.

A man shrieked.

The crones pointed again. Lightning flashed, revealing a gnarled squat thing about twice the size of a man, its arms the thickness of tree trunks. Scores of twisted goat horns crowned its skull. A misshapen perversion of man and beast, it had the muzzle of a horse, a snake's eyes, a boar's tusks, and a mess of bony ridges on its face.

Lightning struck again. Tanaka watched as the thing eviscerated a man in one blow. Its claws tossed the man's innards. Something else scurried out of the Cossack's steaming guts when they hit the ground. The small creature's compound eyes, scales, and stubby legs reminded Tanaka of a twisted chimera of insect, crab, and reptile. Its pincers gnawed on the dead man's viscera.

The storm continued into the night until Tanaka was the only survivor. The others lay dead, their bellies splayed open in the same manner as the other desecrated corpses he'd found along Southern Manchurian Railway.

When the storm ended, the spectral hags floated toward Tanaka, hovering over the ground at his eye level. One laid her hands on his, removing the nails binding him to the wooden structure. She lowered him to the ground, put her hands on his forehead and granted him a vision.

In his mind's eye, Tanaka beheld the railroad tracks of the Southern Manchurian Railway cleaving the bleak landscape, running northeast. Frozen rivers bisected the rail line at various points running from south to north. A network of trenches scarred the desolate plain in a defensive line from west to east, just south of a tributary Tanaka recognized as the Sha River. To the north lay a second river, the Hun, and beyond the Hun, a town.

Mukden.

Like a hawk, Tanaka focused his mystical vision on specific areas of the battlefield, observing the guidons and banners of individual units. He found himself outside time and viewed the Russians' positions with total clarity.

Just as quickly as his vision began, it ended, and Tanaka found himself lying on the cold soil just before morning twilight, surrounded by mutilated corpses. The white hags watched him.

"Feed us," they said, before dissolving into the ether.

While the ghost women had vanished, Tanaka's perfect knowledge remained, and he was giddy with the chance to restore his honor.

As he surveyed the carnage, everything around him was dead save for his pale horse tethered to the crossed railroad ties. Strangely, he felt neither warm nor cold, and he could no longer see his frosty breath.

Tanaka wondered why the *raijin* and *raiju* had spared him and his mare. But ultimately, he decided it was pointless dwelling on such abstract and arcane notions. He had more pressing concerns like delivering his intelligence to General Nogi. Tanaka climbed on his mount and headed west toward Third Army.

⮑

Tanaka had ridden all day and night to reach Third Army's field headquarters. Like iron filings to a lodestone, he quickly sought out and found General Nogi Maresuke's banner rippling above a simple canvas field tent.

The general was a man of contrasts bridging tradition and modernity. A samurai's son, he'd fought to put the samurai down during the Satsuma Rebellion. When the enemy had captured his regiment's banner, he'd fought with suicidal bravery to recover it until his commanders had ordered him to stop. Losing a banner in combat was a terrible shame for any officer. Were it not for the Emperor's forgiveness, General Nogi would not have survived to capture Port Arthur from the Chinese in 1894, and from the Russians in early 1905.

When Tanaka approached the elderly general, the man's eyes cast a sad, pensive look. The general averted Tanaka's gaze and looked toward the horizon. "It's not natural for a father to outlive his sons," he said.

Tanaka didn't know how to respond to the general's frank expression of emotion, and he wanted desperately to comfort the general. Everyone in the Imperial Army had made heroic sacrifices in this war, but General Nogi had lost more than most. Both his sons had died in this war; one in the Battle of Nanshan, and the other in the fanatical assault on Port Arthur's Hill 203. Tanaka had great respect for the old man, and would not begrudge him his moment of grief.

General Nogi turned, raised an eyebrow, and said, "You look awfully pale, Tanaka-kun. And it seems your face has taken a beating. I'm happy to see you're still alive." He paused for a moment and then said, "What news have you from Unit 108?"

Tanaka bowed to his commander. "Nogi-sama, may I borrow a map?"

"Myake-kun!" the general yelled. A soldier materialized as if by magic, and produced one. The general handed it to Tanaka. Tanaka traced several symbols on the map representing Imperial Russian units down to the regimental level.

Nogi's eyes widened. "How did you come upon such detail? We haven't been able to get anyone that close to the Russians, especially in the center of the front. There must be several hundred thousand men there."

"A shade over three hundred and forty thousand," Tanaka said before realizing that his supreme confidence must've sounded odd to Nogi. After all, it was implausible that one man could single-handedly obtain such detailed and far-ranging intelligence.

Nogi stared at the map. He then pulled out a small book from his cargo pocket, cross-referencing it against Tanaka's drawings. After several minutes, the general glanced up at Tanaka. "What you've shown me is consistent with much of the detail we have. How were you able to gather this intelligence?"

Tanaka nearly told Nogi the truth, but quickly decided against it for the general would never believe him. Instead, he lied. "I could cover quite a bit more ground disguised as a bandit."

Nogi's eyes focused on Tanaka's as if the elderly general were probing for some hint of deception. But Tanaka held firm. Nogi nodded. "Excellent work, Tanaka-kun. I'll ensure you're properly recognized for your efforts. Dismissed."

Tanaka saluted. Nogi returned the salute. Tanaka spun on his heels and made to exit the general's field tent.

"Wait," Nogi said, "Come back."

Tanaka turned and walked back inside. The general smiled. "I'd like to shake your hand," Nogi said, extending his arm.

Tanaka gripped the general's hand. Nogi's broad smile crumbled. His brows furrowed. "Your...hand, it's ice cold."

Then, with a deep foreboding, Tanaka withdrew his hand and lifted his tunic, exposing his abdomen. Nogi's face twisted into a grimace. When Tanaka touched his belly, it was splayed open in the manner of *raijin*'s victims.

The instant Tanaka realized what he'd become, his corpse collapsed inside the general's field tent. His grim task completed, he passed through death's veil into *Yomi*, where his body would rot for eternity.

Over the next several weeks, tens of thousands of souls would join him, feeding *Izanami*'s insatiable hunger on an industrial scale as the Russians and Japanese invented new, more efficient ways of killing.

END

Afterword

"Mukden" is a historical retelling of the prelude to its namesake military engagement. The Battle of Mukden, which took place in early 1905, was one of the largest land battles in history prior to World War I. This story is the second historical fantasy story I've ever written.

The tale is the sequel to "Necromancer", which first appeared as "Hill of Souls" in *Outposts of Beyond* in 2015. It continues to follow the arcane journey of Japanese soldier Captain Tanaka Hideki, a member of an occult organization known only to Japan's senior leadership as Unit 108. His mission is to work with local Chinese bandits to determine the size, location, and disposition of Imperial Russian forces operating along the Manchurian rail line, but along the way, he discovers something far more sinister.

To craft the story and build the world, I spent a great deal of time researching the events, personalities, and weapons of the Russo-Japanese. I also tried to weave a rather Lovecraftian aesthetic throughout the story, invoking it with a sense of dread and hopelessness.

This story first appeared in *Weirdbook* in February 2017. It also won an Honorable Mention in the Writers of the Future Contest's first quarter of 2015. I hope you enjoy the story as much as I enjoyed researching, writing, and crafting it.

About the Author

Sean is a technology and finance professional, and nationally bestselling award-winning author who writes science fiction and horror as well as nonfiction. Over fifty of his short stories in publications such as *The Year's Best Military and Adventure SF*, *Year's Best Hardcore Horror*, *Terraform*, *Galaxy's Edge*, and *Vastarien*, among others. He is the editor of the *Weird World War III*, *Weird World War IV*, and *Weird World War: China* anthologies. He is also the host of the YouTube channel, *Through A Glass Darkly*, where the paranormal meets military science fiction and fact.

Sean was a research associate at the Harvard-Stanford Preventive Defense Project where he worked on energy security issues. He won the 2006 Policy Analysis Exercise Award at the Harvard Kennedy School of Government for his work on policy solutions to Iran's nuclear weapons program. Sean also spent time at Booz Allen Hamilton as an intelligence analyst focusing on strategic war games and simulations for the Pentagon. Before graduate school, Sean was a cavalry officer in the United States Army where he trained American forces for combat operations in Iraq and Afghanistan at the National Training Center.

Sean holds a Master of Business Administration from Harvard Business School, a Master in Public Policy from the Harvard Kennedy School of Government, and bachelor's degrees in History and Electrical Engineering from Stanford.

www.ingramcontent.com/pod-product-compliance
Lightning Source LLC
Chambersburg PA
CBHW070830250626
47159CB00003B/722